CHOSEN FEW

Dale Dye

Also by Dale Dye

PELELIU FILE
LAOS FILE
RUN BETWEEN THE RAINDROPS
PLATOON
OUTRAGE
CONDUCT UNBECOMING
DUTY AND DISHONOR

CHOSIN FILE

DALE DYE

WARRIORS PUBLISHING GROUP
NORTH HILLS, CALIFORNIA

CHOSIN FILE

A Warriors Publishing Group book/published by arrangement with the author

PRINTING HISTORY
Warriors Publishing Group edition/September 2012

ISBN 978-0-9853388-0-0

PRINTED IN THE UNITED STATES OF AMERICA

10 9 8 7 6 5 4 3 2 1

For the boys bellied-up at Johnny Basket's Bar in St. Louis, Missouri who told the war stories that fired my imagination and started me running to the sound of the guns.

To a sorely missed buddy, Corporal Barry Jones USMC, Fox Company, 2nd Battalion, 7th Marines, who told me what the Frozen Chosin in the Freezin' Season was really like.

And to Julia who bravely and lovingly fights at my side.

Semper Fidelis!

Dale Dye

On a clear, crisp autumn morning in Southern California, Shake Davis stood on the firing line and tried to read the wind. A brisk, salty breeze blowing in from the ocean caused the red range flags to flutter, and prompted the Marines on his left and right to fiddle with the ACOG scopes on their M-4 carbines. Shake ignored the flags and looked downrange at the ground where the breeze was barely moving the leaves and grass cuttings spread over the one hundred meters he would have to cover when the klaxon signaled the start of the exercise. The M-16A4—strapped to his body by a single-point tactical sling—was box-stock with no advanced combat optical gunsight fitted. He was obligated to run the course using only iron sights because he'd let his battleship mouth overload his rowboat ass during a beer and bullshit session with a group of hard-chargers from the Marine Special Operations Command, who doubted his contention that age and experience trumps youth and enthusiasm.

No reason why they should believe it, Shake mused, and decided a slight right hold-off on his point of aim would compensate for the breeze at ground level. The Marines he'd been lecturing and coaching for the past week were all combat veterans—survivors of multiple tours doing the gut-level dirty work in Iraq and Afghanistan. These guys were skilled shooters who'd popped real rounds into real bad guys and they'd be running their A-Game this morning because the targets appearing randomly in each firing lane would not be shooting back at them, and because they wanted to show an old retired fart that they had the right stuff.

Shake ran his eyes over the rifle one last time and reached down to check the custom Kimber .45 caliber pistol in a drop-rig holster on his left thigh. If he got his ass kicked soundly and severely in the exercise, it would serve him right. It must have been the beer that prompted him to challenge these people to a shoot-off that involved running and gunning through a course requiring each man to fire his carbine dry, and then smoothly transition to a sidearm and finish the course scoring hits on each and every target along the way. He'd started out to make a point about using whatever was at hand in a tight situation and not relying on high-speed bells and whistles to get the job done. As the level in the beer keg dropped and the war stories got wilder, he'd felt just confident enough to bet he could clean the course using a standard-issue rifle with iron sights and his favorite slab-side .45 just as well or better than these young operators using tricked-out M-4's and nine-millimeter Berettas.

"You ready for this, Gunner?" A smiling staff sergeant—the same man who embarrassed him at the beginning of his visit to the MARSOC command with a long and lurid recitation of Shake's combat record over 30 years in the Corps—took the rifle and turned his back. The drill for this course of fire required a coach to load each man's shoulder weapon with an unknown number of rounds, so the shooter could never predict when his magazine would run dry. Staff Sergeant Art Kybat inserted a magazine, hit the bolt release to chamber a round of 5.56-mm ammo, flipped the selector lever to safe, and handed the rifle back to Shake Davis. "No tellin' how many rounds you've got, Gunner. Could be thirty; could be two. When she runs dry, transition to that hog-leg of yours and continue the attack. Any questions?"

"Just one." Shake took the rifle and checked the selector position. "How come a good Staff NCO like you let your guys talk me into this shit?" Kybat chuckled and checked the other coaches on the line. "These guys are all rooting for you, Gunner. They may run their suck about time in The Sandbox and all that, but they really love having you here. Guys like you done a lot more with a lot less and they know it. We got a message from Camp Lejeune this morning. They want you out there as soon as you're done here."

"My wife might have something to say about that." Shake shouldered the rifle and tried to find a comfortable position on his left side. The heavy flak gear he was wearing made it a difficult proposition. "She's got this thing where she thinks being retired means I don't do stuff like this anymore." Just as he finally found a way to accommodate the buttstock and keep his right arm firmly under the balance of the weapon, Kybat tapped him on the shoulder.

"It's a little different when you're wearing the SAPI plate carrier, Gunner." Kybat retrieved the rifle and demonstrated what looked to Shake like a very uncomfortable and awkward shooting position. "If you do it the old rifleman way, you're exposing vulnerable body parts to enemy fire. The way we do it now is to move and shoot dead face-on to the threat—like this." Kybat crouched and floated a few steps forward to demonstrate. He moved smoothly in a sort of gliding step with his upper body almost motionless. "This way, you only expose the upper-body parts that are covered by the small-arms protective inserts. The support arm kinda goes out to the side—like this."

"You guys can actually move and shoot like that?" The position seemed all wrong to Shake, who had always been taught to address a target by executing a half left or right face, and then shouldering the weapon with his support arm vertical under the balance of the piece. "I'm gonna wind up waddling downrange like a ruptured duck!"

The Range Safety Officer gave the stand-by signal and Kybat handed the rifle back to Shake. "Do it your way, Gunner. Any man who survived as many firefights as you, don't need to fix something that ain't broke." When the command to unlock came over the loudspeakers, Davis flipped the selector switch to semi-auto and assumed a firing position that he hoped was a reasonable compromise between what he'd been shown and what he felt would help him get rounds on target. Kybat raised his hand and checked the line again to insure everyone was ready. "It's a real privilege to have you here with us, Gunner. Now get out there and get some."

When the starting horn sounded, Shake trundled forward with the rifle firmly in his shoulder and his head up and swiveling, looking for targets. He had no idea how many rounds were in his rifle and no idea how many targets were set to pop up in his firing lane. If he was carrying a short load in the M-16, he only had seven rounds in his pistol to engage any remaining targets with the required double-tap. And all targets had to be engaged and hit to score a clean run on the exercise. The first pop-up to his right front surprised him, but he was able to swing smoothly without stopping and put two rounds into the silhouette, causing it to collapse. The next target, about 15 meters further along, emerged from behind a mound of dirt and only revealed a partial shape like a man aiming in from the prone position. Shake kept moving, held slightly right on the part of the target he could see, squeezed the trigger, and it collapsed. So far, so good.

The third target popped up in a rickety window frame about halfway down the firing lane. Shake advanced firing and scored one hit before the bolt slammed back to stay. He was out of rifle ammo and fought the instinct to dive for cover while he reloaded. There were no reloads in this drill. He slung the rifle to the rear of his body and snatched the .45 out of its holster as he advanced on the target with his eyes locked on the Kimber's front sight. The first round out of the pistol caused the target to disappear, and Shake took a second to try and guess how many targets might show in the 40 or so meters he had left to the end of the lane. Whatever the number, he now had exactly six rounds of .45 ACP to double-tap all of them. At that point things got interesting.

Whoever was running the target controls back at the line shack decided to up the ante in Shake's firing lane. Targets seemed to be popping up every time he took another step forward. He hit one on the left and two on the right in quick succession before the slide on his pistol locked back, indicating an empty magazine. He was completely out of ammo and ideas when the final target popped up just five meters from the finish line. Maybe it was adrenaline or the instincts of an old warhorse. Shake Davis didn't give himself time to contemplate. He hit the final target with a flying body block and beat it into submission with the barrel of his empty pistol. He was still flailing away at the brutalized target when the klaxon signaled the end of the run.

He was flat on his butt and breathing hard when he realized he was surrounded by a group of laughing, cheering, and applauding Marines. "You cleaned it, Gunner!" Staff Sergeant Kybat could barely get the words out between hoots of laughter. "I ain't ever seen it done that way, but the rules say all targets must be hit—and you damn sure hit that last one."

* * *

There were only a few other drinkers at the bar of the Oceanside steak house. Shake was glad to have a little time alone as he swirled bourbon over ice and contemplated having another one before calling a cab to take him back to his motel. It had been a great week, and he didn't much mind the major dent he'd put in his personal plastic buying the MARSOC shooters a steak dinner after they cleaned up on the range. *Truth is*, he thought as he signaled for another drink, *I love just being around these young Marines. And another truth is*, he told himself as the second snort arrived, *it's good to know I've still got it. That's my ego talking. I know it and I don't give a shit. For a beat-up old bastard who will never see the soft side of sixty again, I can still hack the load.*

The lovely and talented Mrs. Chan Dwyer Davis, his bride of the past three years, had made him solemnly promise no more jumping out of perfectly good airplanes or swimming out of fully functional submersibles, but she understood why he wanted so badly to accept the invitation from the Marine Special Operations Command to visit, talk shop, swap war stories, and generally inspire all the young operators to great sacrifice and even greater dedication. It was what the Corps called the *moto factor*. You get a visit from a retired Marine Gunner like Shake Davis with a colorful reputation and a combat record stretching back to before most of them were born, and there's a certain motivation to it. *And so be it. If that's an ego trip, I'll buy the ticket and take the ride. Retired is one thing—don't give a shit anymore is another thing entirely.* Marines aspire to live up to their history—to match the deeds done by their predecessors—and that can be a powerful multiplier even as they are writing their own colorful chapters in military history.

It's like I told Chan, Shake thought as he stared at his craggy countenance and thatch of snow-white hair in the mirror behind the bar. *I ain't dead and I ain't crippled and I sure as hell still care about Marines. If there's something I can do to make what they've got to do a little easier or a little more palatable, then I need to do it.* Fortunately, his 30-year pension and Chan's hefty salary as a senior analyst at the Defense Intelligence Agency provided enough slack for Shake to travel and play a little bit without worrying about paying the bills.

He decided a third drink wouldn't hurt as the bartender was pouring short anyway. He ordered and then reached into a jacket pocket to look at the message Staff Sergeant Kybat handed him before herding his team of operators back toward the base. Apparently, he'd gotten good reviews from his visit at Camp Pendleton, and the word had been passed through the special operations back channels. He was now officially invited by the Commanding General of the MARSOC command at Camp Lejeune for an extended visit and some consultation on the special operations training syllabus. That was right in Shake's personal wheelhouse, but he'd need to call Chan and get her blessing before he accepted. She was a terrific woman and a wonderful wife, but there was only so much absence on the part of her husband she'd tolerate.

For a former Military Intelligence officer who'd been at his side through some interesting adventures, Chan had a remarkably strong nesting instinct. She cherished their time alone in the pricey townhouse they'd bought in suburban Virginia and was always finding domestic chores for him to handle. Shake didn't mind—in fact he relished pleasing her—but there were only so many leaky faucets and creaky floorboards he could fix before he started getting antsy. He supposed it was something in the genes she inherited from her Thai mother, but Shake had quickly come to understand that he'd married a woman with very strong opinions about marital stability and a relatively placid domestic life.

He was reaching for his cell phone when it began to vibrate and the caller ID indicated Chan was either missing him or reading his mind. *Could be either or both,* he thought with a grin, and punched the button to activate the call. "*Sawadee*, Spouse...how you doing?"

"I'm missing you." Chan sounded a bit distracted but Shake decided that might be his escalating hearing loss—or the booze. "How's it going out on the Left Coast?"

"All is well, Chan. I'm sitting in an Oceanside bistro boozing it up to soothe my damaged ego after an embarrassing day on the range."

"Range? As in firing range? I thought you were out there just shaking hands and motivating troops with tales of past glories."

"I did all that—and somehow it developed into this deal where I had to compete with a bunch of young, muscular, and enormously talented special operations door-kickers. It was entertaining for them—embarrassing for me."

"Well, you better come home." Something in Chan's voice put Shake on alert. It wasn't her usual stop-screwing-around tone.

"I got this invitation from the MARSOC guys at Camp Lejeune. I was going to ask you about heading over there and..."

"Better send regrets, Shake. You're needed here."

"Anything wrong, Chan?"

"I can't talk about it on the phone but there's someone here who wants to talk to you in the worst way. Guess who it is and you'll know why I'm sounding so weird."

Shake belted at his drink and motioned for another. "Does his name start with a B and rhyme with Bayer?"

"Yep. He dropped by the house last night looking for you. He's out of the CT business these days and holding down a very big desk at Langley. There's something up involving Mike but he wouldn't say much more. You better catch the next thing smoking out of LAX for Dulles."

"I'm on my way—first flight I can book in the morning. I love you, Chan."

He stabbed disconnect, swallowed the drink that had just arrived, and shoved his credit card at the bartender. He had no earthly idea what the senior CIA man who called himself Bayer wanted, but if his best friend Mike Stokey was involved there was no option. Shake Davis would do whatever was necessary to help.

"He's way the hell off the reservation." The man who called himself Bayer dropped into a chair, stared into the electric flames in Chan's fireplace, and sipped at the stiff scotch Shake had just poured for him. "Mike has run off the edge of the map and that makes me very nervous, for a couple of reasons."

"That how come you wanted to meet at the house instead of the office?" Shake was fresh off a cross-country flight and drinking ice water to fend off grogginess. He reached down and scratched behind Bear's floppy ears. The huge Golden Pyrenees nuzzled at Shake's hand and whined for more attention. "It shouldn't come as a surprise to anyone in Clandestine Services that Mike goes his own way. He always has."

"Mike's good at what he does for us—none better in my opinion—but he tends to run too close to the edge. You know that better than I do from personal experience, Shake."

"He's got a way about him, that's for damn sure." Shake decided he was sufficiently recovered for a drink and made his way to the bar thinking about his close calls with Mike Stokey in Vietnam and most recently in the South Pacific. "If you don't like the way he operates, why don't you just retire his ass? He's getting too old for spook games in the field anyway."

"I've been seriously considering that. I was going to discuss it with him personally when he got himself launched on this most recent thing. There comes a time with guys like Mike when they step over the line and either wind up dead or serving time in some dark, dank gulag as a pawn in a very embarrassing international power play." Bayer polished off his drink and held out the glass. Chan got up to get him a refill, and Bear padded after her hoping for a treat from the jar they kept on the wet bar. Shake just sipped his drink and stared at the fire. There was no use pushing Bayer. He'd drop the other shoe when he was ready.

"You need to get a saddle for that damn dog, Shake." Bayer watched the gentle giant sit with his muzzle resting on the top of the bar. "Either that or a bigger house so he can get a little exercise."

"Bear's a great shitbird deterrent." Shake waved a hand in the general direction of the neighborhood. "We take him for a walk and he clears the area for blocks. Nobody screws with Mister Bear."

Bayer thought for a moment and tugged at the knot in his tie. "What I say here goes no further. I guess I don't have to tell you that. I'm not here in an official capacity because this situation hasn't been reported up the political chain, and it needs to stay that way if possible." Bayer leaned forward with his elbow on his knees and took a deep breath. "So, here's the deal. Mike's been involved with an investigation into North Korean nukes. He's been at it for the past six months or so, working out of Seoul, mostly. A couple of weeks ago, he inserted into the Liaoning Province of southeastern China to help set up a drone reconnaissance operation."

"That's part of what used to be called Manchuria, right?" Chan handed Bayer a fresh drink and dropped into a chair with a glass of chilled Chablis. "Was this with or without Chinese cooperation?"

"Unofficial all the way. We've got a sort of understanding with some people in the PLA." Bayer sipped his drink and seemed to be pondering how to phrase what he wanted to communicate. "I can't get into the weeds with you on this but we've been running a surveillance program way under the radar—and by that I mean without any Congressional or State Department oversight at all. We're on the good side of certain high-level Chinese military assets that want no part of a nuclear armed North Korea. They can't cooperate with us in the open, but they can turn a blind eye to a little drone base just across the Yalu from their troublesome neighbors. We use that secret site to launch a UAV over specific areas we want to investigate, and share the Intel that's developed. It's a win-win for the PLA and nothing gets reported officially to their civilian bosses in Beijing."

"And just as crucial for you, I'd guess..." Chan grinned at Bayer, sharing a little humor among intelligence insiders. "...is that neither the President nor the Secretary of State gets wind of you guys conducting a sub-rosa, non-sanctioned operation with the Chinese—not to mention sharing the Intel dump. They would not be pleased."

"I think it's safe to say that's an accurate assessment of the situation." Bayer was not grinning. "The thinking at certain levels in the community was that taking the risk involved was better than getting caught with our pants down should the North Koreans do something stupid. The situation in that country is desperate, and they don't have the best international track record for restraint. The politicians may have other priorities, but Intelligence professionals need to stay focused on real threats. As you're aware, that sometimes means doing what's necessary to protect the nation whether those actions are officially sanctioned or not."

"When the going gets weird, the weird turn pro," Shake chuckled. "So you guys set up this unofficial recon base and run the op off the record. It ain't the first time and it won't be the last, I guess. Aren't drones mostly flown and controlled from sites here in CONUS? How come you need a base in China?"

"Too few assets and too many demands." Chan sipped at her wine and got the nod from Bayer. "The long-range, high-endurance drones controlled out of Creech in Nevada are major theater combat assets. Everybody wants time on targets within their area of operations, and priority goes to the Middle East right now. The high-level national Intel demands from CIA, DIA and the like get laid off on satellite reconnaissance assets, but that's usually a cat-fight between the agencies for time on the birds."

"The quick-fix is to station a smaller UAV nearer the target and control it in theater." Bayer popped the latches on his briefcase and spread a map of the Korean Peninsula on the coffee table. "We very quietly brought a stealthy, off-the-inventory reconnaissance drone into Seoul with the mission of getting it, plus a small control and support crew, up around the Yalu to over-fly specific areas in North Korea. As our Korean or Chinese assets fed us Intel, we could get the drone over the area and get a good idea of what was or was not happening with the North Korean nuke projects. That's what Mike was working on—last we heard from him."

"When was that?" Shake bent to look at the map and recognized some of the terrain. It was an area very familiar to Marines who knew anything about the Korean War—and that was *all* Marines from their first history class in boot camp.

"Six days ago." Bayer spun the map and pointed at a spot on the Chinese side of the Yalu River. "Mike was the contact guy with our North Korean assets. He cobbled together Intel from agents in Pyongyang, and then helped develop targets for surveillance. Apparently, something tripped his trigger, but he didn't bother reporting anything to me. I found out he was gone when I heard from our guy running the UAV out there. That's Dick Liccardi, a former Air Force tech-Intel guy and one of the best drone drivers in the business. Dick says Stokey crossed the Yalu with a couple of Koreans he had on the payroll and headed for this area right here."

Shake and Chan leaned over the coffee table and stared at the map. "I think I know what tripped Mike's trigger." Shake pointed at a patch of blue just east of the spot marked by Bayer's finger. "That's the infamous Chosin Reservoir. Back in the winter of 1950, the entire 1st Marine Division was trapped up there, surrounded by a pot-full of pissed off Chinese. They had to fight their way out..." Shake traced a line on the map running in a southeasterly direction. "...from up here at Yudam-ni all the way back to Hungnam, and then eventually to the port of Wonsan where they were evacuated. It's a huge deal in Marine Corps history: The Frozen Chosin in the Freezin' Season, an epic fighting withdrawal. Every Marine studies that fight."

"Well, all that's interesting, but I believe Stokey was motivated by something more than a nostalgic trip to an old Marine

Corps battlefield. Liccardi reports they ran three missions over the area at Mike's specific request. I've been all over the data and photo-imagery with the experts: Nothing but water in the reservoir and a bunch of snow-capped mountains on either side of it. There's a hydroelectric plant to the north and a few settlements for the people who presumably keep it running. Some trucks running in and out of there but that's hardly unusual—or suspicious. I think Mike got wind of something else happening in that area and decided to check it out personally—in defiance of strict orders to the contrary."

"And the telemetry shows no sign of nuclear activity?" Chan was suddenly in full analyst mode. "I'm presuming you had the UAV rigged with the appropriate sensor packages?"

"Yes—and it was working for the other sites we investigated. There was just nothing suspicious from the over-flights in or around Chosin—or what the NK's call Changjin. I'm betting Mike was working on human intelligence, something he got from an agent on the ground. And I've been hoping for the past week we'd either hear from him or he'd get back across the Yalu for the reprimand he so richly deserves."

Shake sat back and thought about a very dangerous and nearly disastrous mission he'd run just three years before retiring from active duty. The real reason for Bayer's unofficial visit was becoming clearer by the minute. "I'm guessing you want someone who is familiar with the area to go looking for Mike. And that someone would have to be both unofficial and deniable if he gets caught operating in North Korea."

"Whoa—just stop right there." Chan smacked her wine glass on the coffee table hard enough to crack the delicate stem. "First it was Vietnam, and then it was that deal out on Peleliu. Every time you get your ass in a crack, you reach out for Shake and he damn near gets killed doing dirty work he's got no business being involved in. Well, I've got news for you. Shake Davis is an old retired poop and he's not about to go into North Korea for you or anybody else. Mike Stokey can pull his own damn fat out of the fire this time!"

"Easy, Chan." Shake put one hand on her knee and scratched at Bear's ears with the other. The dog was sensing trouble and, for that matter, so was he. "Let him finish before you tear his head off."

"I know all about Iceberg, Shake." Bayer glanced over at Chan to see if she recognized the code word. Apparently, she didn't. Chan sat with her arms crossed and a very angry look on her face. Bayer shrugged and nodded at Shake. "You want to tell her?"

"Operation Iceberg..." Shake swallowed what was left in his glass and set it down on a coaster. "It was while I was doing a 3rd Force Recon tour out in West Pac. We got sent down to Korea to work with a long-range patrol outfit called the Imjin Scouts, part of the Army's 2nd Infantry Division. We had some South Korean Special Forces augments, and we were just running little cross-border deals up along the DMZ to keep the North Korean commies honest. The serious recon stuff was being done by Air Force SR-71 Blackbirds and U-2's flying out of Okinawa. We were fat, dumb and happy until one of the U-2 drivers had to ditch. They got the pilot, but there was a lot of highly classified shit scattered all over around the Chosin Reservoir area. We got alerted to get up there very quietly, and either recover the important pieces or destroy it all in place."

"You never mentioned any of that." Chan got up to replace her wine glass, feed Bear a treat, and try to calm down a little. "I don't remember anything from any of the classified files I've read. And I've read almost everything I could about the weird crap you did on active duty. How do you explain that?"

"Well—things did not go exactly as planned. And I'm guessing the potential for an international shit-storm got most of the official reports dumped into a shredder as soon as they were submitted."

North Korea—Operation Iceberg

It was hard to see much beyond 100 meters in the pitch dark and blowing sleet off the coast north of Hungnam. And the pitch and roll of the small inflatable boat caused by heavy, wind-driven chop in the Sea of Japan made it hard to focus. Shake got only occasional glimpses of the dark smudge marking the rocky stretch of beach along the desolate, uninhabited area they'd selected for the landing. There were three ROK Marines somewhere on that beach, making sure it was safe for the second boat carrying Shake, two more Korean Marines, and one very seasick U.S. Air Force NCO to come ashore.

Shake tugged on the line securing the IBS sea-anchor and maneuvered the boat more bow-on to the heaving swells. It didn't help damper the motion much, but at least he could keep the shoreline in sight and have a better chance of spotting the pre-arranged signal from the recon party: Green for go, red for recover, and get the hell out of Dodge.

"See anything yet?" Master Sergeant Doug Bland, one of the most highly-skilled avionics technicians in the Pacific Air Forces, sounded like he was ready to heave another load of whatever was left in his stomach over the side. Shake had been feeding him Dramamine and electrolytes almost from the moment they left the submarine off the coast of North Korea but it hadn't done much good. To avoid surface radar and patrol boats, the sub had to launch them well offshore in heavy sea conditions. The Marines were used to it, but Master Sergeant Bland most definitely was not.

"Nothing yet." Shake took his eyes off the coastline long enough to look back over his shoulder at Bland huddled along the gunwale of the IBS. "Drink some more of that stuff in your canteen. We're gonna need you healthy once we get ashore."

Bland spit some bile over the side and Shake saw sets of white teeth showing through the camouflage on the faces of the two Korean Marines huddled back near the muffled outboard engine. *They do this kind of thing all the time*, he thought as he turned his attention back to the shoreline. *Here we sit off a very unfriendly coast, all set to waltz right into the enemy's back-yard, and they're laughing at a seasick American. Just another walk in the park for these guys.*

"Assuming we actually get ashore..." Bland shifted position and screwed the cap back on his two-quart canteen bladder, "...how long to the crash site?"

"We briefed all that, Doug. About thirty clicks up and down the high ground—maybe two days in and two more out. You should be back at Hickham in a week. A lot depends on the weather."

"And this horseshit weather is good, right? Reassure me."

"North Koreans don't like to be out in it any better than we do. Weather is the reason we decided not to insert by air ourselves. And as long as the weather stays bad, we don't have to worry so much about helicopters and roving patrols. Should be a piece of cake; we get in while their air assets are grounded, you do your thing at the crash site and we're gone. Forecasters in Seoul said this stuff will hold over the entire Korean Peninsula for at least a week."

"And we all know how accurate the fucking weather weenies are." Bland tugged at the hood of the South Korean Army parka he was wearing and shivered. "See anything yet?"

"Yeah—here we go." As the IBS topped a swell, Shake caught sight of a flashing light down low on the beach near a tall rock formation. "Green to go." Shake nodded at the Korean Marines and felt the boat steady as they fired up the outboard and jammed it into gear. "Let's get this show on the road."

As they neared the crashing surf-line, Shake signaled for the ROKs to secure the outboard for a rough landing and patted Master Sergeant Bland reassuringly on the shoulder. "Just hang on and let us do the grunt work. When I say go, get over the bow and run for those rocks to your right." Bland seemed like a nice enough guy, and Shake wanted to make the unfamiliar mission as easy for him as humanly possible. He also wanted to be very

sure—as he'd been cautioned by a serious two-star in Seoul—
that nothing happened that might cause Master Sergeant Doug
Bland and all his state-of-the-art avionics expertise to fall into
North Korean hands.

"Above all, it's your responsibility." The general had been
emphatic and crystal clear in a private session with Gunner
Shake Davis: "Under no circumstances—none whatsoever—is
Master Sergeant Bland to be captured by the North Koreans."
Shake was fairly sure he understood what that meant. As the IBS
plowed through the breakers and crunched onto North Korean
soil, he was also determined to accomplish this mission without
having to kill a fellow American.

* * *

It had been a brutal hump over the North Korean mountains
through biting winds and blowing snow, but the crash site at
last lay just below their perch on a rocky crag southeast of the
Chosin Reservoir. The homing device in the U-2's instrument
package was still perking, and Bland's hand-held scanner led
them right to it with only an occasional assist from Shake's map
and compass work. There was no one in sight around the
scattered field of aircraft debris and the weather was still
shitty—what aviators ruefully describe as zero-zero: no ceiling
and no visibility.

Shake checked his watch and determined it would be dark
in less than an hour. He decided to rest the team and go after
the sensitive pieces of the wreck at first light. Hiding in mountain snow-holes the first night after landing hadn't given them
much of the rest they needed for the hard push through the cold
and wind to reach their objective. The Korean Marines seemed
no worse for wear, but Bland was wobbling on shaky legs and
showing signs of altitude sickness. If the weather stayed as
horrible as it looked at this point, they could afford to rest
before searching for classified gear and then using the sack full
of thermite grenades they carried to destroy the U-2 wreckage.
There was no doubt in his mind that the North Koreans would

be out patrolling—looking for the crash site. Hopefully, they'd wait until the weather cleared. By that time, Shake wanted to be long gone, leaving nothing but a useless, burned-out pile of scrap in their wake.

"Go now? Or wait?" The Korean Marine team leader crouched next to Shake and offered a plastic sack of the malodorous stuff he was chewing. Shake knew from painful previous experience that the snack was winter *kimchee,* the fiery-hot pickled cabbage that the Koreans swore could keep a man from freezing in the worst sub-zero weather.

"Not much chance of air assets in this weather." Shake fingered out a chunk of *kimchee* and popped it into his mouth. "Let's rest until dawn when we can see what we're doing and then hit it. Shouldn't take us much more than an hour or two."

Sergeant Sam Jackson of the Korean Marine Corps' Deep Reconnaissance Company eyed the weather, sniffed the air, and glanced to his right where Bland was curled up under a white poncho liner dead asleep. "Your zoomie is going nowhere for a while." He smiled at Shake and shrugged. "Maybe best we wait. No foot patrols, so we should be OK. I'll take first watch."

On the trek through the mountains, Shake admired the stocky Korean sergeant who moved like a machine but didn't say much beyond what was necessary. What he did say was either a quick bark in Korean or a perfectly phrased comment in American English. It didn't take long for Shake to recognize a competent professional soldier and about as tough a man as any he'd ever seen operating in dangerous, difficult conditions. In the mission brief, he'd introduced himself with a shy smile, read the surprise on Shake's face, and filled in the blanks. "Dual Citizen. Dad was a soldier stationed at Camp Humphreys; Mom was working in the NCO Club. I went to school in LA for a while and then came back to Seoul, decided I liked Korea and joined the Marines—theirs, not yours."

"You do this kind of thing a lot, Sam?" Shake looked around their little hide-site at the Korean Marines who seemed perfectly relaxed, either already asleep or casually brushing snow and moisture off their weapons.

"We jump the fence all the time, but usually not so far north. My guys have a lot of time in the islands off the west coast in the Yellow Sea and areas just north of the DMZ, but it all comes down to the same drill: Either whack the NKs and run, or lay chilly in their backyard and keep an eye on them. They do the same thing to us—just not as well."

"Is that how come we haven't seen any foot patrols so far?" Shake could feel the heat from the winter *kimchee* igniting in his belly and crawling up his esophagus. The steam from his breath in the frigid air smelled horrible.

"It's a combination of things. The NKPA troops stationed out here aren't the cream of anybody's crop, and they don't get paid enough to get real excited about traipsing around looking for what's left of a crashed airplane in the cold. Add to that, the stupid bastards in Pyongyang probably have no idea it was a spy plane carrying classified gear. They'll get around to patrols when the weather clears or some hard-ass arrives to kick them out into the snow."

"Let's hope that doesn't happen anytime soon." Shake pulled his white poncho liner out of his rucksack and mashed the sack of thermite grenades into a pillow. "Wake me in two hours and I'll relieve you."

* * *

"We got a problem."

Shake snapped awake and sat up to see Sgt. Sam Jackson kneeling nearby, staring down the slope toward the crash site. He checked his watch. It was still an hour before what he'd calculated as nautical dawn, and there was no noise except for the muted sounds of the Korean Marines packing up their gear and weapons. It took him another few seconds to understand Jackson's concern. There was no wind and there was no snow. The weather had taken a decided change for the better—or worse from their perspective.

"When did it happen?" He crawled over to join Jackson who was monitoring a burst transmission on the encrypted radio that was the only link to their mission control. "About an hour ago." Jackson motioned for his radio man to pack up the unit and stood stretching his muscles. "Seemed like a good reason to break radio silence, so I asked for a quick update. The weather front blew out to sea. It's stormy off the coast, but here we got nothing but blue skies and pleasant conditions, perfect for helicopter operations and foot patrols."

Shake swept the surrounding hills for signs of daylight and glanced over at Bland who was sitting up looking distinctly groggy and bedraggled. "Better get your shit together, Doug. Weather's changed and we need to get moving in a hurry." Bland struggled to his feet and stood staring down-slope toward the crash site, pondering the new development.

"Sam, let's leave a couple of your guys up here on the high ground to listen for rotor blades and watch for patrol activity." Shake shrugged into his fighting gear and shouldered the sack of thermite grenades. "The rest of us will hustle down there and start searching for classified gear."

"I'm thinking we go with Plan B on the classified gear, Shake." Bland shrugged into his equipment and packed away the sensor unit. "It's up to you but I don't think we should fart around trying to recover anything at this point. Best burn it all and get the hell out of here."

"We start that many fires and somebody's gonna see the smoke in a hurry." Sgt. Jackson dispatched two of his Marines toward a high pinnacle off to their right where they would have excellent observation of the entire reservoir area. "I don't know if they've got helicopters, but it won't take long for that NKPA detachment at the power plant north of the reservoir to get here."

"Sergeant Bland's right on this one, Sam. We'll have to take our chances. We can't afford the time to sort through the wreckage, and if they get on our case, we don't want to be running for the coast carrying extra gear." Shake led the detachment down the slope toward the wreckage. "We'll do this by priority. Doug, you find the most important stuff and we'll burn that first."

Master Sergeant Doug Bland seemed completely recovered from the insertion ordeal as he sprinted from one piece of wreckage to another. None of the others understood the jargon he used to identify things that caught his eye, but they all responded to his direction and quickly slapped thermite grenades where he indicated. By full dawn, the area was blazing with intense flame and covered with a pall of black smoke that rose into the clear, cold air over the crash site.

"I think we got the critical stuff." Bland was scanning a laminated check-list in the pale light of the sun rising above the mountains to the east. He turned to Shake and pointed at a long wing section about 50 meters away from the blazing remains of the U-2 cockpit. "I need to make a second sweep and then we can burn the rest of it."

Shake checked the ammo bag and counted three thermite grenades remaining. He looked to the north and saw nothing in the air or on the ground on the other side of the Chosin Reservoir. Jackson was running back from a pile of electronic black boxes that he'd just ignited, and Shake caught his attention. "What do you think, Sam? One more sweep? Or head for the hills?"

Jackson glanced up toward the over-watch position and waved his arm to acknowledge a signal from his sentries. "No option, Shake. There's a helicopter approaching from the east!"

He heard the chop of the helicopter's rotors echoing off the surrounding mountains. It wouldn't be long before it reached the crash site. Any troops the bird might be ferrying would be on the ground before they could get back up the slope to their hide-site. Shake had to figure something out and he had to figure it out in a hurry. He pointed at a boulder formation about 30 meters from the burning crash site. "Sam, put your guys in position behind those rocks. If the helo lands and puts troops on the ground, fire 'em up!"

Master Sergeant Doug Bland was running for the rocks with the Korean Marines when Shake grabbed him and pulled him in the opposite direction. Bland didn't argue, and followed Shake with a burst of adrenaline powering his legs. They were charging through the snow toward an icy overhang Shake had spotted near a piece of flat, snow-covered ground on the edge of the crash site. He'd made enough combat assaults and helicopter insertions to know that if the pilots landed, they'd do it on level ground upwind of the smoke and flames. That's where Shake wanted to be. And if his short-fuse plan didn't work—well, at least he'd have Master Sergeant Bland close at hand.

Shake could see the helicopter coming in low and fast by the time they reached the area he hoped the pilots would chose for an LZ. The bird was an old Soviet Mi-8 and there were troops gawking out the cargo door. "Get your white poncho liner and pull it over you." Shake fumbled in his rucksack for his own poncho liner and pointed into the shadow cast by the overhang. "Get right back in there and hold on to the liner so the rotorwash doesn't blow it away."

He whipped his poncho liner over his head and snuggled in under the overhang beside Bland. It was crunch time. The Mi-8 was doing a low-level, low-speed pass over the crash-site. Shake had no doubt the pilots intended to land when the helo turned upwind with the nose pointed at the ground. He had to make a decision. Either Bland could cut it or he couldn't. If it turned out to be the latter, Shake didn't want to think about what he might have to do. He reached into the ammo bag and pulled out two of the remaining thermite grenades. Then he racked the bolt on the Swedish K submachine gun he'd chosen for the mission and shoved it toward Bland.

"Doug, listen to me. I know you're not trained for this kind of shit, but we're in a bind here. When that helo lands, Jackson and his Marines are gonna open up on them. The pilots will try to get the bird airborne, and we don't want that to happen. I'm gonna try to get a couple of these thermites into the helicopter, but I'll need a distraction. When I give the word, we take off and you spray the hell out of the cockpit area with this." Shake snapped the folding stock into place and handed the weapon to Bland who looked at the little nine-millimeter sub-gun like it was an alien artifact. "There's nothing to it, just point and shoot.

Long as you keep pressure on the trigger, she'll fire. All you gotta do is keep 'em busy for a little while."

"I'm your man." Bland picked up the Swedish K and pointed it in the direction of the helicopter floating in toward a landing in a shower of white rotor-wash. "And I'm as ready as I can be—under the circumstances." Shake admired the look of determination on the Air Force NCO's face and hoped he wouldn't have to use the pistol under his parka on anything but the North Koreans leaning out of the helicopter now settling on its landing gear. Guys like Master Sergeant Doug Bland— volunteers way the hell out of their element—deserved better.

The helo was carrying a standard ten-man NKPA rifle squad. They spread out and advanced on the burning wreckage with their AK-47's at the ready as the pilots kept the rotors turning with the engines in ground idle. It wouldn't take them long to pull pitch after Jackson's Marines engaged the dismounts. Shake shrugged free of his poncho liner and pulled the pins on two thermite grenades. He nodded once at Bland, and then surged out from under the overhanging snow ledge. He was plowing through knee-deep snow toward the helicopter when he saw rounds smack into the Plexiglas of the cockpit. Bland had the pilots' undivided attention and Shake could see the shocked look on their faces as they shouted into the radio mikes attached to their helmets. The Mi-8 Hip was spooling up and getting light on the gear as he lobbed the first thermite into the open cargo bay. He spun to the left and dunked the second grenade into an open ventilation panel next to the co-pilot who scrambled to retrieve the smoking missile.

Shake hit the ground, nearly buried in blowing snow, as the helicopter lifted into the air with its engine screaming and the rotors cracking at the thin, high-altitude air. He glanced to his right rear and saw Master Sergeant Bland following the departing helo with the blazing muzzle of the Swedish K. As the helo rose, Shake could see North Korean troops falling under Jackson's fire. He rolled onto his back and screamed for Bland to get down as the shuddering North Korean helicopter violently exploded and spun burning into a snow bank on the icy edge of the Chosin Reservoir.

The helicopter wreckage added more smoke and flame to the turmoil above the crash site. Shake was fairly confident the aircrew hadn't had time to radio details about what happened just before they died, but the huge plumes of black smoke would be easily seen from the ground. That meant the NKs would be launching more air assets and foot patrols to investigate. It was time for a very fast exfil and the quicker they got themselves hidden in the mountain passes, the better chance they'd have to make it back to the beach without being intercepted.

Sgt. Sam Jackson was checking the North Korean bodies that lay sprawled and leaking blood into the snow. The Korean Marines had been deadly accurate and thorough in engaging the squad from the helicopter. "Got 'em all," he said to Shake and motioned for his men to start up the slope, "but it won't be long before there's a bunch more out here hunting for us." The good news—if there was any at this point—was that the submarine could hang around for as long as it took for Shake and his team to make it back to the beach. The North Koreans would spend their time and assets searching for infiltrators on the ground, and the reported weather out at sea would likely keep their coastal patrols in harbor for a while. The key was to move quickly and avoid being spotted from the air. They could figure out the rendezvous details once they got close to the beach. Assuming they made it that far.

* * *

The exfil trek through the mountains was torture for everyone. Under better circumstances, Shake and Sgt. Jackson would have preferred to wait and move at night, but they had to put as much distance as possible between themselves and the crash site which was crawling with NK patrols by the time they reached the first range of rugged peaks surrounding the Chosin Reservoir. In daylight, they had to move cautiously and avoid leaving tracks that would point toward their destination at the coast. By the time they'd reached the mountain passes, the air was buzzing with low-flying helicopters and high-flying fixed-wing reconnaissance aircraft.

Sgt. Jackson showed everyone how to rig their white poncho liners as capes that could be quickly deployed as snow camouflage when aircraft threatened. His Marines were experts at finding routes that wouldn't leave tracks in fresh snow. They were just as good at covering tracks when they had to break trail. Everyone walked as fast as possible in file, and when they could see their own tracks, Jackson's Marines hauled boulders into play and rolled them back along the trail. Rolling rocks were nothing unusual in the mountains and they covered manmade tracks as well as a road-grader.

Everyone was thoroughly exhausted by nightfall, but Shake knew they'd have to keep going. There was no time for rest and the dark would give them a chance to move at top speed. Master Sergeant Bland seemed to be holding up well. Either he'd become acclimated or sheer adrenaline was pushing him to new levels of endurance. As they crested a peak and started down the other side, Sgt. Jackson spotted an overhang and signaled for a halt. He maneuvered toward Shake with his radio man in tow.

"Should be good transmission up here," Jackson checked his watch. "Maybe we make the rendezvous point on time or close to it if we push on through the night. I'm gonna send a pos-rep and let 'em know we're on the way."

Shake nodded and snapped on a red-lens penlight to check what he thought was their position on his map. "It'll be a hard push but at least we won't have to worry about covering our tracks. I'd damn sure like to be out of here before daylight." If they stayed lucky, they might be able to make the beach, recover the boats they'd buried in sand and shale rock, and get out to sea before dawn. Letting the sub know they were OK and outbound was a good idea. At least the boat would know to hang around looking for them even if they were late by a couple of hours.

Jackson got an acknowledgement to his burst transmission and waved for his Marines to start moving. Shake caught up with Master Sergeant Bland and jabbed him on the shoulder. "You did real good back there, Doug. I owe you a beer and a bunch of abject apologies for all the stupid shit I've said about Air Force weenies in the past."

"I'll take the beer, but you can keep the apologies." Bland handed Shake the Swedish K he'd been carrying since the fight at the crash site and shook his head. "I'll take Air Force weenie all day long if I never have to do something like this again."

Shake was trudging along near the back of the file, ignoring the fire in his thigh muscles and mentally sketching out the medal recommendation he intended to make for Bland, when the signal to halt was passed and everyone dropped to a knee. After a couple of tense minutes, Sgt. Jackson maneuvered back along the file and knelt beside him. "Point man spotted something up ahead in the pass." Jackson pointed toward a flashing amber light on a peak to their left. "That's likely a beacon the NKs put in as a navigation aid. It wasn't there on the way in."

"Is that a problem?" Shake stared at the beacon and then checked his map with his little penlight. "We're only a couple of hours from the beach."

"Maybe; maybe not." Sgt. Jackson looked at the spot on the map that Shake indicated. "That beacon was probably installed sometime today. The NKs don't usually put stuff like that out here and then just leave it on auto-pilot. Could be they left a maintenance or security crew with it."

"Can't we detour around?"

"Not if we intend to make the beach before dawn. We wind up having to spend an extra day and we might not make it to the rendezvous at all."

Shake checked his map. Off to the left of the beacon site, it showed a jumble of tightly-packed contour lines—a sheer drop. If they bore off to the right, they could avoid passing too close, but it would be a long, hard trek. "Yeah, I see it. We go for the pass and we make the beach tonight. We go around and we'll be stuck hiding all day with bad guys following our tracks." Shake snapped off the penlight and made his decision. "You take the lead. Let's give it a shot."

About halfway through the pass, Sgt. Jackson's point man was challenged by a North Korean sentry. Everyone froze as NKPA sentry and South Korean Marine engaged in a tense conversation. And then the night exploded with muzzle flashes. All the incoming fire was small arms from the left side of the pass. In the staccato light, Shake saw Sgt. Jackson sprinting forward, firing on the run, then watched him fall next to two motionless forms in the middle of the trail.

He grabbed the nearest Korean Marine and pulled him toward the left. Bland was prone in the snow as rounds whipped over his head and caromed off the rocks to their rear. "Doug, stay down! Don't move unless you hear from me!" From his perspective, sprinting to the left of the trail with the Korean Marine chugging along behind him, Shake could see the NKs had formed a firing line parallel to the trail. He could see no muzzle flashes above or below that line. If they could turn the flank from slightly above, they might be able to get all the shooters in one quick sweep. Shake stopped and tried to count the enemy weapons firing into the darkness. He estimated no more than six AKs with the shooters practically shoulder to shoulder. He pointed toward a rocky crag and outlined his plan with no idea whether the Korean Marine at his side spoke English or not.

"We'll go for those rocks right there. You open up on them and I'll sweep down the line." Shake made a firing motion with his weapon. The man was an experienced professional. Even if he didn't understand the words, he'd grasp the concept quickly enough. They sprinted across the trail and started climbing.

When they reached the rocks, the NK shooters were still burning through magazines. In the still mountain air, Shake could distinctly hear the snap of magazines being replaced and bolts being racked to the rear. He made out only two weapons returning fire and that meant the team had taken casualties in the initial exchange. He pointed toward a gap in the rock formation and motioned firing. The Korean Marine got the picture and maneuvered to set up his best shot. Shake snapped a fresh magazine into the Swedish K and set the bolt to fire when he squeezed the trigger.

The Korean Marine raised his hand to let Shake know he was ready, and then began firing quick, accurate shots into the backs of the North Korean shooters. Shake bolted away from the rocks and began to trigger short bursts into the NK troops as he moved behind and parallel to their firing line. It was over in moments. Between his shots and the fire from his cover man, it looked like they got all the NK troops. Shake swept the hillside above the pass for stragglers as his new partner methodically fired insurance rounds into each of the bodies. Shake tumbled down off the low ridge and ran for the place where he'd left Master Sergeant Doug Bland, hoping he'd find him alive and intact.

Bland was alive but not quite intact. He was hugging his left leg and fumbling with a first-aid pack. "Felt like a snake bit me." Bland tore at the bloody patch on his trousers and probed at the flesh underneath. "Something hit me hard just after you guys left. I was too fucking scared to move." Shake snapped on his penlight to take a look. The entry wound was just below the knee and looked like a keyhole from a ricochet. "Probably a round glanced off the rocks." He took a battle dressing out of the first-aid pack and helped Bland bind the wound. "Can you walk?"

Bland stood, slowly put pressure on his left leg and winced. "Hurts like a sonofabitch but I don't think it hit anything vital. I can walk but it ain't gonna be very fast." Shake just nodded and headed up the trail to find Sgt. Jackson. They were now officially in deep shit, and he was afraid the news wasn't going to get any better.

Jackson and another man were busy stripping the uniforms and equipment from two fellow Korean Marines who lay motionless along the side of the trail as Shake approached. Jackson pointed at the man who had been on point. "Corporal Park never should have tried it. He's from Pohang down on the southeast coast. That sentry heard his accent and knew we were no lost patrol. He sensed bullshit and opened up. Corporal Joon was coming up to give him a hand and got nailed in the effort." It was a moment before Shake noticed Jackson favoring his right side and spotted a dark stain showing through his snow parka.

"Looks like you're hit, Sam. How bad is it?"

"Don't know for sure." Sgt. Jackson probed at the stain and winced. "Cracked a couple of ribs, but I don't think the round penetrated. We need to push on."

"No chance carrying your guys, Sam. Plus you're hit and Sgt. Bland took a ricochet through the leg. We better look for some place to hole up."

"No, we push on. The NKs will be all over this area at dawn. We need to make the beach before daylight. And there is no need to carry the dead." Sgt. Jackson said something in Korean and his two remaining Marines began to maneuver the naked bodies of their dead comrades into a pile. "We should have one thermite left." He pointed at Shake's ammo bag. "Let me have it."

When the survivors were ready to move with one of the Korean Marines supporting Master Sergeant Bland, Shake nodded silently at Sgt. Jackson. He knew what was coming and he didn't really want to see it, but ignoring it seemed disrespectful. He stood quietly and watched as Jackson pulled the pin on the thermite grenade and then shoved it between the two bodies stacked one on top of the other. When he pulled his hand away, the safety lever snapped and in seconds the dead men erupted into a funeral pyre.

"A necessary procedure." Sgt. Jackson watched the blaze consuming his casualties for a moment and then started moving. "Minus the uniform and gear, one Korean looks just like another. Just a couple of crispy-critters and nobody's the wiser." There was nothing more to say and a lot of miles to travel before daylight. Shake fell in on the other side of Master Sergeant Bland and helped him limp as fast as possible down the long mountainside toward the beach.

"That's about the size of it." Shake gathered glasses to refill and started toward the bar. "We made the beach just before dawn and found the boats intact. We sank one on the other side of the surf line and puttered around in the other until the sub spotted us. The weather in the Sea of Japan was genuine dog-shit but they finally got us aboard about five miles out, and we headed back south."

"I never heard anything about that." Chan looked across the coffee table and shrugged at Bayer.

"No, you didn't." Bayer rose and went to help Shake mix drinks. "What you and everyone else heard over the next couple of weeks was the North Koreans bitching and moaning about the South Koreans staging a raid on their territory. Not word one about the aircraft, probably because there wasn't enough left of it to make an issue over, and because Kim Jong-Il saw there was more leverage to be had by accusing his southern brothers of horrible war crimes. They released a bunch of pictures, including the burned bodies, and got a little play in the international press. It was nothing unusual for the place and time. Most importantly, they didn't get any of the classified gear—thanks to Shake and his guys."

Shake carried his drink toward the fireplace and slumped into a chair. "And Master Sergeant Bland got the Meritorious Service Medal—plus a Purple Heart. I still hear from him every once in a while. Leg healed fine. He's working for the FAA out in Colorado someplace."

Shake raised his glass. "And here's to Sergeant Sam Jackson of the Korean Marines. May Buddha bless him wherever he is these days."

* * *

Bayer left after another hour. What he wanted Shake to do was clear, but by no means a done deal as far as Chan Dwyer Davis was concerned. They talked it over with decreasing heat for another two hours before Chan gave up and stalked toward the bedroom.

"You're gonna do what you're gonna do, Shake Davis." She turned at the threshold and pointed a finger at him. "But I want it on the record that I'm against this stupid deal—and if you get yourself killed or captured, I'll never forgive your dumb ass." The slamming bedroom door sounded like a gunshot and sent Bear sprinting for comfort in Shake's lap.

"So what are we gonna do, partner?" Shake maneuvered into a more comfortable position beneath his over-size dog and ran his fingernails down Bear's long, bony spine. "Do we help a buddy or ignore all that and insure domestic tranquility?"

Shake was still trying to interpret the look in Bear's liquid brown eyes when he finally fell asleep.

"Some ops are deep-cover, off the radar, full-black..." Bayer plopped a cardboard box on the rented kitchen table of the CIA safe house located just outside the back gate of the Quantico Marine Base and collapsed into a chair. "...and then there's this deal."

Shake slid into an adjacent seat and began to pick at the flaps on the box. "No support from your outfit—is that what you're trying to say?"

"C'mon, Shake. I'm not asking you to do something like this completely on your own hook." Bayer tore a sheet of paper from his notebook and slid it across the table. "Memorize this number and then destroy the paper. There's a new type of cell phone we've developed—untraceable and hard as hell to monitor in a certain band-width. That number is my phone. Yours is in the package. It's state of the art. You won't be getting any no-signal indications with that thing, and the battery is rated for twelve hours continuous use. You can contact me directly either by voice or text. If you're in a crowd or worried about being overheard, there's a list of phrases in the package that will mean nothing to anyone but me and you. When you really need something, I'll bust my butt to get it for you."

"Can I use it to call anyone else?" Shake opened the package and pawed through the contents. Beside the high-tech phone, all the rest appeared to be documents of one kind or another.

"Call anyone you want. We'll pick up the tab. It works just like a regular cell with international dialing capabilities except when you call my number. If you do call anyone besides me, the call can be traced or monitored, so be careful using it."

Shake set the phone on the table and rummaged around in the paperwork until he found a well-thumbed standard U.S. passport. He flipped to the ID page and recognized the picture as a duplicate of the one in his regular passport. All the other personal data was genuine, including the first name he hated and his lack of middle initial. "So, for the purposes of this exercise I'm Sheldon NMI Davis of—Port Huron, Michigan?"

"Back story is already in place. If anybody checks, you're a consultant with the Blue Water Area Transit System—a retired military guy and logistician hoping to peddle your expertise to South Korean ferry services. There are plenty of them up and down both coasts, so you've got a credible reason to travel anywhere."

"Except north of the DMZ—which is where you want me to go."

"You're gonna meet a guy in Seoul. Name and rundown on him is in the package. He works for us but his cover is ship-building. He's negotiating with the Chinese for a commercial contract to build container ships in Korean shipyards. He'll get you to Beijing where he'll introduce you to one of our PLA contacts. That guy gets you delivered to our drone base up on the Yalu. That's where the fun begins."

"Uh-huh. And I'm telling you right now, my friend, that fun is not going to involve me going into North Korea by my lone-some. I intend to pick up some experienced help."

"There's no way you can take any U.S. assets, ours or mili-tary, into North Korea with you. That's a firm no-go and non-negotiable. Hell, Shake, if we could afford a risk like that, we'd just cobble together a SEAL Team or some SF guys or some of our Clandestine Services people and go look for Mike. We can't do it that way—and you know why given the current Admin-istration."

"I get the picture, but I'm still not going across the Yalu alone. I've got some ideas that will keep your nuts out of the fire, but let's get something straight here. I'm doing this my way or not at all. The only reason we're having this conversation is because it's Mike and he might be in serious trouble. Everything else is a side-issue as far as I'm concerned."

Bayer stared at Shake for a long moment and then nodded. There was no wiggle-room and time was getting tight. The longer they waited and argued, the more likely Stokey would wind up either dead or captured. There was still no word from him, and the people at the drone site reported no contact of any kind. UAV flights over the Chosin Reservoir area had been increased, but the bird spotted nothing that might provide a clue to Stokey's status.

"We still haven't heard anything from Mike." Bayer stood and made his way toward a coffee pot on the kitchen counter. "One of the Koreans he took with him was carrying an encrypted burst-transmission radio. They've been monitoring the freq twenty-four-seven: Nothing from them and no response to calls. I hope to Christ you don't wind up finding three frozen stiffs."

"Mike's not dead—at least not yet."

"How do you know that?"

"I called his sister Barbara down in Texas. She hasn't heard from him."

"Stokey is gonna call his sister on the phone if he's in trouble?"

"It's a deal Mike set up a while ago—just after the Peleliu thing, in fact. He paid some guy—probably somebody from your outfit—to build him a little satellite transponder. He carries it everywhere. If he's in really deep shit, he pushes a button and Barbara gets a message that says something like "having a wonderful time; wish you were here." The message contains his GPS coordinates. Barbara gets that message on her cell, she calls me. If he hasn't mashed that button yet, he's OK."

"Does it work the other way around? Can she send a message asking for his location?"

"Nope. Mike didn't want anything like that. It's an emergency beacon only. No two-way communication, no text, and only the one message he can send. I'll be talking to Barbara regularly and she'll let me know if she gets any kind of hit from the transponder."

"You'd think he'd have that thing hooked up to us. We can do more for him in an emergency than his sister, for Christ's sake."

"It's Mike, so go figure. You said it yourself last night. He plays close to the edge. There's probably a whole bunch of shit he's got set up that you don't know about. What he told Barbara was to contact me immediately if she got the message. You can read what you want into that but I think he set it up so you wouldn't jump off the deep end and interfere with what he wanted to do."

"That sounds about right." Bayer checked his watch. "I've got to get moving. You're booked on a KAL flight, business class, Dulles to Seoul in the morning. Boarding pass and flight details are in the package." Bayer shrugged into his coat and paused at the door. "And I've already heard from Chan. That girl has got some mouth on her when she's pissed off about something."

"She understands why I'm doing this." Shake shook Bayer's hand and opened the door. "That's not to say she's real happy about it—but she understands."

"Do me one last favor." Bayer stepped outside the safe house and glanced up and down the suburban street. "Keep the DIA inquiries to a bare minimum. That kind of thing can set off alarm bells and we don't want that, do we?"

Shake shut the door and picked up his new cell phone to give it a test. Chan needed the number and she just might have had some luck finding the man he wanted to see in Seoul.

* * *

"Are you still pissed?" Shake reached across the dinner table and squeezed Chan's hand. He'd made one of their favorite meals in hopes of decreasing the pressure on the home front. She hadn't said much all day and he decided not to press the issue for fear of making things worse. He'd said what he needed to say about loyalty and friendship last night and that hadn't ended well.

"I'm not pissed off, Shake. I'm worried." She reached down to pet Bear who was sensing the tension and moping around the dinner table. "In fact, frightened is a better word. I don't want you to feel like your Man Card is being threatened, but you're too old for this stuff. What I'm afraid of is that you'll let your balls override your brains. You're planning to go into some really bad areas in really bad weather and the North Koreans are not what you'd call predictable players."

"You've been around me long enough to understand I know my limits, Chan. You don't survive doing the kind of stuff I used to do without knowing where the line is."

"Used to do is the operative term." She picked up a scrap of sirloin with her unoccupied hand and made Bear sit up for it. "I just don't understand why Bayer can't get someone else to solve his problem."

"You mean someone younger, right?"

"I mean someone who is not my husband; someone who can be relied on not to write a check his ass can't cash just because he's trying to help a friend."

"Here are a couple of points to ponder." He reached for her other hand and hoped she could read the love in his eyes. "Except for eighty-year-old Korean War vets, I'm one of the only guys who have ever been in that area, so I know the terrain and I know the tricks to surviving in it. I'm also the guy who knows Mike best and that means I'm the guy most likely to find him in a hurry. Plus—I'm very much in love with you and more than a little motivated to survive this thing so I can come home to you. I won't take any stupid chances and I'm hoping I can add a little insurance thanks to the digging you did for me this morning."

"What makes you think Sam Jackson would be willing to go back into North Korea with you?" Chan was showing hints of a smile and he could feel some of the tension draining out of her grip on his hands. "Our sources in Seoul said he's been out of the military for ten years. He's working for the South Korean tourist industry, based down around Pusan. He's probably got a wife and a bunch of kids."

"I'm not suggesting he'd go along personally, but a guy like Sam Jackson is never really out of the military, Chan. You read the report. He's mostly involved in setting up visits and reunions for Korea vets coming in from the States. I'm betting he's still hard-wired into the South Korean military establishment. He'll know some reliable operators willing to go with me."

"And I'm betting it will wind up being two old poops trying to relive youthful adventures. Just promise me faithfully that you'll look before you leap, Shake. Mike might check in or turn up at the UAV site by the time you get everything set up to go looking for him."

"If that's the case, I'll eat some *kimchee*, drink a little *soju* and catch the first available fight home."

"Is that a promise?"

"It is. And if you'll help me finish packing, I'd like to engage in a little bedroom exercise to tone my aging muscles for the ordeal that lies ahead."

They retired to the bedroom, but Shake had to finish his packing in the morning before Chan drove him to Dulles.

Changjin (Chosin) Reservoir, Democratic People's Republic of (North) Korea

At dusk, Mike Stokey crawled out of the snow-hole on the high ridge north of the Chosin Reservoir, and focused his binoculars on the lights of the little settlement in the valley between his perch and the hydroelectric plant he'd been observing for the past two days. The rumble in his stomach told him he'd have to risk sending Lee back down there tonight. He'd feel safer sending someone else on a second trip to buy food from the villagers, but there was nobody else. He certainly couldn't go, and his only other option was buried under a ton of snow and ice in the mountains to the west. The avalanche that killed one of his two NK assets and buried their only radio beyond retrieval almost made Mike scrub the mission, but he decided to push on and see if he could make sense of what he was hearing from people on the CIA payroll in Pyongyang.

Sun Myung Lee crawled out of the rancid hole, pissed noisily into a nearby snow bank, and flopped down beside the American CIA operative who was a very valuable man. Lee didn't much care whether the red-headed American found what he was looking for in this desolate, dangerous area where a reasonable man would not go, but he was willing to do a lot of unreasonable, potentially fatal things for the money he was being paid. Over the past two months, he'd earned more money than he could make in a lifetime teaching school in the little village on the banks of the Yalu. In a few more months—assuming he survived—Lee would be able to pay the high price the smugglers demanded to get him and his family safely out of North Korea. His education and his ability to speak English would land him a good job in the south, just as it had landed him this lucrative job working for Mr. Mike Stokey.

"What do you think, Lee? We need more food. Can you make another trip down to the village tonight, or is that too risky?" While he waited for an opinion, Stokey eyed the low clouds scudding across the reservoir pushed by an arctic wind. They had adequate cold weather gear and clothing, but if the temperature dropped much below the current frigid levels or if a big snowstorm blew down from the surrounding mountains, they might be trapped out here for weeks. He reached under his parka and felt for the little transponder he wore on a chain around his neck. If that happened, he might have to send the signal to Barbara. She'd call Shake Davis, but Stokey had no earthly idea what good that would do in present circumstances.

"I think it's safe enough for me to buy some rice and vegetables tonight." Lee rolled over in the snow and pointed toward the settlement. "There is a merchant who lives there near the market place. He was more than happy to see the extra money."

"No questions asked?"

"Of course he asked questions. This is a small village and strangers are not common. I told him I was a driver on one of the trucks we've been watching. My accent is the same as his and I asked him not to talk about his new customer if he wanted me to return with more cash. He completely understood the need for discretion."

"Damn, Lee—you speak excellent English." Stokey handed over a roll of North Korean *won*. "Where'd you learn?"

Lee counted out a few bills and handed the rest back to Stokey. "My father was a language scholar. He worked for the state news agency in Pyongyang. He always said knowing English would pay dividends someday. It appears he was correct."

"Is your father still around?"

"He is still around Korea—buried somewhere near Pyongyang, I believe. He was executed along with my mother for translating a Christian bible. I was in the Army at the time."

"And you wound up teaching school in that village...what's it called?"

"Uiju—on the banks of the Yalu River and well away from Pyongyang. There was no future for me as the son of so-called traitors. They tossed me out of the Army, but my commander was kind enough to let me get lost in a hurry. I wound up in Uiju where my grandfather lives, and kept what you would call a very low profile. They needed a school teacher and I could serve, so the village elders decided to take a chance on me. I can't say they were sad to see me leave."

"How come you didn't make a run for the south?"

"It's not so easy, Mr. Stokey. The people of the south are very suspicious of anyone who arrives unannounced and unexpected from the north—especially a former soldier. I have a wife now—and a son. When I go, I'll take them with me. That requires a great deal of influence or money. I have none of the former but you are kindly providing the latter."

Stokey checked his watch and glanced up at the snow-filled clouds gathering over the Chosin Reservoir. It would be full dark in about 30 minutes and they'd likely be digging out from under a butt-load of new snow by morning. "You know anything about science, Lee?"

"I was a technician officer in a missile unit. We worked with what I believe you call SCUDs. I was never very good at it, but I knew the basic scientific principles of missile ballistics. Is that helpful?"

"I don't know. Did you ever hear of something called a Marx generator?"

"I am certainly familiar with Marx—Karl Marx, one of the big thinkers in communism, but I thought he was mainly an economist. Did he also work in the physical sciences?"

"Beats me—but the people who are telling me things out of Pyongyang are all excited about something called Marx generators—and they claim that's what these trucks have been hauling away from Changjin." Stokey pondered some of the information he'd gotten from the female technician at the UAV site. She said variations of the Marx generator were sometimes used to generate Electro-Magnetic Pulses when the Air Force wanted to check survivability of various aircraft components in a nuclear attack.

"And what is a Marx generator used for?"

Stokey shrugged. He didn't understand the science and he was lost in the ozone by the time the technician started rattling on about things like flux-compression generators but he understood a thing that could be used to generate EMP could be used as a weapon. He'd always connected EMP with nuclear detonations, but the techie said there was something called non-nuclear EMP which might explain why the UAV was getting no nuke readings around Chosin.

"Apparently, it's a device that can produce tremendous electric power in a single surge." Stokey re-focused his binoculars on the plant entrance where a first shift of sentries was trudging out into the blowing snow.

"Changjin is a hydroelectric generating plant," Lee said. "That would seem to fit. What does a Marx generator look like?"

"I haven't got a clue, Lee. But I'm gonna find out before we leave here."

Seoul, Republic of (South) Korea

The differences in efficiency and ambience between the oppressive, dingy international terminal at Dulles and the slick, traveler-friendly atmosphere at Seoul International was refreshing after nearly fourteen hours in the air. Shake cleared through arrivals with nothing more than a cursory glance at his documents by the paramilitary South Korean immigration agents. He picked up his bag, turned over his arrival paperwork, and headed for a sign that advertised buses and the airport taxi rank. It was a completely different and much friendlier experience than his last arrival at the old Kimpo Airfield when he was travelling baggage class as an active duty member of a Marine Corps Mobile Training Team.

He looked over the hotel courtesy buses loading tons of baggage brought into Korea by citizens fresh off a stateside shopping vacation, and decided he'd rather make his way into Seoul by taxi. He had a card inscribed with the name and address of his hotel written out in Korean, but the slick little hustler running the taxi rank spoke English.

"Welcome to Seoul. Intercontinental? Good choice." The cab honcho blew a whistle loudly enough to make Shake wince and pointed at a vehicle about halfway down the rank. "Cash or credit card is no problem. Tip's up to you." The hyper little character snatched at the door of a late model KIA and held out his hand. Shake tossed his bag into the cab and handed over a U.S. ten-spot. Some things had changed drastically since the last time he was in Korea, but everyone was still on the hustle.

While the cab driver banged gears and swerved his way through airport traffic, Shake pulled out his contact list and cell phone. Mr. Pak Chun Song of the U.S. Central Intelligence Agency via Daewoo Shipbuilding and Marine Engineering answered after three rings. "It's Shake Davis, sir. I'm headed for the Intercontinental Hotel."

"Welcome to Seoul, Mr. Davis. I've been expecting to hear from you. Why don't you get settled and we'll meet in the morning? Is this a good number for you?"

"It's my mobile phone. I'll have it on all the time while I'm here. I'm looking forward to meeting you in person."

"Are you OK for breakfast or lunch tomorrow?"

"Breakfast would be fine. I think we should get started as soon as possible. What time would be good for you?"

"I'll call you at eight in the morning, if that's not too early. We can eat and get started on your itinerary. How's that?"

"I'll order room service and see you in the morning. Thanks for your kindness."

Shake punched off the call and sat back to marvel at the changes in the area since the last time he'd been in Korea. With a little squint at the neon as they rolled into midtown Seoul, it was easy to believe he was approaching Times Square in downtown Manhattan.

* * *

Sam Jackson was more than a little shocked when Shake struggled through the phone tree at the Korean Tourist Agency office in Pusan and finally got him on the phone. In fact, Shake had to discreetly refer to a few details of their last time together before the former Korean Marine believed he was actually talking to his old American comrade on the line from Seoul. They exchanged small talk for a while, and Shake discovered that Chan was right about his domestic situation. Jackson was married and had two teenage kids. The girl was studying computer science in Seoul and the boy was in his second year at the Korean Naval Academy at Chinhae. Sam had left active service as a major six years earlier, but his son was bound to carry on the family tradition as a Korean Marine officer.

Shake offered to fly down to Pusan for a visit, indicating that he had some matters to discuss, but Sam Jackson wouldn't hear of it. He insisted that he needed to fly up to Seoul on business anyway. He'd catch a flight in the morning and meet Shake for lunch at the hotel. "If you are planning to bring some veterans over for a reunion, Shake, I'm your man. I've still got some good contacts in the military here and I can set up some very interesting things for you."

"It's something like that, Sam. It would be great to team up with you again." Shake hung up happy to hear that he was right about Jackson's contacts. For what he wanted to do, they'd likely need some high-level help.

* * *

Pak Chun Song arrived shortly after a liveried waiter rolled a breakfast service cart into the room. Shake shook his hand and poured coffee for them. The South Korean agent took a seat at the breakfast cart and pulled a chromium device from the inside pocket of his jacket. He placed the little box near a tureen of scrambled eggs and pressed a button. He drummed his nails on the table for a few seconds and then nodded. "White noise," he said. "This hotel is pretty safe but you learn after a while in Korea that it's best to take no chances. We can talk now."

"I appreciate the help, Mister...what do I call you? Pak or Song?"

"I go by Pete—Pete Pak when I'm doing business. The other stuff is too hard to explain for people who aren't brought up in the culture."

"I guess you've gotten the brief from Bayer?" Shake spooned eggs onto two plates and handed one to his visitor. "I'd like to get your take on a few things that have got me a little confused."

"I'll try to help." Pete Pak sniffed at his eggs and motioned for Shake to continue.

"My wife is a former military intelligence officer now working for DIA, so she's fairly savvy about these things. We got to talking before I left the States. She thinks maybe the Chinese are playing both sides from the middle on this North Korean situation. What's your take?"

Pak thought for a few long seconds, looking over his shoulder at the door of the hotel room as if he half expected someone to come charging through it. Then he lowered his voice, re-checked the white noise transmitter and leaned over the breakfast cart. "Your good wife is fairly perceptive if that's what she thinks. Let me give you a little background. On the sur-face—in showcases like the Six-Party Talks—China makes noises like it doesn't want a nuclear-armed North Korea on its borders. The real story is a whole hell of a lot more complex. The Chinese civilian leadership loves the fact that the west is shitting peach-pits over a nuclear-armed North Korea."

Shake frowned and nodded. It was beginning to sound like Chan had it figured correctly. Pak picked up the narrative. "Look at it this way and it's not hard to understand. As long as North Korea can threaten with nukes, America keeps pumping aid into South Korea and that keeps the hope of a re-united Korea pretty much out of the question which is just right for the Chinese. So, Beijing makes public noises like they are trying to keep a lid on Kim Jong Il. They come off like progressive peacemakers—and that gives them increased leverage with the rest of the world in things like trade balances, currency manipu-lation, human rights questions—not to mention Taiwan."

"And China gets away with running that scam..." Shake poured more coffee and thought it over for a moment. "...because the U.S. Administration is not paying proper atten-tion, right? China gains a military-strategic advantage while Washington focuses on more immediate problems—like Iraq, Afghanistan, Iran and counter-terrorism."

"It's hard to focus on a tiger in the forest when you've got a pissed-off lion in your front yard." Pak added pepper, dug into the eggs, and uncovered a plate of crisp bacon. "If that's what your wife told you she's right on the money. Too damn bad the right people aren't listening to smart observers like her."

"I'll tell Chan she got the nod from an expert. How do you want to play this current situation?"

"I'm working on a contract to build container ships here in Korea for some Chinese customers. When we've got the clear-ances set, we'll catch a flight to Beijing and have dinner with a senior PLA contact. He's PLAN and the Chinese Navy observer on the ship-building deal. The military in China has got its fingers in everything, so a meet with him won't draw too much attention. I'm not sure exactly how it will pan out, but he's agreed to get you up to the site on the Yalu."

Shake bit into a slice of buttered toast and decided he didn't have much choice but to trust whatever Bayer and Pak had set up. "And you're fairly confident this guy won't just turn me in for a promotion or a little leverage with his seniors?"

"No guarantees in this business, Shake. But this Chinese Navy Senior Captain—Ming Yao Chi is his name, by the way—is both patriot and pragmatist. He's not in it for money. I spent a lot of time developing a relationship with him. He can be touchy—but the bottom line is that he wants his country to succeed and prosper. He figures the best way to make that happen is to get away from all the communist dogma and keep China moving toward a position of influence in the global economy. That's how I got to him initially. I convinced him things like this shipbuilding deal would make China a bigger player in seagoing commerce."

"How come a patriot like that cooperates with an American intelligence operation inside Chinese territory? If it's not money, what is it?"

"Senior Captain Ming Yao Chi happens to hate North Koreans. I don't know exactly why but it has something to do with his family. Apparently one or more of the Ming Yao Chi clan spent time as military advisors to the North Koreans, and it was not a pleasant experience. You mention North Korea to him and the heat in the room goes up rapidly. My guess is he thinks anything that's bad for North Korea is good for China. We pitched the idea to him by showing him some very convincing evidence that Pyongyang was making progress in weaponizing their nukes."

"And we took the risk of staging a drone base in China based on the sentiments of a... what? Senior Captain in the Chinese Navy is about the equivalent of a lower-half rear admiral, right?"

"He may be only a Senior Captain in the Chinese Navy, but Ming Yao Chi is well-connected and influential throughout the PLA. The way I figure it from watching him maneuver is that he's essentially the errand boy or mechanic for a bunch of more senior PLA guys who share similar sentiments about North Korea and a basic distrust of their own bureaucrats. Plays like a win-win so far."

"Well, Pete, I'm gonna have to take your word for it and trust your judgment. When do you want to leave for Beijing?"

"I'm working on your visa now. You'll go in as a consultant on my staff. Probably take the better part of two days to complete the paperwork and pay the necessary bribes."

"That works for me. I'm due to meet an old friend here in Seoul this afternoon. He may be able to help with what I need to do."

"Hold it right there." Pak held up a hand and smiled. "This is a need-to-know deal. The less I know about what you're doing once you reach the site the better. And I wouldn't recommend you share your plans with Captain Ming Yao Chi. You know the drill. The more compartmented these things are the safer it is for all involved."

"Noted." Shake refilled their coffee cups and once again pondered what he'd been worrying about ever since he boarded the plane at Dulles. He really didn't have a plan to tell anyone about even if he wanted. He was hoping Sam Jackson would help him come up with something that would work. He needed to get on with this thing and find Mike before the North Koreans did.

After Pete Pak left with a promise to call as soon as the Chinese visa was settled, Shake made a call to Stokey's sister. There was still no word from Mike or his emergency transponder. Barbara noted Shake's new number and promised to call, anytime night or day, the moment she heard anything. By noon on his first day in Seoul, Shake decided there was nothing more for him to do until he could talk to Sam Jackson and formulate some kind of plan. He locked his passport and a few other sensitive documents in the room safe and headed for the hotel bar to meet Sam Jackson and see if OB Lager was as good as he remembered.

W hen he returned to the observation post, Lee carried a burlap bag half-full of sticky rice, turnips, winter *kimchee*, and dried sweet potatoes. He also had an interesting question that he posed inside their rank snow-hole as Stokey lit a fire big enough to make the frozen food chewable and small enough to keep the roof from melting.

"Why would the North Korean Navy be visiting the hydroelectric plant at Changjin?"

"Navy? I don't know." Stokey bit off a piece of sweet potato and thought it over for a moment. "We're a long way from the ocean or any port out here. What makes you ask?"

"Two more big trucks arrived while I was down in the village." Lee massaged a ball of rice, popped it into his mouth and chewed vigorously. "They were accompanied by a staff car. In the staff car were two senior NK Navy officers. I recognized the uniforms and collar tabs."

"They didn't spot you, did they?"

"No. I was busy with the merchant who told me the Navy officers sometimes buy liquor from him. This is not their first visit to Changjin. The merchant thinks the officers are some kind of electricians. He has heard them talking about technical things."

"What kind of things? Did he say?"

"He did not say and I did not think it was safe to ask too many questions. His considered opinion is that the Navy officers have something to do with electrical power problems, and that's why he doesn't think it unusual for them to be visiting the electrical power plant. I don't agree."

"Why not?" Stokey was listening intently and trying to mate this new information with the tip about Marx generators he'd gotten from reliable sources in Pyongyang. If large-scale electrical generators were being manufactured at the Chosin site and shipped somewhere for some reason, what did the North Korean Navy have to do with it? Something was not right; something was glimmering around the edges of his perception, but he couldn't bring it into focus. "Maybe the best electrical power experts just happen to be Navy officers and they've been sent out here to deal with some problem."

"It doesn't work that way in the NKPA, Mr. Stokey." Lee poured melted snow water to make tea and dug in his pack for sugar. "If the Navy is visiting Changjin, it's because they have a specific interest in something that's happening here. Otherwise, it would be civilian technicians. I believe whatever has been leaving Changjin in trucks belongs to the Navy, and these officers have come to check on progress—or lack of it if that is the case."

Mike Stokey accepted a cup of steaming sweet tea and thought for a moment. Then he reached around for his pack and pulled out a plastic-wrapped bundle. Inside was an IR illuminator and a sophisticated camera fitted with an infra-red lens. Used as a system, the package could light a subject and make it visible to the camera's memory card in full dark. It was time to stop observing from a distance. He needed to get down to the hydroelectric plant and take a few pictures of whatever was being hauled away from Changjin. The presence of NKPA Navy officers suggested that whatever that cargo was, it was bound for North Korean ports. It might be torpedoes or missile components or whatever the hell Marx generators were, but it was time to find out and get the information back to the analysts who might have a usable take on what was up at Changjin.

"The next convoy that arrives—I'm going to meet it with this." Stokey held up the camera unit. "Let's figure out how to make that happen without getting me killed or captured."

Seoul, Republic of (South) Korea

S am Jackson was easy to recognize when he strolled into the Intercontinental lobby. He was trussed up in a trench coat over a suit and tie, but he moved with that same fluid grace that had marked his movements through the snow-covered mountains of North Korea. He still looked fit and lean as he swept the lobby with the same shrewd, calculating glance Shake remembered from their time together. Shake stood and waved, watching his friend brush rainwater from a shock of brush-cut hair that was just beginning to show patches of silver.

As Shake watched his old comrade shed his coat and hand it to a bar manager who treated the new arrival with the type of deference reserved for someone familiar and influential, Shake motioned for a waiter to deliver the fresh beer and huge plate of Korean appetizers he'd pre-ordered. He owed Sam Jackson a lot and here he was after many years of little or no contact about to ask a huge favor. Lunch and a few beers was the least he could do for the major guidance he was seeking.

Jackson grasped Shake's hand in a firm grip, just holding on with no shaking for a long moment as he grinned and looked into the American's eyes. "It's been too long," he said in the familiar American English Shake remembered, "Entirely too long. You look the same, my friend. No change—except maybe the married life has softened some of the edges."

They slid into the booth across from each other and lifted the frosty beer mugs. "To old friends and old times," Shake toasted for them and made room for the steaming plate of Korean delicacies that arrived at the table. "Sam, you look terrific. Fill me in on life and times since we did all that dumb stuff north of here."

The catch-up conversation lasted through three beers and a huge lunch in the hotel dining room. Everywhere they went, the staff seemed to know Sam Jackson and treat him like a valued customer beyond the normal level of polite service. When the waiter arrived with the check, Jackson merely waved a hand and the man rapidly disappeared. "Please, Sam, let me buy. I owe you a bunch."

"Not gonna happen, Shake. Not as long as you're in Seoul." Sam grinned and motioned for the waiter to re-fill their glasses. "I do a lot of business with the major hotels here. Korean War vet visits and that kind of stuff. I run a tab and get a big discount."

"Well, I guess I'll just have to add this to what I owe you for getting my ass out of the Chosin in one piece."

"As I recall at least one part of that incident..." Sam Jackson sat back and lit a cigarette with a battered old Zippo lighter. "It was the other way around. If you hadn't flanked the shooters in that mountain pass, I'd still be up there. Those bastards had me nailed and I wouldn't have lasted much longer laying out in the open."

"Chalk it up to piss-poor North Korean marksmanship, Sam. The guy who made it happen was your Corporal Soon. You ever hear from him?"

"Corporal Kim Soon is now Colonel Kim Soon of the Korean Marine Corps. I see him all the time. He remembers it all very well and always asks about you." Sam laughed and made a motion like firing a rifle—the same one Shake had used that frigid night in the North Korean mountain pass to communicate with his covering shooter. "He does this every time he sees me. You had no idea he spoke English about as well as you do."

"Well hell, Sam—he never said much to me until after it was all over. Glad to hear he's OK. What have they got him doing? Holding down a headquarters desk?"

"Not a man like Soon. He's doing some...well, he's got a command. A very important area in a chain of disputed islands off our western border. He's a serious operator these days."

Shake toyed with his drink and decided they'd just about run the small talk into the ground. "Sam, I've got a serious problem and I don't know how to get it solved. Can we go somewhere a little more private? I need some good advice and I think you're the man who can give it to me."

Sam Jackson pondered for a moment and then stood. "It's too wet to walk. Let's go up to your room."

* * *

"He's in there somewhere near the Changjin Reservoir." Sam Jackson stared at the map and poked at a spot of blue. "And you don't know exactly where?"

"My best guess is that he's somewhere near the hydroelectric facility, Sam. His bosses think he got a tip about something going on there and decided to check it out for himself. He's an old and true friend—and he's also a guy who takes too damn many chances. I need to get in there, find him and get him out before he gets killed or caught."

"Understandable." Sam sat back and lit a cigarette. "If he gets nailed or captured, the NKs either have a hostage or they have some serious leverage to scream about violation of their sovereignty, crimes against humanity, American war-mongers, and all that same old stuff they've been spouting for years." Sam bent to re-examine the map. "And you say he had two men with him—both North Koreans?"

"That's what I was told—two North Koreans that he's got on the payroll."

"Have you considered they might have turned on him?"

"We'd have heard about that from the North Koreans, wouldn't we? They'd be making all the noise you just mentioned."

"Probably right." Sam stood and walked toward a window overlooking the rain-swept streets outside the hotel. "So, supposing you get to this site on the Chinese side of the Yalu, what then? Are you planning to just cross the river, head for the Changjin and look for him?"

"That's about the size of it—unless you've got a better suggestion."

"One suggestion I have is that you don't try this on your own. I think we can help with that—or Colonel Soon can help with that. Suppose I could arrange for some Korean Marine special operators to go along with you?"

"That would be a huge help, Sam. The last thing I want to do is get in a fight or wind up being chased through those mountains by the North Korean Army. Think you might be able to get something like that done?"

Sam returned to the map and studied it for a while before stabbing his finger at a spot on the Chinese side of the Yalu. "You say the UAV site is here?" Shake looked at the familiar spot north of the Chinese area marked Dandong and nodded. "Somewhere right near there. They told me it's just a couple of native huts to cover the crew and electronics and a short strip in a fairly desolate area. Apparently, the drone is relatively small, and they don't need much room to launch and recover. The Chinese military people in the know have apparently got the site locked down tight."

Tracing a line southwest from the UAV site, Sam pointed at a cluster of dots near the area where the Yalu River spilled into the Yellow Sea. "Colonel Soon commands a Special Forces operational detachment right here on Yeonpyeong Island." He thought a while, lit a cigarette and stared at Shake for a long moment. "I'm trying to decide how much I should tell you given where you'll be going."

"Sam, I wouldn't be asking if I could see any other way. I don't want you to put yourself on the line or compromise yourself in any way. I'm not about to try and help one friend by making trouble for another one."

Sam nodded, smoked silently for a while and pulled out his iPhone. Shake just sat quietly and watched his old friend think. After scrolling through a few things on his phone, Sam put the device on the table and crushed his cigarette into an ashtray. "Have you ever heard of *Angibu*?"

"Sounds like something you ordered for lunch." Shake could see Sam was still pondering. "But I'm betting it's something else, right?"

"*Angibu* is the ROK Agency for National Security Planning; the ANSP. It's what used to be called the Korean CIA." Sam lit another cigarette and ran a hand through his hair. "I do some part-time work for them. They drafted me shortly after I left active duty. What that means is that I'm probably going to have to let my superiors know about this UAV business operating out of China over North Korea—assuming they don't know about it already."

"Oh, shit, Sam—I had no idea. That may blow the whole deal. Is there any way we can keep this quiet for a while—at least until I can check with the people who sent me out here?"

"I said I was going to let my superiors know about what you told me. I did not say when. Suppose I was able to get you some serious help in finding your friend. Would you be willing to propose a sharing of the Intel? We help you get your buddy out of North Korea. Your people reciprocate by sharing what they discover with the drone flights?"

"Sam, that's way above my paygrade. I'm just a hired hand in this thing. I don't know who knows what about anything at the upper echelons. If I'd known you were still a player, I'd never have asked you for help. I'm really sorry about this."

"Put all that aside for a minute, Shake. Look at it this way. For all practical purposes, America and South Korea are allies, right? We cooperate on all sorts of different levels. I know for a fact that we share Intel with the CIA and vice versa. We've been all over each other since the Seoul Summer Olympics back in 1988. So, maybe this would be just an expansion of that cooperation. Your country wants to keep tabs on what the NKs are doing in their nuke program and so do we. Maybe your country didn't want us to know about this new operation, but now we do—so what's the harm?"

"The man who briefed me said that this program is unofficial, not sanctioned by our government. That's the harm. You make a request through official channels to share Intel and suddenly people who aren't supposed to know about all this start asking questions and heads start to roll."

"Seems to me if your guys can run a risky, deep mission like this unofficially, they can share the profits unofficially. I think I can guarantee you nobody in *Angibu* wants to do anything to compromise a program like this. If we share and it's got to be back-channel, low-level and unofficial, that's fine. We know a thing or two about operating outside official channels."

"Sam, I've got to make a call."

"So do I, Shake." Sam Jackson stood and nodded.

"Listen, Sam, please don't do anything until I can talk to my guy back in the states. I may have screwed the pooch completely here."

"Make your call, Shake. I'll wait until I hear from you. The call I need to make is to Colonel Soon. He'll be delighted to hear you're back in Korea."

"Keep talking, Shake." The man who called himself Bayer carried his personal cell phone out of his office and headed for a glassed-in atrium at the end of the corridor. "I'm moving to another area where it won't bother anyone when I start screaming."

"I swear to God I had no idea my guy was connected with any Intel operations." The connection was clear as a bell and Bayer could hear the agony in Shake's voice. The man was clearly upset and Bayer decided to control his initial reaction to the call. He took a deep breath and clicked into damage control mode. "I warned you about this kind of thing, Shake, but that's water under the bridge at this point. Tell me the rest."

"Sam Jackson is the Korean Marine who was with me on Iceberg. I wanted to ask him for some good hands to make the crossing with me. The dossier Chan dug up said he was working for the Korean Tourist Bureau. I figured he was still connected with the ROK military but I swear I had no idea he was an Intel player. I'd never have approached him for help if I'd known that."

"And what he's proposing is that we keep everything under the radar—and we share the UAV Intel dumps with—who? How does he plan to hook all this up without someone in the government on his end finding out about it? Answer me that. You know how these things work, Shake. The more people who know about an operation, the more likely that operation will be compromised. You realize at this point there's probably a whole lot more at risk than just Stokey's misbehaving ass, don't you?"

"All I know is what Sam Jackson told me. And I trust him. He says he can work it out to keep the operation off the radar if we're willing to share the Intel dumps. I've got no idea how he intends to do that but I believe he'll do what he says."

"And you figure he can come through with some valuable assistance?"

"Invaluable is the word, Bayer. If he lends a hand, we can get this done, get Mike out of there intact and nobody's the wiser."

"Where is he now?" Bayer was thinking rapidly and mentally reviewing the list of South Korean sources and operatives he knew about in and out of the *Angibu*. He needed to turn around, get to his office and call that list up on his computer. It would take some time to work through the classified interlocks and filters to find what he needed.

"He's down in the lobby, I think. He said he'd wait to hear from me."

"He's heard all he needs from you." Bayer spun and stormed back toward his office. "I need about twenty minutes to think and go over some data here." He entered his office, flopped into his chair and began to tap on his computer keyboard. "In a half-hour, find your buddy and get him somewhere secure. Then put him on this phone with me."

Bayer didn't wait for Shake's response. He was busy working through the system to access the CIA's top secret dossiers on South Korean *Angibu* contacts.

One hour to the minute after the initial call to Bayer at Langley, Sam Jackson emerged from the bedroom and handed the secure phone back to Shake Davis. He eyed the ice bucket containing six bottles of OB Lager and pried the caps off two of them. "Your man Bayer is a hard-ass."

"He is that." Shake crushed out the fifth cigarette he'd chain-smoked since Sam disappeared into his bedroom with the phone. "I could tell you some stories about the shit sandwiches he's made with me in the middle."

"Fortunately, he's also a reasonable guy and a thorough professional." Sam handed Shake one of the sweating beer bottles and dropped into a chair. "I think we've got a deal."

"What's that mean—or do I need to know?"

Sam sipped beer and shrugged. "It's fairly simple and straightforward. He knows some people over there who know some people over here. They communicate; they cooperate. The obligation for me to make an official report is now overcome by events. Certain people in *Angibu* will unofficially find themselves in receipt of some unexpected and very valuable intelligence. Where it comes from remains an official mystery."

"Sam, I don't know what to say."

"Say nothing." Sam waved a hand and reached for his cigarettes. "The thing to do now is concentrate on getting into North Korea and finding your friend Mike Stokey. I've had some thoughts about that."

"There was a message from my local contact while you were on the phone." Shake pulled a hotel message form from his pocket and scanned it. "Apparently, my visa is all set. We leave for Beijing around noon tomorrow on the Daewoo Shipbuilding private jet out of Seoul International. Do I still go ahead with that trip?"

"I think so. You need to get to the site and wait. Some of our people will meet you there."

"Some of your people? Who?"

Sam Jackson scooted forward in his chair and drained his beer. "I spoke with Colonel Soon. I'm going to Yeonpyeong by ferry tomorrow to confer with him, but he's already screening his commandos for a couple of good men who will go with you to Changjin."

"Yeah, good—but how do they get into China?"

"One revelation deserves another." Sam rose and went to retrieve another beer. "Look at the map. Yeonpyeong Island is located in the Yellow Sea off the western coast. From there, we run regular reconnaissance missions using stealthy surface craft and submersibles. We've been doing it for quite a while now. At this time of year, the Yalu is deep enough to allow navigation all the way up to the Dandong area. Your Korean Marine escorts will arrive near the drone site via submersible craft. They will have your cell phone number and send you a message with an exact position once they've made their way as far up the river as they can go."

Mike Stokey and his partner Lee had to wait impatiently for nearly two full days for the next convoy of trucks to arrive at the Changjin hydroelectric plant. The vehicles rolled toward the reservoir, already showing large patches of ice on its banks, and turned onto the road leading into the plant. Just before noon, all three trucks were parked in the usual loading area as Stokey studied them closely through his high-powered binoculars. At his shoulder, Lee snapped pictures with a telephoto lens fitted onto a high-resolution digital camera.

"See the markings on the fenders, Mr. Stokey." Lee fired off a few more frames and then let the camera hang from the strap around his neck. "They are from the Wonsan Naval Base on the east coast." Stokey focused on the fender markings, but he didn't recognize the symbols and Korean characters. He did know the trucks were the same fairly bog-standard NKPA six-ton cab-over types they'd been observing ever since they arrived at Changjin. Each truck carried a three-man crew in winter fatigue uniforms. He couldn't see enough to determine if they were army or navy, but the Krinkov AK-74 carbines they carried told him they were definitely not civilians.

"Probably the same drill, Lee. They'll go in and get warm, probably get something to eat, and then start loading the trucks." Stokey checked his watch. "If they hold to the regular pattern, they'll spend the night here and leave early in the morning."

"And you intend to take pictures of the cargo tonight?"

"We do it just like we planned." Stokey took the camera, inserted a thumb-drive, and depressed a button to download the photos they'd shot over the past week. In the camera's memory card were photos of cargo being loaded on previous convoys, but they weren't worth much. He needed to know what was inside the containers. "If these guys are like most soldiers and sailors, they'll be least alert an hour or two before dawn. Around midnight we move in closer and wait to get a feel for guard shifts. Then I get into the truck park, take some pictures, and join up with you. We should be back up here before daylight. Then we pack up and head west at nightfall."

"I still think you should let me do the picture-taking." They'd been over the point a number of times, and Stokey remained adamant about it. This was the most dangerous part of the reconnaissance mission, and he was not about to sacrifice another hired hand if something went wrong. It was his mission and his responsibility to take the biggest risks.

"That's not gonna fly, Lee. We've been over it and that's that. If something goes wrong, you take the photos and head for the Yalu. Turn what we've got over to Mr. Liccardi at the site, make your report, and collect your cash. The amount we agreed on is stowed in my gear back there." Stokey ducked into their snow-hole to change batteries in the camera and check the IR gear. When he was satisfied the photo equipment was set, he pulled a Makarov semi-auto pistol from his pack and screwed a sound suppressor into the muzzle threads. It had been risky to bring the weapon onto the site after the Chinese made it clear that all firearms were forbidden. He'd been forced to hide the parts in a pile of electronic spares, but now he was thankful that he'd decided to take the chance. That little weapon, eight rounds of 9x18mm Soviet ammo, and the razor-edged Gerber Mk II fighting knife strapped to the inside of his right calf were all he had to fight his way out if it all went into the crapper.

Stokey had learned a long time ago through punishing experience that over-thinking a thing like that or worrying about what might happen led to self-doubt and that led to fatal mistakes. He pulled off his boots, slid into his arctic sleeping bag, rolled over, and willed himself to sleep.

The dinner meeting with Senior Captain Ming Yao Chi was fairly frosty where Shake was concerned despite the hot, spicy food served in the private dining room of a small but well-appointed restaurant near Beijing's commercial district. The Chinese naval officer spoke enough stilted English to ask a few questions about Shake's military service. He nodded politely when Shake told him he'd mainly been a desk-jockey concerned with logistics, but something in the man's dark eyes said he didn't believe much of what he heard. The majority of the evening passed with the Mandarin conversational load carried by Pete Pak and their host. There were guards posted outside the private room, but beyond their ominous presence the whole event seemed like any dinner meeting between any businessmen in virtually any world capitol. Not a word was spoken—at least none in English—about the ultra-secret UAV site or Shake's upcoming journey to it.

Pete Pak was all smiles and calm demeanor when Ming Yao Chi excused himself and stepped out of the dining room to handle a phone call. "You're on for tonight—right after we leave here. He's turning you over to one of his English-speaking officers. He'll take you to the hotel. Pack only what you absolutely need—nothing that won't fit in a backpack or a single valise. Leave anything else with the concierge. I'll take care of it."

"Then what happens?"

"Then you go where they tell you to go and do what they tell you to do. That's all I know and it's all I need to know."

"OK, that works." Shake pondered the instructions. He'd spent a long and expensive day before leaving the States buying an excellent array of cold weather boots and clothing. It all fit snugly in a single mountain rucksack. What he'd really wanted to carry with him was a solid set of climbing and survival equipment, but that might have prompted uncomfortable questions about what he was planning to do with it. He made a mental note to call Sam Jackson when they got to the hotel and have the Marine escorts bring an extra set of whatever gear they planned on carrying.

Their host returned to the private dining room followed by a waiter who served some sort of iced Chinese delicacy for dessert. Senior Captain Ming and Pete Pak continued to chat casually over brandy, but Shake refused any sort of spirits. He'd even passed on the beer during dinner. He wanted to be stone sober for whatever was in store for him at the hands of the People's Liberation Army or Navy in the next couple of hours. When a waiter stuck his head inside the door to see if there was anything else, Senior Captain Ming waved him off, checked his watch, and stood. He shook Pete Pak's hand and motioned for Shake to follow him out of the dining room.

Waiting outside was an unsmiling uniformed PLAN officer wearing blue and silver shoulder boards that Shake thought designated a Lieutenant Commander. The man made no move to shake hands or otherwise acknowledge the American visitor. Ming pointed at Shake and said something in Mandarin. When the escort officer nodded his understanding, Captain Ming took his Navy overcoat from a hook and shrugged into it. He stared at Shake for a long, uncomfortable minute as if he was having second thoughts and then nodded. "Go with this man. No questions, no cameras." And then he abruptly strode out the door of the restaurant slapping his high-peaked, Soviet-style officer's cap on his head and holding onto it against a blustery winter wind.

"This way, please." The escort officer turned on his heel and led the way out through the main entrance where a PLAN staff car idled with an enlisted driver at the wheel. Shake slid into the warm interior of the vehicle as the escort officer opened the door. When the escort was settled in the backseat next to Shake, he mumbled something to the driver and they cruised off into

downtown Beijing traffic heading, Shake hoped, for the Peninsula Hotel.

"My name is Davis." Shake held out his hand where it remained ignored by the escort officer for a long moment. "I am
aware of that." The officer eventually gave Shake's hand a
perfunctory pump. "You may call me Yang."

"We're headed for the Peninsula Hotel, right?" Shake tried
to see something he recognized in the brightly lit streets but
nothing looked familiar.

"That is correct. You will collect one bag and nothing else.
No cameras of any kind. When you are ready to go, return to the
lobby entrance. I will be waiting for you there."

When the staff car deposited him under the gilded arches of
the Peninsula's main entry, Shake scrambled out and pushed
through the crowded lobby heading for the elevator banks. He
caught the first car, stepped in, and pressed the button for his
floor. As the elevator rose smoothly, he listened to the gabble of
Chinese from his fellow passengers and reached for his cell
phone. He hadn't thought about the camera built into the
phone. If they searched him and decided to take the phone, he
was in trouble. The no-nonsense escort officer didn't seem like
the kind of guy who overlooked such things.

Shake unlocked the door to his room and tried to organize
his thoughts. He needed to pack a go-bag to take with him and a
stay-bag for Pete Pak to handle. He had to contact Sam Jackson,
check with Stokey's sister, put in a quick reassuring call to
Chan, and then figure some way to hide his cell phone. He
made quick work of the packing, changing from business suit
into casual clothing and a heavy jacket that he hoped wouldn't
attract too much attention. Then he tossed his cold-weather
gear, some extra socks and underwear, and a shaving kit in his
old, comfortable mountain rucksack. Everything else went into
his wheeled suitcase. He dialed open the room safe and stuffed
his passport in a jacket pocket. What few incriminating papers
he'd saved were quickly shredded and flushed down the toilet.
Next, he staged his ruck and suitcase near the door and
punched up Sam Jackson's private number. Sam was on the

line after the second ring and Shake felt fairly confident by the time he disconnected that his old friend understood the vaguely-worded message about extra climbing and survival gear. Barbara Casburn—née Stokey—in Texas had still not heard from Mike, and Chan was half-asleep when she answered his call.

"*Sawadee*, Sweetheart, and greetings from beautiful Beijing in the People's Republic."

"It's three a.m. here, Shake. Are you OK?"

"I'm fine Chan. Just heading out and I probably won't be able to call for a while. I just wanted to hear your voice and tell you I love you."

"Well, I love you too." Chan knew better than to ask questions or push beyond whatever message Shake wanted to send on an open line. "Have a good time—and call me first chance you get."

"I will, honey. Don't worry. It's going just fine."

"Be careful, Shake. And say hello to Mike for me."

Shake killed the call and checked his watch. He'd been up in the hotel room for forty-five minutes and it was time to get rolling on the next leg of the journey. He carried both bags down to the lobby and turned the suitcase over to the concierge, marked with Pete Pak's name for eventual pick-up. Then, he headed for the lobby shop and searched around among the toiletries until he found what he wanted. He paid cash for a box of gauze pads and a roll of adhesive tape and then headed for the men's restroom on the other side of the lobby.

In one of the stalls, he dropped his trousers, wrapped the cell phone in gauze and strapped it tightly to his thigh, high up in the crotch where it nestled snugly against his balls. The aloof escort officer didn't look like the kind of guy who would probe too far on a pat-down and he would likely shy away from direct contact with another man's genitals. If not, he was in for a bad time. Before he left the restroom, he trashed the remaining gauze and tape and then pulled a little Canon digital camera out of his ruck. It was a Christmas present from Chan but at this point, Shake figured it was a worthy sacrifice. If he was reading

Lieutenant Commander Yang correctly, the best defense might just be a good offense.

The staff car wheeled up immediately when Shake pushed through the revolving door. The driver got out and opened the trunk. Shake shrugged off the pack and handed it to the driver who tossed it carelessly into the trunk and slammed the lid. Shake ducked into the car and waited for the driver to get back behind the wheel. When they were rolling on a highway heading east out of Beijing, he reached into his jacket pocket, pulled out the digital camera and handed it to Yang.

"You said no cameras. That's the only one I've got and I didn't want to leave it around the hotel for somebody to steal. I thought you might like to have it."

"I have a camera." Yang was underplaying but it was clear from the look in his eyes that the expensive little Canon was an attractive prize. Shake just shrugged and settled back in the seat. "Well, now you've got two. It's yours if you want it."

Yang tucked the camera in a pocket of his overcoat. He said nothing more until ninety minutes later when he leaned forward and spoke to the driver. The car pulled over to the side of the road and Yang took a length of dark cloth out of his pocket. "You must wear this for the remainder of our journey." Yang motioned with the cloth toward Shake's face. "Do you agree?"

"Sure." Shake let the escort tie the blindfold around his eyes and settled back wondering what it was Yang didn't want him to see. He was fast asleep 15 minutes later.

He wanted to check his watch when the whine of turbine engines spooling up woke Shake from the nap he'd been taking behind the blindfold. Whatever his escort didn't want him to see had something to do with aircraft—very likely helicopters if Shake was right about the source of the turbine noise. The PLAN staff car made a hard right turn, and Shake grabbed the hand rest to keep from sliding into Yang's lap.

"We have arrived," Yang said when the car stopped. He unlocked the door and said something to the driver who switched off the engine and walked around the car toward the trunk. "You may remove the blindfold, but do not get out of the vehicle until you are ordered to do so." Shake fought off the temptation to render a salute and bark "aye, aye, sir." Instead, he untied the blindfold, blinked at the lights shining from a nearby aircraft hangar, and shifted at his crotch where the hidden cell phone was causing a major irritation in his scrotum area. The driver came around the car, plopped Shake's rucksack on the hood, and proceeded to root around in it looking for contraband. He found nothing of interest, re-cinched the pack-straps, and lit a cigarette.

Shake's watch indicated nearly midnight. They'd been on the road for the better part of four hours and he had no earthly idea where he was other than somewhere in China east of Beijing. The buildings and ground support equipment outside the hangar indicated they were on some sort of air base or airfield. His ears told him a helicopter was spooling up somewhere nearby, and he guessed the next leg of his journey was going to be by air. He sat quietly until Yang finally returned and motioned for him to get out of the car. The escort officer put his hands behind his head, spread his legs, and motioned for Shake to assume the position.

As he'd hoped, the pat-down was perfunctory, and Yang's hands got nowhere near where Shake had strapped the cell phone. When it was done, Shake breathed a sigh of relief, put his hands down, and waited while Yang conferred with the driver. The enlisted man retrieved the pack and handed it over as Yang motioned for Shake to follow him out of the shadows. When they stepped into the pool of light from the hangar doors, Shake saw a helicopter sitting on a ready-pad with its anti-collision lights flashing. A crew chief, connected to the aircraft by a long communication cord, was conducting a walk-around inspection while the pilots in the cockpit ran through their pre-flight checklists.

Shake stood waiting for instructions as the pilots engaged the rotors which began to turn with an odd mechanical groan. The helo was familiar. Shake had studied the capabilities of any number of friendly and threat rotary-wing aircraft when he was on active duty and he recognized this one as a Chinese Z-9B or what NATO called the *Haitun*. It was basically a knock-off of the Aerospatiale Dauphin, a four rotor-blade, long-range transport model with an encased tail-rotor. The *Haitun* could be configured as a gunship, but this one stood sleek and unarmed as the rotors turned up to ground taxi speed while the crew chief hopped into the open cargo bay and motioned for Shake to come aboard.

Yang gave him a polite shove and motioned for Shake to head for the aircraft. "Good luck to you, sir. And thank you for the camera."

Shake walked toward the helo, refusing to duck as most people instinctively did when they approached a helicopter with rotors turning. He had no idea whether he was about to make a safe journey at the hands of competent pilots carrying out secret orders or be tossed out of the helo somewhere over the vast Chinese hinterlands never to be heard from again, but he was not about to look like an amateur on the way. He crawled into the vibrating aircraft, nodded at the grinning crew chief, and strapped into one of the sling seats. The aircraft rolled forward on retractable landing gear for a distance, and then leapt into the air as the pilots pulled pitch.

The crew chief slid the door closed and sat looking at Shake curiously for a few minutes as the aircraft clawed for altitude. Then he flipped the night-vision goggles mounted to his helmet into place and stared out at the black sky. Shake shifted his rucksack into a footrest and sat back, feeling the vibration of the rotor blades through the sling seat and hoping Mike Stokey was doing at least as well as he was.

Changjin (Chosin) Reservoir, Democratic People's Republic of (North) Korea

From the close observation point less than 50 meters from the hydroelectric plant's truck park, Shake and Lee conferred on the plan one last time. They'd been in position since 2200 and it was now 0200. During the long, cold hours they sat behind a large rock formation observing the sentries on duty around the Changjin motor pool, they had finalized the move Stokey was about to make.

There were four sentries on watch in this area. They were relieved by new guards every two hours. The men currently gathered around a warming fire burning in a 55-gallon drum were the third set of guards they'd observed. They were certainly not very alert or motivated. Lee guessed their main function was to discourage pilfering by people from the nearby village.

The guards yawned continuously as they chafed their hands and shrugged at the AKs carried muzzle-down on their shoulders. The standard drill seemed to be that the sentries spent most of their watch standing around the warming fire, and only occasionally made a cursory walking tour around the perimeter of an unfenced square where the three target trucks and a number of other smaller vehicles were parked. Lights stood at each corner of that perimeter, and Stokey could see a steady shower of fresh snow falling through the pools of yellow light. It was a miserable night on the banks of the Chosin Reservoir and the sentries didn't seem worried about an officer or sergeant of the guard—if there was such a thing—checking posts.

"I'll make my move after the next guy takes a walk. As soon as he gets back to the fire, I'll move down the drainage ditch, go in from the west side, and see what I can get." Stokey checked the pouch containing the IR illuminator and camera fitted with the special lens that could read the light. He had a set of infrared sensitive goggles tucked under his parka. "I'm only going to be in there for fifteen minutes." Stokey carefully exposed the luminous dial on his watch and set the bezel. "When I've got what I need, I'll meet you back here."

He covered the watch with the elastic cuff of his parka, and returned his attention to the sentries who were doing little jigs around the fire to keep their feet warm. His main concern was noise. The containers aboard the cargo trucks had access hatches at the rear that were secured with heavy-duty lever latches. Stokey had experience with that system, and knew how noisy it could be. Even if he managed to quietly open a hatch, there was the problem of squeaky hinges. He patted his pocket and felt for the small spray-can of break-free lubricant he'd carried down off the mountain and hoped there was enough remaining in the can to soak the latch and hinges.

At 0210, one of the sentries turned away from his watch-mates and shambled toward the truck park. The other three remained huddled around the fire, only occasionally looking out into the dark and blowing snow. Stokey knew from long experience that as long as there was a fire, soldiers would gather around and stare at it. It was human nature, and the damage the bright light did to night vision never seemed to be a concern. When it came to huddling around a fire, soldiers of all sorts were like moths.

It was 0230 when the walking guard returned to the warming barrel and Stokey crawled to his left into the shoulder-height drainage ditch that ran along the right side of the truck park. There was a layer of thick ice on the bottom of the ditch, and he moved slowly to be sure it would take his weight and not produce a noisy crunch.

At 0255, Stokey was halfway up the right side of the truck park and well out of sight of the sentries around the fire. He bobbed up quickly to get his bearings and wished for the hundredth time that he'd been able to get some more sophisticated night vision equipment for this mission. It was coal black this far from the standing lights, but he could see snow falling harder against the dark outline of the nearest truck parked just 20 meters away from the edge of the ditch.

Stokey donned his IR goggles, snapped on the illuminator, and looked around for activity. The weird amber-yellow glow reflected from everything covered by the illuminator was invisible to the naked eye which was good. It was not very helpful in discerning detail for a man wearing IR sensitive goggles which was bad. It was long outdated stuff, and Stokey hadn't used IR equipment since his early days in the Marine Corps before light-amplification technology gave birth to modern NVGs. There was no helping the low-tech drawback at this point.

He swept the IR illuminator over the containers and spotted one that had a crushed corner, probably suffered in sloppy loading onto the trailer. He thought that shake-up might have dislodged some of the rust in the latching mechanism and decided to make the damaged container his target. Stokey crawled out of the ditch and headed for the rear of the selected truck. He gave the break-free container several vigorous shakes and then sprayed the latch mechanism and hinges.

Forcing himself to wait a few anxious minutes while the break-free soaked into the metal, Stokey swept the illuminator around the perimeter. He saw no signs of movement and thought he heard laughter over the soft sigh of a frigid night wind. He needed to get moving before a sentry decided it was his turn to brave the snow and cold for a perimeter stroll. The latch resisted for a time until Stokey put his shoulder into the effort. When the locking device finally lifted, there was little sound beyond a mild clunk. He pulled the latch toward him and cautiously swung the container door open. A quick scan with the illuminator showed that he was looking at a box within a box.

The exterior container was constructed with walls of thick metal sheeting. He'd planned to climb inside, pull the door shut after him, and take his pictures, but there was no room inside the container. Through the IR goggles, he saw something that looked as much like a cattle-feeding trough as anything else he could imagine. It was a long box, open on the top, with sides that were about waist high. He stripped a glove and felt the material. It seemed to be some sort of high-tensile plastic or fiberglass material. Stokey put a foot on the truck's trailer hitch and strained to see what was inside the box.

It was something electronic. He could tell from the carefully soldered wiring and plug connections. Running the entire length of the container were two rows of what looked like large resistors or transistors. Stokey had no idea which, but they all seemed to be wired together like batteries in series and plugged into a long plastic tray that covered the bottom of the box. He snapped a series of pictures as he carefully maneuvered the illuminator in concert with the camera lens. As he finished the available angles and stepped down from the truck, a familiar marking caught his eye. It was the three-bladed symbol for radioactive material. Stenciled below it were some Korean characters plus a grouping of letters and symbols: Cs137 and 2MV. He quickly took pictures of the markings, stepped to the ground, and swung the container hatch shut as quietly as he could.

As he turned toward the drainage ditch to make his break, Stokey saw a cone of yellow light sweeping the alleys between the parked vehicles. He heard snow crunching beneath boots and realized he was caught. One of the sentries was making rounds and he'd seen something that made him curious. Maybe it was the tracks in the snow between the ditch and the truck. Maybe it was some noise he'd made. Whatever it was, the sentry was curious enough to investigate. There was no time to think about that. The flashlight was sweeping over the front of the truck and the sentry would be on him in seconds. Stokey grabbed the trailer hitch and used it to lever himself under the truck between one set of dual wheels and the vehicle's differential. The Makarov was within easy reach inside his parka but Mike was thinking beyond that. If the sentry spotted his boot-prints, he'd certainly look under the truck. If he shot the man, there would be no question but that an armed intruder had been poking around the hydroelectric plant and the trucks carrying the mysterious cargo. Stokey needed a better Plan B and he needed it in a hurry.

Shuttling around at the rear of the truck, the sentry swept his flashlight over the ground. Stokey could see the man's snow-covered boots and heard him rattle the latch on the container door. If the man decided he needed help and called for his buddies, the Makarov might be the only option. As the beam from the flashlight swept over the rear tires of the truck, Stokey cocked his right leg, reached for the Gerber MK II, and slid it silently out of the leather sheath.

The guard crouched and swept the light under the truck. His eyes got wide and wild as he spotted the intruder lying in the snow. He recoiled immediately and banged his head painfully on the truck's trailer hitch. In seconds, the man would be screaming for help. Stokey lunged forward, pushing hard with both legs and drove his dagger-point blade into the man's throat just under the chin. There was a strangled gurgle as Stokey followed his knife hand out from under the truck, straddled the sentry, and smacked his free hand smartly on the butt of the knife to drive the angled blade up into dying man's brain-stem.

Quickly re-stowing his photo equipment, Stokey cleaned the knife blade on the dead man's parka and then dragged him toward the drainage ditch. He tumbled the body into the cut and then jumped in behind it. He needed to get back to Lee and get them as far as possible away from Chosin before dawn. When the security people at the hydroelectric plant discovered the dead sentry, they'd be all over the surrounding hills looking for a killer or a spy—probably both—and the heat would be on for real. Time was the enemy and distance was their friend.

Lee was holding position in their close reconnaissance site when Stokey flopped down beside him breathing hard. "Sentry spotted me," he gasped. "I had to take him out. I dumped the body in the ditch but it won't be long before the others find it. We need to move—and we may not have time to get our gear and cover our tracks." Stokey was up and ready to move when Lee grabbed him by the sleeve.

"We should buy some time, Mr. Stokey. Leaving gear behind in the site is a bad idea. If they find evidence that foreigners were here, they will call out all assets to find us."

"I can't help that now. We need to get moving west."

"If they catch us—if they get the camera or capture you—all this will have been for nothing."

"It's like I said, Lee, we've got no choice."

Lee stripped off the native Korean coat he was wearing. It was a padded, home-spun garment like almost all North Korean country people wore during the winter. "I'll leave this here. They'll find it as soon as they start searching. They'll conclude it was left by someone in the village who got caught trying to steal and killed the sentry. While they investigate, we will have time to collect our gear and cover our tracks."

"That's gonna buy serious trouble for some innocent people." Stokey weighed the options and decided they didn't have much choice. It was a horseshit them-or-us situation but it wasn't the first time he'd been faced with that kind of hard choice. "Leave the coat. I've got some spare gear up on the mountain. Let's get up there, sanitize the area, and head west. "

A pale sliver of light was just showing along the eastern horizon as the Chinese helicopter banked into a hard series of turns and began to bleed off altitude. Shake caught an occasional glimpse of dark water and realized they were somewhere near the infamous Yalu River. There were no lights that he could see as the pilots tightened the descending spirals and brought the aircraft into a landing attitude. As the crew chief hauled open the door, a blast of frigid air howled into the cargo compartment. Shake leaned over to take a look at the rapidly-approaching ground, but there was nothing to see beyond a few snow-covered hummocks that reflected the helicopter's landing lights. When the aircraft dropped into ground effect, everything below disappeared in a blinding swirl of white.

As they bumped into contact with the earth, the crew chief motioned for Shake to dismount. The aircraft was still turning with enough power to keep it light on the landing gear, so this was apparently a quick delivery and not a prolonged stop. He grabbed his rucksack and jumped down into ankle-deep snow. Before he even had time to run out from under the rotor-fan, the pilots pulled pitch and the aircraft nosed over clawing for altitude. Shake took a knee with his back to the blast from the departing helo and looked around for someone to clarify his situation.

Wherever he'd been so unceremoniously dumped, it looked desolate and deserted. He was on a flat piece of ground that stretched for a couple of hundred meters in either direction. If he was where he wanted to be, this flat strip would be the short runway for the UAV. And if he hadn't been simply marooned to fend for himself, there should be someone around involved with the drone mission. He stared at the two large hummocks that were the only irregularities on the horizon, shouldered his rucksack, and walked toward them. As he got nearer, he spotted what looked like a series of spikes protruding from the top and sides of the snow-mounds. On closer examination, they were aerials, antennae, and some other piping that looked like exhaust vents. *Very likely*, he thought, *I'm in the right place and the people I need to find are somewhere under all that snow.*

Shake could see neither entryway nor any footprints around the mounds which were tucked up against a forest of snow-covered pines. He stripped the ruck off his shoulders and dug around to find a reliable little Surefire Defender flashlight, snapped it on, and swept the beam over the snow. With the exception of the piping and the antenna arrays, he could see no evidence of human presence. The mounds must be where the control and monitoring equipment are located, and there had to be some people around to maintain and operate that gear. Shake shouldered his ruck and began to walk around the area looking for an entrance.

"Hold it right there!" The command sounded very much like it was backed-up by a weapon. Shake froze and stared into the stand of pine trees. His ears told him that's where the body issuing the orders was located, but he could see nothing but trees and snow in the gloom. There was a slight rustle on the edge of the forest, and Shake detected movement near one of the trees.

"Your name better be Davis." A man rose from the snow, draped in a white parka and holding a compound bow at full draw with an arrow notched and ready to fly.

"That's me. You need me to prove it?" Shake was relieved to see the stocky individual relax the tension on his bow string and shove the arrow into a quiver at his waist. "Not necessary. We got word we were gonna have a round-eye visitor." The archer stepped out of the forest and approached Shake with his hand extended. "Dick Liccardi," he said. "I'm sort of the honcho around here."

Shake shook the man's hand and tried to make out his features in the shadow beneath the hood of a white parka. Liccardi was stocky and powerfully built, but it was hard to see much of his face beyond a luxurious mustache that looked like something from one of the Super Mario Brothers. Shake had spent some time fooling around with archery and understood that all the little bells and whistles attached to the bow resting at the man's side would only be useful to someone who knew what he was doing. "Glad you didn't decide to let fly with that thing. Looks like it could do some serious damage."

Liccardi motioned for Shake to follow and trudged toward the rear of the nearest snow mound. "Our hosts nixed any firearms on the site. I told 'em I was gonna use this to hunt..." He waved a hand vaguely in the direction of the forest. "...and supplement our meager rations. They didn't seem to have a problem with it. I actually got a feral hog last week. I think we've still got some of that pork left if you're hungry."

At the rear of the snow mound, Liccardi lifted a white cloth and mashed a button that resulted in a muted bell tone. "Doorbell," he said. "Let's 'em know the visitors are friendly." A circular section of snow at the base of the mound lifted and Shake saw blue eyes behind a pair of wire-rim glasses peeking out from under it. "Open up, Larry. Our visitor has arrived." The snow-covered lid slid open on a track to reveal a flight of stairs leading down toward a storm door about six feet below ground level. Liccardi introduced Larry Saski as the chief of maintenance at the site. "Larry designed all this," he waved a hand in the air, "and showed us how to build it."

"Only took a couple of weeks," Saski said as he shook Shake's hand. "The hard part was the digging, but the Chinese helped with that." Saski pushed open the storm door, and Shake was greeted by a welcome blast of warm air. Inside the underground bunker, two technicians were fiddling with a cluster of cable connections. Shake was surprised to see one of them was a pretty, petite woman with a crop of shag-cut brown hair framing her face. She looked vaguely familiar.

"Gunner Davis, welcome to our little home away from home." The woman smiled with a sparkle of mischief in her brown eyes and crossed the crowded little space to shake his hand. "We've met before." Shake was unable to place the face and the woman standing before him wrapped in a cable-knit sweater and padded vest didn't seem inclined to elaborate.

"You owe me five bucks, Julia." The other technician looked up from the piece of equipment he was monitoring. "I told you he wouldn't remember." The speaker reached around in his seat to offer his hand. "I'm Tom Young, Mr. Davis—telemetry, communications, part-time cook, and sanitation engineer— which is the term we use for the guy who empties the chemical shitters around here."

Liccardi took Shake's rucksack, tossed it in a corner, and indicated a seat near a card-table that was littered with technical manuals and paper plates. "The mystery girl is Julia Dewey, back-up UAV pilot and data-link technical whiz. She claims to have met you in the Marine Corps." Shake sat down and tugged at the zipper on his jacket, still unable to place the woman's name or face.

"No reason you should remember, Gunner." She dropped into a chair across from him and laughed at his obvious discomfort. "I was a buck sergeant at the time. You were checking in on some mission at El Toro. I drove you in from the Orange County airport in a HUMVEE."

"Now I've got it." Shake relaxed and gratefully accepted a hot mug of coffee from Larry Saski. "You were pretty chatty as I recall: Gave me a rundown on the base and the whole purple-suit concept. It's good to see you again, Julia." He looked around the room. Over the coffee aroma he could smell a coppery tang from the banks of electronic gear that sat humming all over the space with much of the intricate innards exposed. "You just never know where you're gonna run into another Marine."

"I went to school after I got out." She waved a hand at the glowing equipment and complex cable-runs. "Pretty intense stuff, avionics, computer science, satellite technology—and then I got a job out at Creech working in the UAV program."

"And I drafted her for this deal." Liccardi dropped an affectionate hand on her shoulder. "She's the best there is at data retrieval, and she's turning into a good stick on the bird."

"Where do you keep it? I didn't see any aircraft when I arrived."

"That's because you're not supposed to, Mr. Davis." Larry Saski grinned and leaned against a bare dirt wall that was covered with what looked like parachute material. "We launch and recover the bird out of here, but when it's not airborne, we keep it tucked up inside that patch of woods you saw behind the site. Some of those trees ain't what they look like."

"The bird is a specially-modified Northrop-Grumman Model 410." Liccardi pointed at the photo on the cover of one of the tech manuals at Shake's elbow. "For this mission, the techno-geeks designed a version that has folding wings. We haul it out of the woods, load the sensor package, unfold the wings, and launch. When we bring it back in, we just reverse the procedure, recover, download, and shove it back up under the trees."

"Nobody's the wiser after we finish raking the snow." Tom Young shrugged into a parka that he pulled off a wall-hook and started for the door. "And we are some serious snow-raking mammy-jammers around here. Chow in about an hour, Mr. Davis. Can I set an extra plate?"

"Please do—and I'd feel much less like a turd in this punch-bowl if everyone just called me Shake."

* * *

The first thing Shake Davis did when Liccardi showed him to the crew living quarters beneath the adjacent snow mound was drop his trousers and remove the cell phone from its painful nest near his balls. Liccardi watched him rub talcum from his shaving kit on the tender spot and grinned. "You probably didn't need to bother. There's no coverage out here. We have to do all our comm through the transceiver sets and that can be iffy depending on the weather."

Shake depressed the power switch and watched the iPhone screen illuminate. It took a few seconds, but the phone eventually showed five bars and the international connection symbol. He tossed the phone to Liccardi and grinned. "That's a new model developed by the folks at a certain unspecified federal agency denoted by one consonant and two vowels. Bayer said I wouldn't have any coverage problems and it looks like he was right."

"Too damn bad Mike didn't have one of these." Liccardi examined the phone and the available apps with admiration. "We're still monitoring the net and making a call about once an hour—but nada. I've gotta figure the radio he was carrying is broken or something like that. He was supposed to check in every other day at a pre-arranged time. We got two no-sweat situation and position reports from him and then nothing since. That's when I fired a rocket up to Bayer."

"Bayer said you're former Air Force." Shake re-buckled his trousers and flopped on one of the rigid bunks lining the walls, "And you've got an intelligence background?"

"Guilty as charged. I was mostly tech-intel but I know how the other part of the game is played."

"So what's your take on what Mike was after? According to what I heard, you guys didn't have any hits on the nuke sensors around Chosin. What makes him want to take the chance on a personal recon in North Korea? I've known him for a long time. He usually doesn't do risky stuff without a good reason."

"I don't know what to tell you, Shake. Mike fed us leads that he developed from humint sources, but he kept a lot of stuff to himself. He'd disappear for days sometimes and we never knew where he was. I nearly shit myself the day he walked in here with two North Koreans in tow. He had us feed 'em a meal and then pulled an envelope out of his gear and proceeded to pay 'em big wads of cash. I talked to one of the NKs. The guy was a school-teacher from some little ville on the other side of the Yalu and spoke excellent English. Apparently Stokey made a couple of crossings to find these guys. I told him I thought it was risky as hell, but he claimed he knew what he was doing. That's another thing that's got me worried. Could be one or both of those guys wasn't as reliable as Mike claimed."

"If he got burned or double-crossed by one of 'em having second thoughts, we'd be in the middle of a big stink out of Pyongyang by now." Shake lit a cigarette and kicked off his boots to change socks. "If it was something like that it would be all over the TV or the State Department would be dealing with a ransom-hostage situation and Bayer would know about it. The North Koreans know how to play that game. I gotta figure Mike is still as OK as he can be that deep in bad-guy country. What I'd like to know is why he felt like he needed to conduct a personal reconnaissance. What the hell was he after? "

"He spent a lot of time with Julia before he left. I didn't catch a lot of it, but Mike was quizzing her about technical stuff. What I heard had to do with high-power electronics. You should talk to her."

"How about right after we eat? I'm a bit parched after the affairs of this fucking day."

"We're gonna run another mission over the Chosin area this afternoon," Liccardi laughed and pointed at a narrow little shower stall at the far end of the barracks bunker. "Get a shower with whatever warm water we've got left from the sun heater. You can talk to her before we launch."

Shake quickly stripped down for a much-needed wash. He was naked, shivering, and digging for a towel in his ruck when Liccardi paused at the barracks door. "I guess you'll give me what details you think I need—but are you planning on going across to look for Mike?"

"That's why I'm here, Dick. There's nothing complicated about it. We need to get him out of North Korea before he gets killed or caught. It's as simple as that."

"And you'll let me know how we fit into that scheme, right? I'm feeling a little uncomfortable in an essentially uncomfortable situation, you know? This mission and these people are my responsibility. Mike is on the roster as just another technician. If the Chinese find out he's a company man and operating across the Yalu out of here, I'm not sure what they'd do."

"I'll tell you everything I can, but it's all a little fluid at this point. The Chinese know I'm here, obviously, but I'm fairly certain they don't know why. We'll keep it that way if at all possible. I'll hang around with you until I hear from some guys who are supposed to meet me around here. After that, I'm on my own hook and you just continue the march. All I really need right now is a shower, some chow, and a place to re-charge the phone."

* * *

"One more thing." Shake stood at the edge of the pine forest with his phone watching Julia Dewey and Larry Saski hand pump JP-5 into the fuel cells of the UAV staged on the runway strip. "Talk to Chan and tell her I'm fine. Also have her dig around and get what she can on Marx generators, especially as they might relate to EMP."

"What's that about?" Bayer sounded a little less frustrated than he did when he first picked up the secure phone and discovered there was still no word from Stokey. "Have you got some kind of a lead?"

"Maybe. Apparently Mike spent some time with one of the technicians out here trying to find out about Marx generators. She said he sparked to the possibility of them being used to generate EMP. As usual, he didn't bother to let anyone know what he was thinking, but it could be he was looking into some kind of connection between that stuff and whatever's going on up around the Chosin."

"I'll call Chan and get into it with the tech-intel guys. Meanwhile, don't lose focus. Your business is to find Mike and get him out of North Korea. That's crucial. Pete Pak reports he's starting to get weird rumbles out of his PLA contacts. This whole deal could implode in a heartbeat. We'll worry about what Mike was doing over there once he's back under control."

"There's a plan in place. I don't want to say too much about it right now but I should be on the other side of the river in a day or two. They're about to launch another mission in a few minutes. Maybe they'll spot something this time."

"Keep me posted. A call a day with updates; that's all I ask."

"It's gonna be mostly text messages from now on—first one tomorrow." Shake punched out of the call just as the UAV engine began to turn. He could see the flaps and other flight control surfaces being tested by Liccardi who was manipulating the bird from inside the bunker. The little drone, showing its full 30-foot wingspan and an array of sensor pods, rumbled into a downwind position for take-off. Shake hustled toward the control bunker where he'd deposited his navigation gear. He needed to plan a route to the Chosin Reservoir and get it plugged into a GPS. The call from the Korean Marines could come at any time. And he wanted to talk to Liccardi about borrowing that bow.

T he Korean petty officer on the bow planes announced the boat was steady at the ordered depth, and the quarter-master of the watch hit an overhead switch to raise the periscope. The captain of the Son Won II Class diesel-electric submarine stepped up to the scope and made a quick 360-degree sweep for North Korean patrol boats. Passive sonar monitors declared the area free of threat vessels, but the captain was an experienced hand at clandestine operations in the Yellow Sea and not the kind of sailor who took unnecessary chances in those waters no matter how much reassurance he got from his technicians.

"Fifteen seconds, Captain." The quartermaster on the other side of the instrument let his CO know how much time the periscope mast had been exposed above the surface. The captain rarely needed or exceeded 30 seconds of visual observation. He was used to sailing quietly on instruments off the North Korean coast, but the current mission and their position just southwest of the mouth of the Yalu was a little too close for comfort. He oriented the scope toward the coastline and saw nothing but whitecaps: No patrol craft, no commercial vessels, and no fishing junks.

Now, if only it stays that way for a few more hours. The cap-tain stepped away from the eyepiece and nodded for the quartermaster to lower the scope. If the area remained clear until dark, he'd maneuver as close as possible to the shoal-waters and launch the 65-foot mini-sub latched onto his deck plates aft of the sail. "Resume previous depth and speed." The captain turned to his conning officer and pointed at an LED screen showing a navigational chart of the area. "Stay within the pre-plot and notify me immediately about any sonar contacts."

On his way aft to alert his three passengers that the mission looked like a go unless something changed before nightfall, the captain intercepted his diving officer heading for the sub's tiny wardroom. "All systems are in good shape, Captain. We've double-checked power plant, electronics and maneuvering gear, and the nav system has been synched and tested. My crew just finished loading most of the Marines' gear. Does it look like we launch tonight?"

"So far, I see no reason why not. What about the lithium-ion batteries? Any problems?"

"I think we've got that beat, sir. Whatever it was that caused the battery fire on the American version back in 2008, we haven't had any problems with it. We should probably let them in on our modifications one of these days. It seems only fair since they gave us the plans and prototype after they cancelled the Advanced SEAL Delivery System."

"That's a problem for someone else to solve." The submarine captain clapped his diving officer on the shoulder and edged past him in the narrow passageway. "Our problem is getting three men with more balls than brains off this boat and headed up the Yalu."

The submarine's passengers were gathered around the access trunk leading to the mini-sub's interior and going over a nautical chart with the navigator when the captain arrived. He motioned for them to continue what they were doing and watched as his navigator traced a northerly line along the Yalu with his finger. He called out river depths, and the lone civilian on the landing team carefully recorded them on a GPS device. The man looked calm, capable, and competent at what had to be more than twice the age of the two hard-faced Marine Commandos who sat nearby stuffing equipment into a big pack. When the captain got his mission brief at Yeonpyeong, Colonel Soon said the man with the odd name for a Korean was a former Marine with *Angibu* connections, vast experience, and a solid reputation. That was all he needed to know beyond the fact that a wise man didn't question Colonel Soon.

"We expect to commence launch operations in a little less than three hours." The captain checked his watch and smiled. "There's time for a good meal before you go. If there's anything else I can do for you in the meantime, just let me know."

At 2035 by the submarine's master chronometer, Sam Jackson and his two Korean Marine mission mates sat comfortably in the min-sub with all their gear neatly arranged around them. Forward in the bow sat the sub's diving officer and a petty officer from the navigator's crew as his co-pilot for the trip up the Yalu. With final checklists complete, they notified the sub that they were launching and hit the switches to release the modified ASDS into frigid water 85 feet below the surface of the Yellow Sea.

The solenoids tripped and the mini-sub's shrouded screw began to spin silently under impulse from powerful electric motors. The diving officer checked his navigational systems, ordered an increase in the throttle settings, and steered directly for the mouth of the Yalu River. Over the next 90 kilometers, cruising with China off their port side and enemy North Korea off their starboard side, they would have to stay as silent and as deep as water in the river would allow. If they were spotted by the Chinese or the North Koreans, there would be no return trip.

Changjin (Chosin) Reservoir, Democratic People's Republic of (North) Korea

By mid-afternoon, Stokey and Lee were well up into the range of rugged mountains that ran along the western side of the Chosin Reservoir area. Using snowshoes to cross the flat stretches between the peaks and ridgelines would have made for faster travel, but they stuck to the rocky edges where shadows masked their movement and they left no visible tracks in the snow. The white winter camouflage gear they were wearing would provide relatively good concealment from aerial observation, but it wouldn't be much help if the North Koreans began to search with thermal-imaging equipment.

They needed to find a place somewhere up high and fairly distant from the reservoir, hole-up to rest and plan a route, and then push on at dark. Lee did a thorough job collapsing the snow-hole and covering their route out of the area, but there was always the chance that they'd overlooked something. He didn't have much confidence in the ruse to shift blame for the security breach and the dead sentry onto the people of the village adjacent to the hydroelectric plant. That was just a gambit to buy time, and it wouldn't necessarily preclude further searches.

Of course, it could be I'm getting my skivvies in a twist over nothing, Stokey thought as he followed Lee up yet another boulder-strewn traverse. *Could be that stuff in the containers is just some high-tech electronic equipment that uses nuke-juice for power. Could be its just stuff that the fearless leader has ordered up to improve the power-grid in beautiful downtown Pyongyang.* In that case, the NKPA wouldn't shed much sweat finding the culprits. On the other hand, if the gear being built and shipped out of Changjin was destined to support some major North Korean power play involving EMP, it was a whole different deal. It could be a version of the old shell game. While the North Koreans rattle nuke-tipped missiles with one hand, with the other hand they are quietly preparing to strike with a different weapon that nobody thinks they've got. *If that's the case*, Stokey decided, *the NKPA will employ some serious operators to find out what happened. And in that case they'll start scouring the mountains with patrols and air searches before long.*

Lee paused in the shadow of a large rocky formation and waited for Stokey to join him. He pointed at a section of dark, ominous clouds on the western horizon. "Have you noticed it's getting colder, Mr.Stokey?" Mike could feel a blustery wind on his numbed cheeks and an ache in his fingertips, but they'd been humping too hard for him to notice much change in the ambient air temperature. He glanced at the clouds and nodded. "I'm guessing that's a snowstorm on the horizon."

"It will be on us in about one hour." Lee nodded and examined the boulders at their backs. "I suggest we take shelter here where there's a little wind-block and the rocks will absorb most of the snowfall." Stokey shrugged off his rucksack and dug for their little two-man arctic snow-shelter. The storm would keep any air searches grounded, but it might also add days to their escape from North Korea depending on the snow dump and how long the storm lasted. They didn't have much reasonable choice if they intended to reach the Yalu alive. And Stokey most assuredly intended to do just that. They'd risked way too much to die frozen stiff somewhere in the mountains of North Korea with what might turn out to be some very important intelligence.

It was pelting wind-driven snow by the time they crawled into the little white nylon shelter and wrapped themselves in sleeping bags. Stokey fingered the emergency transponder under his parka and decided he'd wait at least one more day before calling for help that might never come anyway. He listened to the wind howling down on them out of Manchuria and wondered how those ill-equipped and half-frozen Marines who'd last climbed these hills more than 50 years ago kept going, fighting cold that was just as much a bitter enemy as the swarms of Chinese soldiers bent on their destruction.

S hake was sitting in the barracks bunker examining the closely packed contour lines on his 1:50K map of North Korea with a little magnifying glass when Julia Dewey interrupted his route planning. "Gunner, we're bringing the bird back early. There's a big storm blowing in and it's headed right for Changjin and environs."

"Nothing on Mike?" Shake looked up from his work and decided he could use a cup of coffee. There was still no word from the Korean Marines, and he'd done about all the pre-planning he could without hearing from them. "Or did you have enough time over the target?"

"We had a couple of hours of clear coverage. Dick orbited in a widening search pattern from the reservoir. No nuke hits, no sign of Mike or any kind of signal from him either. There was just a convoy of three trucks headed east and some strange doings around the village near the hydroelectric plant."

"What kind of doings?" Shake stood, stretched, and headed for the door.

"Looked like some kind of major shake-down or a raid. There were NK troops all over the place herding the villagers around. We got it all recorded from the real-time video feed. You might want to take a look."

In the control-room bunker, Tom Young was scrolling through a grainy videotape that the crew had recorded as the UAV orbited over the village next to the Chosin Reservoir. "When we saw all this going on, Dick adjusted the orbit and we kept the bird overhead for a while to see what it was." Shake pulled up a chair as Young cued the tape to the beginning of the sequence. Dick Liccardi stood over his shoulder and pointed at the screen.

"We've been over that village a bunch of times." Liccardi stroked his mustache and tapped a fingernail on the video screen. "Never anything beyond what you'd expect from a little ville or people that obviously support the staff at the plant."

Shake watched armed uniformed figures shove clumps of civilians around like cattle. Others were charging in and out of the huts all along the main road that ran through the village. "Looks like a full-on search. Could be something went missing from the plant and these guys are looking for it?"

"Yeah, could be." Liccardi pulled up another chair and sat. "On the other hand, they might be looking for Stokey. No reason to think that, I guess, other than that we know he's in there somewhere."

"And it could be he either got into the ville for some reason, or he got spotted by one of the villagers." Shake continued to watch the taped activity that reminded him of scenes he'd seen hundreds of time in another part of the world: American troops conducting a cordon and search on a Vietnamese village.

"If that's the case, they didn't find him." Tom Young leaned back in his chair. "I've seen the entire sequence. There's a lot of pushing and shoving, and some of the NK soldiers were in and out of the huts a bunch of times. In the end, they marched about six people off toward the hydroelectric plant. Everyone else went back to business as usual."

"There's one other thing you should know." Dick Liccardi pointed toward an instrument bank in another corner. "We got some indications of unusual aircraft launches. Julia ran a scan for descriptives and they were all recon birds: Tupelovs and Antonovs out of Pyongyang and Wonsan."

"So they're looking for something—on the ground and in the air?"

"That would be my guess." Liccardi shrugged and pushed back in his chair. "The good news is they turned back about the same time we did. Nobody's gonna be flying in the storm."

It was 0745 local time as Mike Stokey crawled out of the arctic shelter and managed to shove through the accumulated snow that had fallen overnight. The howling, frigid wind that drove huge flurries of wet snow across the mountain all night was now just a steady whisper. Stokey stretched and relieved his aching bladder. Snow was still falling at this altitude, but it was now the sort of light, powdery stuff he hoped would cover any tracks they were forced to make moving west toward the Yalu.

At first light when Lee crawled out of the shelter to check on the snowfall, he reported hearing aircraft flying in a north-south pattern over the mountains. Stokey checked the lightening sky, but he could see nothing through the low, dense cloud banks, and that likely meant neither pilots nor cameras could either. He heard the sound of several more high-flying aircraft as they consumed some of their meager remaining rations and noted the air activity was unusual—more than they'd ever heard in the past two weeks around the Chosin Reservoir. Their deflection trick had likely failed. The NKs were looking for someone or something, and the little village was no longer the focus of their search.

They needed to get moving but very carefully with a clearing sky full of eyes and cameras. Visibility at altitude was likely good, but the craggy high ground all around them was still socked in tight. Lee thought they'd be safe enough to move as long as they avoided any peaks, passes, or clearings that would take them out from under the cloud cover. Stokey agreed. What speed they could make was essential. If the weather continued to improve and the cloud cover burned off, it wouldn't be long before they were dodging low-flying helicopters.

After a careful map-study, they decided that the best bet was to continue due west and head for a paved road that ran north-south through a series of switchback ridgelines toward Pyongyang. If they could make that road by nightfall, they could cut as much as a full day off their trek by running parallel over good ground before turning west again and back up into the mountains. On the other side of those mountains was a long, heavily-forested valley that led directly to the banks of the Yalu.

Stokey took a compass bearing and nodded in a westerly direction. They stepped off toward higher ground, crunching through fresh snow and holding a good pace for about a kilometer. At that point, reduced visibility and thinner air forced them into a slow muscle-grinding plod.

Yalu River, North of Dandong, Peoples Republic of China

S am Jackson hopped over the gunwale of the small rubber raiding craft onto Chinese soil and turned just in time to see the mast of the mini-sub sink below the frigid waters of the Yalu. As they'd done hundreds of times before on clandestine missions from the sea, the two ROK Marine Commandos ran the boat up under a stand of trees and expertly camouflaged it with native brush and snow. There were high-flying aircraft orbiting far off to the east over the North Korean mountains, but Sam was fairly certain their landing had not been spotted.

He was gratified to see the Marines wordlessly take up overwatch positions inside the gloom of the little forested stand where they could scan visible stretches of the river and spot anyone approaching across the open country to the south toward the Chinese settlements at Dandong. The Marines seemed to be as competent and professional as he remembered from his own active duty days. They also seemed quite happy to be on dry ground and out of the clammy confines of the mini-sub. Not that the ride was uncomfortable. The little submersible was warm and dry, but like all passengers who have no control over their fate, they suffered from spending helpless hours bobbing up and down as the pilots maneuvered the small craft over and around obstacles while fighting like a spawning salmon against the rushing current of the Yalu.

The mini-sub crew made the nerve-jangling trip without ever having to surface or broach the boat; relying on active sonar and other sensors to avoid underwater obstacles. They were exhausted by the time they half-surfaced just before dawn to launch the landing party at a site where the river was becoming too shallow to hide them. Sam didn't envy the crew the return trip to meet the submarine still loitering out in the Yellow

Sea, but he was confident they'd make the withdrawal with all the skill they demonstrated on the insertion.

Pulling the UHF encrypted radio out of their gear package, Sam rigged a field-expedient antenna, selected the assigned frequency, inserted a plastic encryption key, and hit the transmit button. After an anxious minute, the green light on the radio control panel flashed. The submarine had received the safe arrival message. They would now loiter out there under icy waters waiting for a second transmission from the same source. That would come after the search party returned from North Korea with the American agent safely in hand. Then the captain would order the mini-sub crew to make a second harrowing trip up the Yalu.

Sam Jackson popped a piece of his favorite winter *kimchee* into his mouth, checked their position on his GPS unit, and reached for his cell phone. He punched up the message app and typed in coordinates for their position and a simple message: **STANDING BY HERE.**

It was deathly silent on the winding road except for the crunch of their boots and the ragged pant of their breathing, so Stokey and Lee heard the approaching vehicles long before they saw the flash of headlights cutting through the dark. As they did on two previous occasions when trucks passed heading north, they scrambled up the slope on the right, flopped behind a fold in the snow-covered ground, and waited. They'd made good time humping along the hard surface and Stokey's pace count indicated they could make the turn west in about another hour if they could stay on the road.

Three vehicles approached through the haze of falling snow, and Stokey spotted an aerial-festooned military Jeep or command car in the lead. Crawling behind it at safe intervals for the slick road conditions were two trucks with canvas-covered cargo beds. Stokey ducked as the vehicles negotiated a hard right turn and headlights swept over their hiding place. The only other vehicles they'd seen on the road were civilian cargo haulers, and he tried to keep himself from reading anything peculiar into the appearance of a military convoy.

They remained hidden above the road surface until the sound of the vehicles faded and then Stokey nudged Lee. "Probably nothing to worry about—let's keep moving." They slid down onto the surface of the road, stepped into the tire-tracks, and headed south at a brisk pace. The little thermometer Stokey had attached to his jacket zipper-pull had bottomed out, but as long as they kept moving the cold was not a factor.

Lee was in the lead when they trudged around a sharp turn in the road and ran into a North Korean soldier. They were on him before Stokey recognized the figure bundled in white winter camouflage on the side of the road for what it was. Lee froze in place and said something in Korean as Stokey, standing about 15 meters to his rear, glanced up to a patch of high ground where a flashlight beam glowed in a stand of snow-covered trees. The soldier was as shocked as they were to encounter pedestrians on the road in this remote area, but it didn't take him long to reach for the weapon slung across his back. While Lee and the startled sentry exchanged guttural phrases, Stokey reached inside his parka and retrieved the Makarov. When the soldier aimed his weapon, Lee raised his hands and Stokey slid to the left to establish a clear field of fire. As the muzzle of the man's AK swept in his direction, he triggered two quick rounds, aiming center-mass over the suppressor tube. The sentry folded and collapsed like a rag-doll but not before he triggered a single shot that echoed off the hills like a cannon in the still air.

He heard shouts from the pine forest as Stokey ran forward to retrieve the dying man's weapon and led the way up the slope on the opposite side of the road. They were about halfway up the rise when the flashlight beam caught them, and Stokey heard the familiar bark of an AK firing on full-auto. There was a stand of boulders to their right front and Stokey headed for it, plunging as fast as he could through knee-deep snow. A second burst of fire from the road-bed followed them, and Stokey heard a grunt. Lee was still moving, but he was hobbling and holding onto a spot on his right leg at about mid-thigh.

Stokey spun, clicked the stolen AKS-74 onto full-auto, and triggered a burst into the glare of the flashlight below him. Almost instantly it was full dark again on the slope. The flashlight was rolling along the side of the road casting weird shadows in the opposite direction. He grabbed Lee and supported him as they struggled toward the rocks and cover for whatever was going to happen next.

Nothing happened for a full five minutes. Stokey shifted his gaze from the road where he could just make out two humped and motionless figures laying the snow. "Nobody else in sight." Stokey shrugged out of his pack and retrieved a first-aid kit. "They must have been some kind of outpost or road security derail—and that means somebody's gonna be checking on them shortly." He snapped on a penlight to examine Lee's wound. The only visible blood was a smear around a ragged exit hole just above the knee. "Looks like it was through-and-through. Drop your trousers and let me get a better look."

Lee did as directed and Stokey confirmed his initial judgment. The round hit from the rear and plowed through muscle well away from the bone in Lee's thigh. He covered both holes with antiseptic and quick-clot and then wrapped the wounds tightly with a battle dressing. "It's gonna hurt but we need to get moving."

They plowed uphill at a slow but steady pace, moving west and holding to what terrain Lee could negotiate with his game leg. Even with the steady snowfall covering most of their tracks, the hills adjacent to the road would likely be crawling with patrols by dawn. They needed to find some place to hole up and hide until some of the heat from the deadly encounter abated. Stokey looked up through the drifting snow and saw the dark outlines of a rock formation. He had 50 feet of climbing rope in his rucksack and an idea.

W hen the phone stashed under his parka vibrated, Shake flinched and sent one of Liccardi's hunting arrows wide of the target they'd been using for archery practice. "Scared the shit out of me," he said and handed Liccardi the compound bow as he reached for the phone. The text message on the iPhone screen was what he'd been waiting for, and he headed for the bunker where he could check the coordinates on his map. "Looks like my contacts have arrived," he said to the UAV pilot. "You still willing to let me borrow the bow and some arrows?"

"Sure." Liccardi followed him toward the control room. "You seem to know what you're doing with it. You out of here or what?"

"As soon as I can get a position plugged into my GPS, I'm heading for a meet with some Korean escorts." Shake hustled down the stairs and through the storm door into the control room. "The plan is to get across the Yalu, find Mike, and get the hell out ASAP. We get that much done and we'll be out of your hair." He checked the map and did a quick estimate of the distance between the UAV site and the coordinates sent by the Korean Marines. He had about 15 kilometers to cover on a southwesterly track.

* * *

The GPS he'd been following all morning indicated he was in the right spot or close to it, but Shake saw nothing but a snow-covered stand of trees on his right and the muddy brown waters of the Yalu on his left. He wandered toward the trees and glanced up at the clear blue sky where two aircraft were in high orbit over the North Korean mountains. Given what he'd seen on the video from the UAV mission over Chosin, he didn't like the feel of that. One orbiting aircraft was likely routine, but two of them probably indicated there was an air search in progress. That meant they'd have to do most of their traveling and hunting for Stokey at night.

"Just like old times." Shake froze at the sound of the familiar voice. Sam Jackson stepped out from behind a tree and Shake saw two nearby snow piles transform into men with rifles pointed at him. Sam approached with a plastic baggie open in his hand. "Thought you might want some of this." Shake could smell the winter *kimchee* from a distance but he was too shocked to respond. Sam nodded at the two grinning commandos. "Let me introduce you to a couple of good men. The one on the right is Sergeant Park. The other one is Sergeant Jun. They both speak excellent English so watch what you say."

"I don't know what the hell to say." Shake shook hands with the two Korean Marines. "I didn't expect to see *you* here. Tell me you're not planning on going along on this boondoggle."

"If I did that I'd be lying, Shake." Sam jerked a thumb in the direction of the commandos. "These guys are among the best we've got, but they've never operated this far north. They need guidance from a more experienced hand—and that would be me."

"Sam—seriously—there's no reason for you to risk your ass on this thing. Park and Jun can keep me out of trouble. We'll search around for Mike, hopefully find him in a hurry, and get back here. You guys dial up a ride and we're gone."

"That's all set and on call. We'll come back here with your guy and the mini-sub that brought us in will come back to take us out. From there it's onto a sub standing by out in the Yellow Sea and we're home for dinner."

"I still don't like the idea of you doing this, Sam. It's my problem and my responsibility."

"Just consider me another strong back and another pair of eyes. I'm going along, and there's no use arguing about it at this point." Sam produced a GPS from under his parka and punched the power switch. "I've got the quickest route from here to

Changjin programmed. Let's get the data plugged into your GPS and then pack up. We brought the extra gear you wanted."

"Probably best we cross and start after dark." Shake could see that his old friend was in no mood for further dispute. The two Korean NCOs looked capable and professional, but he was secretly glad to be going into serious jeopardy with someone he knew and trusted. "I'm hoping you guys brought night-vision gear."

Sergeant Park pointed at a spot near where the escort team had stashed their gear. "We've got four sets, sir. Gen Three PVS-14s with fresh batteries. Let me show you what we've got and you can get familiar with it before we launch." As Park and Jun sorted through the gear and answered Shake's questions, they spoke calmly in relatively unaccented English with no apparent concern for the fact that they were on the ground in China and about to venture uninvited into enemy North Korea. Shake decided he was going into a risky situation with good men at his side.

"We brought a weapon for you, sir." Sergeant Jun dug around under a white camouflage cover and nodded at the compound bow strapped across Shake's back. "You can probably leave the bow here—if you want." Sam Jackson reached over to snap the bowstring against Shake's chest. "Were you planning on some kind of Robin Hood deal, Shake?"

"It's the only weapon I could find. I borrowed it from a guy at the UAV site. I'm not sure what I was planning on doing with it, but it seemed like cheap insurance."

"This might work a little better." Sam took a bundle from Sergeant Jun, fiddled with some straps and revealed a pristine and well-oiled Swedish K submachine gun. He pulled out four fully-loaded magazines and handed it all to Shake. "I seem to remember you were pretty handy with one of those."

"It's been a while, Sam..." Shake checked the chamber and inserted one of the magazines. "But I believe I can still remember which end the bullet comes out of."

"If we get in a fight, I'd suggest you use that instead of the bow and arrows."

"And I'd suggest we not get in a fight, Sam."

Just after dark, Shake and his escorts rowed the small boat across the Yalu and hid it along the riverbank on the other side. By midnight they were well up into the Kangnam Mountain Range and heading east at a slow but steady pace.

H anging dangerously close to the end of his climbing rope, Mike Stokey used his penlight to inspect the hole in the cliff face. *It isn't deep but its damn sure dark*, he thought, *and it'll have to do for now*. The other end of the rope was secured to the trunk of a thick tree about 30 feet above where Lee sat resting his aching leg. There was a rock ledge about halfway down the sheer cliff and just above the little cave that should hide them from anyone looking over the edge into the snow-covered valley below the mountain. If they stayed deep enough in the small cut, they'd be invisible to anyone looking up from below the cliff. What happened after they got themselves out of sight, Stokey hadn't quite determined yet. First things first and the key was to avoid detection until the roving patrols he expected at daylight moved to another area in their search for the people who killed the soldiers on the road.

Stokey snapped a pair of ascenders onto the rope, maneuvering the bitter end of the line around his ankle in a fashion that would allow him to push as well as pull in the climb back up cliff face. At the top, he explained his plan to Lee who agreed they didn't have much choice with dawn rapidly approaching. Mike went to the anchor tree and tied a slip-knot in the climbing rope. Then he spliced on a length of parachute cord. Once they were both safely down near the cave, he could simply jerk on the cord and retrieve the larger line, leaving no trace for anyone poking around the area.

Lee seemed to think he could make the descent unassisted, and he gingerly walked down the cliff face as Mike instructed with the rope belayed around his waist and favoring his wounded leg. Mike scuffed up the trampled snow around the cliff edge, checked the line, and then began his own descent. It wasn't getting down that had him worried. It was getting back up with no climbing rope. That would be the problem and he had no really good idea how to solve it.

Dawn was beginning to throw shadows across the eastern peaks as they retrieved the rope and settled into the frigid, uncomfortable cave. After Stokey helped Lee change the dressing on his leg wound, he reached under his parka, found his emergency signaling device and pressed the transmit button.

B arbara Casburn was sound asleep when her cell phone rang. She fumbled on the nightstand and managed to knock over her favorite reading lamp before she retrieved the instrument and discovered a text message. The sender ID read MIKE. She righted the lamp, snapped it on, and sat up to read the message she'd been dreading. It simply said **WISH YOU WERE HERE** and contained a set of numbers. She reached for a pen and jotted the figures on a pad: **40/23N – 127/15E**.

She headed for the kitchen to keep from disturbing Marcus, her sleeping husband, and searched around in the junk drawer for the slip of paper she'd used to record a critical mobile phone number. She punched up the message app and thumbed in a text: **HEARD FROM MIKE**. As directed, she added the local time in Texas and the numbers that she hoped would tell Shake Davis where to find her brother.

"They're searching for us." Lee had been listening for the past few tense minutes to shouted conversations in Korean that echoed clearly off the surrounding rocks. "They seem to think the intruders are either Chinese or South Korean."

"Can you tell how many?" Stokey quietly checked the magazine in the stolen AKS-74 and figured he had about ten rounds remaining from the lethal burst he'd fired to eliminate the North Korean road guard the previous night. Those rounds and the four remaining in his Makarov were all they had to use if they were discovered. Lee held up four fingers but Stokey knew that number only included the searchers they could hear around the cliff edge above them. He glanced out the mouth of the cave and saw blue sky illuminated by bright sunlight. The patrol above them would likely give up on this area shortly, but the clear weather would bring helicopters into the game. And helicopters didn't have to worry about climbing up or down sheer cliffs to conduct their searches.

"There's an officer." Lee pointed upward and listened to a guttural conversation. "He's calling his men lazy cats. He says they will stay out here all day and all night if necessary." Stokey nodded and motioned for Lee to shuttle deeper into the cave as sunlight began to spill across the cliff face. The Korean moved with difficulty. His wounded leg was now swollen, coloring into an ugly shade and badly in need of medical attention. Stokey thought it over and quickly decided there was nothing practical or useful to do about that at the moment. He scratched at a spot on his chest where the emergency transmitter rested and wondered if his signal had gotten through. He'd been an obstinate idiot to insist on one-way communication with the

device. The longer he considered the more disgusted he became.

*What the hell was I thinking? Even if Babs gets the message
and calls Shake, then what? Shake will likely just call Bayer and
report that I'm in trouble and give the CIA my location. So
what? What is Bayer—or anyone else for that matter—going to
be able to do about this shitty situation? It's not likely they'll risk
an incursion into North Korea to rescue one operator who
violated orders and got his ass in a serious crack for unknown
reasons beyond sheer stupidity. About all my super-slick,
super-secret emergency signaling device does is let people
know where to look for the body.*

With the exception of a loyal but wounded partner who really had no stake in the situation beyond a payday, he was on
his own with slim chances of survival. The one thing he did not
want to do is wind up captured. That would be a fate worse than
death for him, and Lee would likely never survive to see his
family much less get them out of North Korea. If the Norks
found them, he was determined to go down in a fight. If they
remained undetected until nightfall, he intended to explore a
bit and see if there was a way up or down the cliff with the rope
and equipment he had in his pack. If he could just do that much
before push came to shove, he'd tell Lee that his part of the job
was done. Lee could make his way back to the UAV site on his
own and collect his money without taking any further risks.
Meanwhile, they just had to hide and survive.

The patrol scouring the area around the cliff edge was gone
about an hour when they heard the first clatter of rotors echoing
off the surrounding mountains. Stokey and Lee shoved snow
toward the mouth of the shallow ice cave and wrapped themselves in the white arctic shelter.

* * *

Shake glanced across the trail leading through the mountain
pass and saw nothing but two irregular humps in the snow
beneath the rocks on that side. Sergeants Park and Jun had

expertly constructed burrows, and if Shake couldn't spot them from 20 feet away, there was no way the circling helicopters would. On his side of the cut there was a long rock ledge where he and Sam Jackson sat in deep shadow that hid them from aerial view.

"This much traffic is unusual, Shake." Sam Jackson pointed at the sky overhead where they'd been listening to North Korean helos scour the area for the past couple of hours. "They've got to be looking for someone or something. I'm betting your boy got busted and he's on the run."

"Yeah, and I'm gonna call that good news for now. They wouldn't be out here looking so hard if they had him already." Shake was more worried about search parties poking around on the ground while they waited out the day hiding from helicopters. "How come no foot patrols so far?"

"Lots of ground and not enough people to cover it would be my guess." Sam squinted at his GPS and noted they had fewer than 30 clicks to cover before they reached the Changjin area. "They're probably doing a grid search. Choppers work an area and if they spot anything suspicious, they call for the infantry."

Shake compared figures with his GPS and wondered absently what happened to stir up the hornet's nest. With no word from Mike, there was no way of knowing if he was running or hiding. "What's got me worried is thermal-imaging. You suppose the Norks have that kind of gear this far out in the boondocks?"

"They've got the gear closer to the flagpole." Sam pulled the bag containing the last of his *kimchee* supply out from under his white parka and offered some to Shake. "Whether the bastards would get it out here and use it depends on what they're looking for and how bad they want to find it."

Shake was examining a map, trying to determine what route Stokey might pick if he was on the run, when his cell phone vibrated. He pulled off a glove and dug around in his layers of winter clothing looking for the instrument. After scanning the terse message he elbowed Sam. "We've got a grid."

They quickly plugged the coordinates into a GPS and hunkered over the map looking for the position indicated as Shake explained the significance of the message from Barbara Casburn in Quitman, Texas on the other side of the world. "You suppose that's right?" Sam Jackson put his gloved finger on a spot showing a thick stretch of tightly-packed contour intervals. "Looks like just a range of sheer cliffs above this deep valley."

"How far is it?" Shake was fairly certain about only one thing. Mike would not have sent the position message unless he was in trouble. And if he sent a position report, he'd likely stay where he was hoping for some sort of emergency response.

"About eight clicks." Sam measured the distance between where the GPS said they were and the spot where Stokey claimed to be. "We should be able to make it tonight, but it would be a lot easier if we had some way to communicate with him when we get into the area."

"We'll move at dark. I might know a way to get his attention."

When he stepped off the elevator and charged into the turmoil within the Agency's Asia Section, the man called Bayer knew the TV reports were true. He elbowed into a circle of analysts who were speculating wildly as reports from network foreign correspondents blared in the background. North Korean Supreme Leader Kim Jong-Il was dead of a heart attack, and Pyongyang was in turmoil. Apparently, his son Kim Jong-Un was moving up into the vacant leadership spot, but none of the analysts seemed to have a good grasp on what that might mean to the ever-shifting geopolitical scheme in Asia. He listened to the conversations intently wondering what it might mean for his sub-rosa surveillance mission and what he might need to do about it in the next hour or so.

"No official reaction out of Beijing so far." A staffer barged into the circle carrying a sheaf of translated news reports from his area of study. "They're likely wondering the same thing we are: How is the North Korean military going to react?" He dumped a pile of print-outs on the desk and scurried back toward the China Desk.

"They'll sit still for it, I think." The senior analyst on the Korea Desk pulled his gaze away from a bank of barking TV monitors. "Kim Jong-Un comes out of the military bailiwick. He's only 28 or 29 but he's a full general and his father has been grooming him for the number one spot for years. The real question is whether or not they'll seat him as leader of the party."

Another analyst waved for attention as he scrolled through reports on his computer. "Seoul just put the entire military on full alert—Army, Navy, Air Force, the whole deal."

"Here's the official statement from Beijing." The senior Korea analyst pointed to a scroll running beneath the shot of a

CNN reporter standing in Tiananmen Square. "No surprise, I guess. They're expressing deepest respect for a fallen comrade and condolences to the Korean people for the loss of a great visionary leader."

"That's not all they're doing." The minion from the China Desk returned waving a sheet of paper. "The PLA just issued orders for a full alert." Bayer left them to their speculation. The death of Kim Jong-Il was an intelligence analyst's wet dream, and the experts on the area would be squabbling over cause and effect for weeks. He had more pressing problems.

Back in his office, he brought his computer screen to life and scrolled through a large batch of incoming phone calls he needed to answer. Almost all of them were from people who would be looking for his opinion on the situation in Korea. He ignored them and brought up the classified communications register. Blinking for priority attention was an encrypted email from Pete Pak, his man in Seoul. Bayer keyed in his personal access code to open the file and discovered that Pak had filed his note from Beijing just a half-hour earlier.

S-H-T-F IN PLA. Bayer read the first line and decided shit-hit-the-fan was probably an understatement. He had serious trouble on his hands. **CONTACTS INSISTING ON IMMEDIATE SHUT-DOWN OF NORK SURVEILLANCE OPS. NO CHANCE FOR NEGOTIATION GIVEN SITUATION IN PY. WE HAVE 24 HOURS TO CALL IT OFF AND PACK UP FOR IMMEDIATE EVAC OF ALL EQUIPMENT AND PERSONNEL. I CAN HELP WITH EXFIL TO SEOUL VIA PRIVATE AIRCRAFT BUT NEED YOUR INPUT. STANDING BY...PP.**

Bayer picked up his remote and triggered power to the TV across the room. It was muted and tuned to Fox News as it always was. The network was showing crowd reaction scenes from Pyongyang. Civilians and soldiers near Kumsusan Memorial Palace and in the plaza near the Arch of Triumph were weeping openly and putting on a well-orchestrated show of national grief. Many of them were carrying banners emblazoned with the portrait of the recently-deceased, unpredictable little comic-opera dictator that most Americans only knew from the movie *Team America: World Police*. He pulled open a desk drawer and found the special cell phone that kept him in contact with Shake Davis somewhere northeast of that turbulent capitol. There was nothing new beyond the text he'd received last night. Davis and escorts were proceeding toward a point indicated by Mike Stokey's emergency transmitter.

Bayer needed to do a couple of things in a hurry, and high on the list was getting his people as far from China and North Korea as possible in the shortest possible time. His desk phone chirped for attention as he was contemplating how best to do that, and Bayer saw the caller was Chan Davis. There was no use dodging. She'd find him one way or another and demand information. He picked up the handset and punched the button to take the call.

"You've seen the reports from Pyongyang." Chan didn't waste time with small talk and she sounded upset which was perfectly understandable. If Bayer knew Shake was already in North Korea, there was no question his wife did too. "What are you gonna do about it?"

"There's no need to panic..." Bayer tried to sound upbeat and confident but Chan Davis was having none of it. "You know that's bullshit and so do I. The whole area is in what amounts to DefCon One and we've got some folks waving in the breeze if you take my meaning."

"I'm in the process of issuing instructions to all concerned. I can't say much more right now. I'll call you and we can meet as soon as I get it sorted out. I'll tell you what I know and what the next step is as soon as I can."

"You'd better." Chan sounded resolute and there was a very icy tone in her voice that put Bayer on edge. "I swear to God, if something happens to my husband on this thing, I'll be talking to some friends at the Post and, believe me, you don't want that."

"Chan, there's no reason to worry right now, and there's certainly no call to make threats."

"That's not a threat. That's a promise. I'll be waiting to hear what's up and I'd suggest you make it quick." The line went dead. Bayer swiveled toward his computer and began to tap out a response to Pete Pak in Seoul: **UNDERSTAND SITUATION. PROCEED WITH ARRANGEMENTS FOR TEAM EXFIL. I WILL CONTACT THEM WITH ORDERS TO BREAK DOWN AND STAND BY FOR IMMEDIATE MOVE TO SEOUL. KEEP ME ADVISED OF PROGRESS AND/OR REQUIREMENTS ON THIS END.**

Bayer sent the message and switched to another classified address for Dick Liccardi and his people at the UAV site. By the time he'd sent the evacuation order, he was feeling a little better. They were losing a potentially valuable intelligence resource, but it was probably time to eliminate the risk and shut it all down anyway. They'd gotten nothing valuable on North Korean nuclear efforts and he'd damn near given himself ulcers worrying about running a dark operation that could blow up in his face at any time. He decided he could afford a half-hour for lunch that would give him a little break to decide what needed to happen with Shake Davis and Mike Stokey.

Bayer strolled into the cafeteria about halfway to a difficult decision. After lunch, he'd order Shake to drop the mission and run for the UAV site where he could be evacuated with the rest of the team. If he hadn't found Stokey by now, he was unlikely to find him before the exfil started. Stokey got himself into this mess and now it was up to him to get himself out of it. A Clandestine Services operator on the CIA payroll was involved in a brutal business full of extraordinary risk. A guy like Mike Stokey understood that.

Ministry of the People's Armed Forces, Pyongyang

Marshal Kim Jun-Yi, Minister of Defense for the People's Republic, was changing into his best dress uniform for the first meeting of the senior staff since the formal announcement of the Supreme Leader's demise. As the mentor and military man most personally associated with the anointed successor, Kim's input at this meeting of the nation's uniformed power-brokers was crucial, and he had no intention of appearing frazzled or over-wrought. There would be no coup attempts, no power plays, and no turbulence in the ranks beyond the anticipated maneuvering for coveted positions in a new regime. Marshal Kim would see to that as diligently as he'd worked for the past decade to insure what he desired was—for all intents and purposes—the same as what Kim Jong-Un desired for the Democratic Peoples Republic.

A senior aide stepped into the Marshal's office and smiled as his boss pivoted to check his appearance in a full-length mirror. "Very impressive, Comrade Marshal, as always." The aide opened his ever-present agenda calendar and read for a moment. "All officers on the list have responded and most are already in the building. The meeting is set for the inner council chamber as you ordered."

"Good." The Marshal walked to his desk and began to sort through a stack of papers. "This should not take long. I have some thoughts for the senior leadership before we call on General Kim Jong-Un and declare him The Great Successor and Supreme Commander. You have the official announcements ready for broadcast?"

"All is prepared, Comrade Marshal. At your order we will release to the foreign press and begin airing the official announcements on statewide radio and television." The aide snapped his calendar closed and cut a quick glance outside the window where a massive mourning demonstration was loudly and colorfully in progress. "And might I add that the demonstrations are going exceedingly well. All the foreign networks are showing them."

Marshal Kim nodded and then snatched at a message form in the pile of paperwork on his cluttered desk. His smile faded quickly and he glanced up at his aide over the rims of his reading glasses. "Still nothing from Changjin?"

"There is nothing of interest." The aide had been faithfully following all reports from the area for the past 48 hours as ordered and had no need to look for updates. "As you know, the State Security agents we sent are convinced the village people had nothing to do with the sentry's death. We are continuing to search the area where the two soldiers were killed with both air and ground assets."

"And you still believe it was the Chinese?" The Marshal checked his watch and lit a cigarette. He was beginning to believe they were chasing ghosts. Nothing had gone missing from the project support facility at Changjin, and the all-out search effort was a drain on scarce assets at a critical time.

"You'll recall, Comrade Marshal, the Chinese scientific delegation that consulted with our academicians on the Marx generator capabilities were suspicious of our intent. There were very high-level queries from Beijing regarding our plans after the delegation returned from Pyongyang."

"And we responded that the generators were intended to improve and supplement our electrical power grid as we told them in the first place when we requested assistance. There were no further questions." Marshal Kim narrowed his eyes and glared at his senior aide. "Or were there?"

"There were no further official queries that I know of, Comrade Marshal. But that doesn't mean there were no further questions. Our Chinese comrades can be very suspicious—even to the point of paranoia as we know from our experiences with missile technology. Perhaps they decided to see for themselves what we are doing at Changjin. It seems to me most likely."

"And if it was indeed Chinese infiltrators, Colonel, what would they have found?" The Marshal walked toward his full-length mirror and took a last look at his turn-out for the crucial staff meeting. "They might have seen generators being built to their specifications. They might have seen those generators being placed in containers to be hauled away on trucks—nothing more suspicious or interesting than that. We are wasting time and assets with this business at Changjin. The aircraft will be needed for more important work soon and I want the Special Forces troops on hand here in the capitol. Call it off."

"I will transmit orders immediately, Comrade Marshal." The aide held the door open for his departing boss. "Am I to presume preparations for the Wonsan operation are to continue?"

"Nothing changes except the leadership," said Marshal Kim Jun-Yi as he strode through the door and out into a tiled hallway. "And that is no change at all."

UAV Site, Liaoning Province, Peoples Republic of China

"What about Gunner Davis?" Julia Dewey spun away from the computer screen showing the evacuation order and glared at Dick Liccardi who was going over a classified equipment manifest with Tom Young. "He's somewhere over in Nork Land. How's he gonna get out?"

"Shake Davis is not our problem right now." Liccardi looked up from the equipment manifest and shrugged. "You gotta figure the people who sent him in there will figure a way to get him out. Meantime, we've got less than 24 hours to pack-up, destroy, or disable anything we can't carry and get out of Dodge."

"There ought to be something we could do." Julia slumped in her chair until Tom Young walked over and tapped the computer screen.

"Damn, Julia! Did you read this thing? Shut it down immediately. Destroy all Block I and II gear, upload all standing mission data on the secure link, burn the shitters, empty the ashtrays, and stand by to get our asses hauled out of here by helo starting at midnight local. What part don't you understand?"

"I don't understand how we just leave Gunner Davis hanging..."

"We're not leaving anybody hanging!" Liccardi put an end to the conversation. "We're shutting down a highly-classified and highly-sensitive mission. It should come as no surprise to anyone that we're getting the bum's rush. We get popped running drone missions over North Korea at a time like this and the live loon replacing the dead loon in Pyongyang might see it as an act of war." Liccardi glared around the control room at his crew for a moment and then nodded. "Let's get hot. Tom, you start on the class gear. Gut everything on the list and destroy the components. Larry and Julia get outside and start on the bird."

"What do you want done with that?" Larry Saski was heading for the door with a reluctant Julia Dewey in tow. "We used most of the packing material building the shelters."

"That proud bird with the cast-iron tail remains in China. Unbolt the wings and gut the sensor package completely. Pull all the navigation gear, take a hammer to anything you're not sure about, and then let the damn thing sit. I want everyone on the airstrip ready to go by midnight."

The man who calls himself Bayer looked frazzled as he stepped into the Davis condo and shrugged out of his coat. Chan took the coat but didn't welcome the senior CIA man with her usual hug. The icy atmosphere wasn't lost on Bayer, who just nodded and headed for a seat near the living room fireplace. He was left alone staring into the fire for long minutes before Chan Davis came out of the kitchen with a pair of drinks in her hands.

Bayer smiled, sipped and shivered. "Damn, I needed that after today."

"You're lucky I didn't slip you a Mickey." Chan slumped into a seat on the other side of the coffee table. "It was a tough choice between scotch and cyanide."

"Have you heard from him?" Bayer put his drink on a coaster and tugged at his tie.

"Two text messages—both vaguely worded because he wasn't sending over your secret-squirrel set-up—one said he was heading into the interior. The other said he'd heard from Mike's sister. I take it all to mean he's in North Korea and he's got some kind of location on Mike. There's been nothing since then."

"That about matches what I've heard. He's sending texts rather than calling and I'm thinking that's because he thinks it's safer."

"Or because he's surrounded by North Korean troops and up to his eyeballs in trouble."

"There's no reason to believe that, Chan." Bayer picked up his drink and drained it. "Can I get another one of these?"

"Maybe." Chan Davis learned forward in her chair and pointed a slim finger at her old friend. "And this time it will be cyanide if you don't tell me you've ordered him out of there."

"I sent the message right after lunch. He's to pull out imme-diately, make his way back to the UAV site and evacuate along with them to Seoul."

"So you're pulling the plug on that deal too?" Chan rose, retrieved Bayer's empty glass and headed for the wet bar. "Good idea. I was at a DIA assessment meeting this afternoon. Every-one seems to be more worried about China than North Korea. We could be looking at some major political power plays over there."

"It wasn't exactly my idea, Chan. The Chinese ordered it shut down but it's just as well. For what we were getting, it wasn't worth the risk and our PLA contacts were fairly adamant. They gave us twenty-four hours to cease and desist. I've got a guy in Beijing who's handling the exfil. They should all be safely back in Seoul tomorrow or the next day at the latest."

Chan handed over a fresh drink and stood staring at the fire for a moment. "And you sent all this info to Shake?"

"I didn't provide details. He's got enough on his mind. I just told him the mission was being shut down and to get back to the UAV site immediately. He's to go with them back to Seoul."

"Did he acknowledge?"

"Not so far." Bayer pulled his special cell phone from a pocket and scrolled through messages for a moment, hoping Chan would not dig too deeply into the question of what happens to Mike Stokey. "But I should hear something shortly."

Chan thought for a moment and then sipped at her drink. "What about the escorts he was supposed to be with? He said he was going in with some South Korean commandos."

"I don't know much about that. Neither does my guy in Seoul. I'm guessing Shake will figure something out. He's not the kind of guy to leave people hanging."

"No, he's not—unlike some people we know." Chan sat on the edge of a chair and glared. "So, here's the way I see it. You tell me where I'm off base. Shake probably doesn't even know about the situation in Pyongyang—because you didn't provide details. He gets an order to pull out of North Korea immediately with no further explanation. There's no word from him on whether or not he's located his best friend who just sent an emergency signal. What do you think he's gonna do?"

"Shake's a professional, Chan—and so is Mike Stokey. They understand in situations like this you can't..."

"Oh, bullshit!" Chan leaned across the coffee table and banged her fist hard enough to make Bayer's drink rattle. "My husband is not going to leave his best buddy lost and alone somewhere in North Korea just because you send him a text message saying game over! If he responds at all, he'll tell you in no uncertain terms to stick it up your ass and stay on the case until he finds Mike and comes up with a way to get them all out of there!"

Bayer toyed with his drink glancing from the dark liquid to the hard glare in Chan's dark eyes. She cut to the chase in a hurry and there was no sense in arguing with what was clearly an accurate assessment of the situation. "I expect you're right. I apologize if I've been a little obtuse about all this. I was hoping to make it a bit easier on you."

"I'm not the one you need to worry about." Chan slumped back into her chair and tried to get her emotions under control. "You need to fire up that high-dollar mobile phone of yours and send him a message. Tell him I'm worried and need a situation report. Don't make it sound like I've retired to the fainting couch. Just tell him to text me or text you or something to let me know he's OK and find out what he intends to do."

"I'll do that." Bayer reached for his phone and punched up the message app.

Kangnam Mountains, Democratic People's Republic of (North) Korea

Senior Sergeant Sun Kyo-Ri of the 3rd Independent Reconnaissance Battalion hitched at his equipment rig and trudged up the mountain road toward the small shelter where his commanding officer was crouched over their long-range radio and a small immersion burner. At his rear, the 15 NKPA Special Operations soldiers he'd just finished briefing sat in silent contemplation of the news from Pyongyang. Sgt. Sun was proud of the stoic way they'd taken his terse announcement about the death of their nation's Supreme Leader, but he'd expected nothing less. They were hard, dedicated, and well-trained soldiers who knew that the fate of their nation often rested on the military's shoulders. The question on Sgt. Sun's mind as he approached his commanding officer was what happens next. Their small unit had been combing the mountains for two full days looking for dangerous infiltrators with no results, and the helicopters had suddenly disappeared with no indication that they would be returning.

"Have you told the men?" Captain Cho Ju-Kyu looked up from a map he was studying under a light clipped to his cap and offered his senior NCO a steaming cup of green tea. Sgt. Sun blew at the hot beverage and nodded. "They have been informed, Comrade Captain. The men are prepared to continue the mission in spite of this tragedy. We can either conduct further sweeps tonight or wait for the helicopters to return at daylight."

"The helicopters will not be returning." Captain Cho lit a cigarette and offered one to his senior NCO. "In view of the situation in the capitol, they have all been recalled except for the one scheduled to pick us up tomorrow." He spread the map and angled his head so that the light shined on it. "The search is being called off. We will remain in our current positions tonight and move to this area at dawn." He poked a gloved finger at a spot and Sgt. Sun recognized familiar terrain.

"The cliff area where we searched yesterday," he said. "There are several good landing zones nearby either on the high ground or in the valley below."

"We'll go for the high ground," Captain Cho folded the map and dismissed his senior NCO. "Set out security and let the soldiers rest. We will move out at dawn for the pick-up area. I have no word about when the helicopter will arrive, so we may be waiting for a while."

"And then?" Sergeant Sun drained his cup and handed it back to his officer.

"And then I expect we will receive further orders. There is a state funeral being planned and we may be part of security for that."

* * *

"I'd say your Chinese friends in the PLA have pulled the plug if they're evacuating the drone site." Sam Jackson stared over Shake's shoulder, squinting to re-read the text on the small cell phone screen. "Unless you know something I don't know." They had been preparing to move out into the encroaching darkness when the message arrived and all four men from the rescue party were huddled around Shake's phone.

"I've got no clue." Shake scrolled through the message again looking for anything in the wording that might indicate why Bayer would order him to cut and run without confirmation that Stokey was located. "It doesn't make much sense to me."

"And it doesn't seem like the right thing." Sgt. Jun shifted under his pack and glanced at Shake. "If this man we were sent to find is important enough to risk the mission, we should at least make every effort to find him before we quit."

"I wouldn't want to think my friends would abandon me." Sgt. Park was not a big talker but it was clear from the look on his face that his vote would be to continue the mission. "And you said this Mr. Stokey was a Marine."

Sam nodded and put a hand on Shake's shoulder. "It's your call, Shake, but we've got a general location now. It seems stupid to just leave him hanging out here."

"I'm not about to do that." Shake looked around at the Asian faces in the gathering gloom. "Here's the way I see it. The UAV shut-down is one thing and this mission to rescue Mike Stokey is another thing entirely. I think we can pull it off, and I'm for pushing on tonight. That's my call but you guys are volunteers; you get a vote." Shake waited for responses and smiled when he got three quick thumbs-up from the men crouched around him.

"Let me just send a fuck-you message and we'll shove off." Shake blew some warmth into his hand and tapped out a response to Bayer's recall order: **WE WILL CM. ALTERNATE EXFIL PLAN IN PLACE.** He hit the send button and nodded at his teammates. "That's it. Charlie Mike, we continue mission."

He put the cell phone back inside his parka after confirming that the little instrument was still showing sufficient battery life. It was working as advertised so far, but he was worried about the effect extreme cold might have on the power source and kept it as close to his skin as possible. He cut power to the phone and then he pulled a small metallic toy out of his pocket. Just before they set off into the dark night and freezing wind, he gave the team a quick run-down on how he planned to communicate with Mike Stokey once they reached the coordinates plugged into their GPS devices.

D ick Liccardi's UAV crew sat in pitch dark beside the runway huddled around a stack of equipment boxes. The team had done a quick and thorough job of packing what needed to go and destroying everything else. A message arrived just before dark indicating they would be picked up by Chinese helicopter sometime between midnight and 0200 for further transfer to an airfield where they would be met by a private jet that would deliver them to Seoul. It was practically the reverse of the method used to insert them three weeks prior, but they'd be going out with a lot less baggage than they brought into China.

Julia Dewey volunteered to stay with the assembled gear when Liccardi ordered a final sweep of the area. When she saw the beams of three flashlights disappear into the pine forest behind the bunkers, she pulled out her cell phone and began to compose a message about the situation in North Korea and the reason for abandoning the UAV mission. When she had the essential details keyed into her phone, she punched up the private number Gunner Shake Davis had quietly given her before he left and hit send. It was the least she could do for a fellow Marine who was about to be cut off deep in enemy territory.

T rudging uphill into a driving wind and being pelted with intermittent snow flurries was hard enough, but Shake and his party also had to make a major detour when Sgt. Park spotted a unit of NKPA troops camped along the main axis of their route. The close encounter added three expensive hours to their march, and it was well past midnight when the GPS indicated they'd reached the top of the cliff very near Stokey's indicated position. They were on a flat, snow-covered plateau overlooking a sheer cliff that jutted up from a valley about 200 meters below. Stokey could be anywhere on the high ground or in that valley. It was graveyard quiet except for the whistle of occasional wind gusts and Shake thought the sound of the small, metallic cricket he held in his gloved hand would carry well enough once he began the double-click signal he hoped Mike Stokey would hear and recognize.

The cricket was a gift from an old WW II veteran of the 506th Parachute Infantry Regiment of the 101st Airborne Division who had jumped with it into Normandy on D-Day in 1944. Shake treasured the keepsake and carried it everywhere as a good luck charm. Stokey had always admired it even as they argued about its effectiveness as a friend-or-foe signaling device. Several years ago on an Ozark Mountains fishing trip, they'd tested it against the roar of croaking bullfrogs, rushing streams and other forest sounds. The little cricket was loud, clear and unmistakable and they'd even worked out a code involving a series of clicks. Two quick snaps meant I'm here; where are you? Three snaps indicated a friend and provided a hint to the friend's location.

During that exercise, Mike had a similar cricket they'd bought in a truck stop and could respond in kind. Shake knew there was no chance Mike would still have that little toy with him, but he might recognize the distinctive clicks if he could hear them and there was not much in the way of options. They couldn't just start shouting for attention with an NKPA unit in the area and there was not enough time before dawn to conduct a methodical search. Shake crawled close to the cliff edge and snapped the cricket twice. The hollow clicks echoing off the nearby rocks sounded like two small-caliber pistol shots.

* * *

Lee was on watch at the mouth of the ice cave when he heard the strange sound that seemed to come from somewhere above them. He shook Stokey awake and crawled painfully toward the mouth of the cave. There was nothing in sight outside or in the valley below but blowing snow back-lit by pale moonlight. "What is it?" Stokey maneuvered to Lee's side and stared out into the darkness.

"It sounded like gunshots—only different; not as loud." Lee had been in pain and unable to sleep so Mike thought he might be hallucinating. He crawled out onto the narrow ledge and stared down the cliff side into the valley. There was nothing moving below their perch and Stokey was wondering if the moon would provide enough light for him to start exploring for an escape route when he heard the two quick snaps. There was something familiar about the sound and he tried to recall why that might be. It was definitely not gunfire and it didn't sound like wood snapping under a load of ice. The sound was rhythmic and metallic—like someone signaling—with a toy cricket.

And then he remembered. Stokey pulled his Gerber fighting knife out of its sheath and snatched at his equipment rig. He crawled out onto the ledge and tapped the knife blade onto one of the carabineers hooked to the suspender straps three times in quick succession.

Shake heard the sound and so did the rest of the rescue team as they scrambled toward the cliff edge and looked down into the valley. There was nothing in sight even as the three metallic clicks repeated. "Down there," Sam Jackson whispered and pointed at a rock ledge that jutted out from the cliff face. "Not far below." Shake craned over the edge, but there was nothing he could see but rocks shimmering in shades of pale green and yellow through his NVGs. Still the response was unmistakable. Stokey was somehow somewhere along the sheer drop below them.

"Mike? That better be you."

"Shake? Jesus Christ, man! I never thought I'd..."

"Save it. What's your status?"

"We're down about thirty feet in a little ice cave. I've got a wounded man with me and no way to get back up this damn cliff."

"Stand by." Shake turned to see Sergeants Park and Jun anchoring climbing lines to a couple of sturdy pines at their back. Those guys didn't need orders or instruction. They knew what needed to be done. He dug in his pack for a climbing harness and then turned to Sam Jackson. "You stay up here with the gear, Sam. We'll rappel down and see what the situation is. Once we get them out of this, we'll either take off or find someplace to hole up during the day and move west at dark."

Stokey hugged Shake while they tottered on the narrow ledge outside the ice cave. Park and Jun were already inside the clammy little alcove muttering in Korean and checking on Lee's mobility. "My God, Shake. I sent that damn signal as a last gasp, hoping either someone would come or at least they'd know where to find the body—but I never thought I'd see you!"

"That was the deal, right?" Shake helped Stokey into his climbing harness and fixed ascenders onto one of the lines. "You call and I come running. It took some doing—and Chan is going to have a sizeable piece of your ass when we get home— but first things first." Shake started his friend up the rope and then ducked into the cave to check on the wounded man.

"His name is Lee." Sgt. Jun nodded at the man lying on the floor of the cave and favoring a very stiff leg. "He's one of our brothers from the north—and he speaks English."

"My name is Davis." Shake examined the leg and decided they would have to carry the wounded man up the side of the cliff. "I'm a friend of Mr. Stokey and we're going to get you out of this."

"I understand—and thank you." Lee smiled through his pain and began to crawl toward the entrance. Shake pushed him down and nodded at Sgt. Park. "Can you guys piggyback him up with ascenders?"

"Can do." Sgt. Jun exploded into rapid Korean instructing Lee on the procedure as Shake ducked out of the cave and started up the nearest line. Over his shoulder he could see the peaks to the east growing visible as dawn approached. They didn't have much time left to either move or find a safe place to hide and wait for dark.

The two Korean Marine commandos buddy-carried Lee up the face of the cliff and quickly recovered all their climbing gear. It was obvious after a brief strength test that Lee would be more of a hindrance trying to walk than if they carried him. The question was whether to take turns carrying him piggyback or rig a stretcher. The consensus was to alternate carrying the wounded man on their backs until they found a hide site for the approaching daylight hours and then proceed with a stretcher after dark when they'd selected a best route back to the Yalu. Sgt. Park gave Lee a morphine injection and then shrugged out of his pack and handed it to Sgt. Jun. When Park had Lee steadied up into a manageable load, he trudged off in a westerly direction.

They made about a kilometer on a steady uphill course, looking everywhere for a safe bivouac, when Sam Jackson took his turn at carrying Lee. The wounded man was managing stoically but Jackson quickly noticed fresh blood oozing through Lee's trousers. "We better stop and change the dressing," he said to Shake as Sgt. Jun broke out a first-aid kit and began digging for bandages. Shake nodded and then looked up at the lightening sky. It was definitely time for them to get out of sight. He pointed at a ridgeline to their left that was shot through with stands of snow-covered boulders.

"We'll head for those rocks and see if we can find a good spot. It won't be long before its light enough for the helicopters to be back on station."

* * *

"Helicopter is getting airborne, Comrade Captain." The radio operator shrugged the transceiver onto his back and glanced at his fellow special forces soldiers lined up in two ranks along the mountain trail. "They estimate one hour or maybe a little more depending on weather."

Captain Cho glanced up at the clear sky hoping he'd be back in his headquarters shortly where he could get some sort of feel for what was happening at the high command in Pyong-yang and, by extension, what he could expect in the 3rd Independent Reconnaissance Battalion due to the regime change. He swept his hand in the signal to move out and began walking east toward the rising sun and the proposed helicopter landing zone. He'd gone less than ten meters when Senior Sergeant Sun caught up to him.

"Flank security, Comrade Captain?" Sergeant Sun had been on watch during the night when they heard strange sounds like pistol shots or a weapon being cocked and he was nervous about Cho's orders to ignore the sounds. Granted they were all anxious to get back and find out what was happening in the capitol, but there was no call for sloppy soldiering.

"Not today, Comrade Senior Sergeant." Captain Cho kept walking at a steady pace. "There's nothing in these hills except snow and wind. We've done our job. Let's get on to the landing zone."

* * *

The best they could do for a daytime hide site was an outcropping of boulders about 30 feet up a slope overlooking a pass between two rocky peaks. Across the pass to their right was a single, old- growth conifer that would provide better overhead concealment, but they avoided that possibility. Everyone agreed that if there's only one obvious hiding place, that's where searchers will obviously look. Shake handed Stokey a pouch of trail-mix and a power-bar as he gazed overhead at the sky turning a clear and cloudless blue. Their position didn't provide much overhead concealment and the weather seemed perfect for low-level helicopter searches. Still, the dark shadow from the boulder formation was the best they could do for now. It was too late and too light to search for a better spot.

They'd been tucked up in the rocks for a little more than two hours and Shake had spent most of that time exchanging information and updates with Mike Stokey. He now had some idea of why Mike crossed the Yalu against orders to check on events around the Chosin Reservoir and that took an edge off of the tirade he'd been set to deliver about careless hot-dogging, unofficial solo operations, and putting a bunch of innocent asses into a potentially-lethal sling. If Stokey was right about what he suspected the North Koreans might be up to with these high-capacity generators and EMP, the risk might have been worth taking. They'd know more about that when they got his Intel back to the analysts.

Shake scanned the sky once more looking for high-flying aircraft or helicopters and then pulled his white camouflage smock over his head to power up his cell phone and check for messages. There were two. One from Bayer and one from a number he didn't recognize. He ignored Bayer's demand for news and confirmation that he was heading out of North Korea as ordered and focused on the part about Chan. Bayer said she was fine but worried. Shake accepted fine to mean less than homicidal or suicidal and realized he was being a shitty husband among his other faults. He should have let her know he was OK long ago. The old single-minded mission focus was a hard habit to break. Shake tapped the keypad: **MISSING PACKAGE IN HAND. ALL OK HERE. PASS TO SPOUSE LOVE AND**

APOLOGIES FOR LACK OF COMM. HEADING HOME VIA ALTERNATE ROUTE. MORE SOONEST FROM OTHER SIDE OF BLUE LINE. He hit send and watched the little bar complete its run to indicate the message was outbound.

The second message caused him to duck out from under his smock and poke Sam Jackson who was squeezed uncomfortably between two big rocks on his left. "Check this." Shake handed him the phone with the message from Julia Dewey displayed. "We might have caught a break. I'm betting the Norks have more important things on their mind right now."

* * *

The aging and over-stressed Mi-8 Hip helicopter bound for pick-up of a Special Operations team was ascending sluggishly and heading for a mountain pass just west of their scheduled landing zone. At the top of the pass, the pilot maneuvered slightly left to insure his rotors cleared the rocky rise on the right side of the aircraft and then pushed the nose over to restore forward air speed. His co-pilot was bitching about lousy power in the thin, high-altitude air and speculating about having to make two lifts when the crewman/gunner in the back came up on the intercom.

"There are some men down in the rocks to the right! Is that our people?"

The co-pilot shook his head and tapped a finger on the map displayed on his knee-board. "Not unless they've moved." The pilot knew the scheduled pick-up point was still some distance to the east. The patrol might have moved. Or more likely they just spotted the infiltrators that had eluded them over the past two days. "Call the patrol leader." He pulled the Mi-8 into a looping turn using a tall tree on his left as a reference point. "See if they've got anyone out here."

Shake knew they'd been spotted when he saw the helo climb, bank and turn. The Mi-8 that passed over them wasn't carrying rockets or gun-pods, but he'd clearly seen a crewman behind a door-mounted medium machinegun pointing at them. "Sam, get everyone under as much cover as you can find. That bastard is coming back for another look!" Shake was trying to think of a way out of their dire situation as he watched the helicopter maneuver against the blue sky. They didn't have a weapon heavy enough to do significant damage to the bird, but the machinegun in the door would hose them all if they decided to open up on the next pass. Even if the bird simply orbited to keep them in sight, the crew would be chattering on the radio, vectoring NKPA patrols toward an intercept.

As he watched the bird maneuver, setting up for a second pass, Shake remembered an anti-helicopter tactic he'd experimented with when he was training anti-Sandinista troops in the mountains of Honduras back in the 1980s. A helo-jock told them about ways to foul main or tail rotors using camouflaged cables. They played with the idea and even damaged a marauding Nicaraguan bird by using a Navy ship-to-ship line-throwing gun that carried a heavy cable fired into the rotor fan. He decided they had nothing to lose with a last desperate defensive shot.

Shake pulled Liccardi's heavy compound bow off his shoulder and began to dig around in their gear. "Sergeant Jun, if you get a clear shot at that door gunner on the next pass, take him out!" Jun nodded, snatched at his M-4 carbine, and moved to a position behind a higher boulder where he'd have a better field of fire. Shake found a coil of high tensile-strength climbing cable and began splicing the bitter end onto one of three heavy hunting arrows attached to the bow. The helicopter was loitering at the end of its turn now, probably taking a little time to verify their position and transmit it to the infantry.

Sam Jackson had pulled Lee under a shallow outcropping. They'd be as safe there as anywhere in the next few minutes. Shake tossed the Swedish K at Mike Stokey and pointed at Sgt. Park. "When it's inbound, fire a couple of rounds and then take off down slope. I need him as low as possible!" While Mike and Sgt. Park got into a position where they could easily bolt out from cover, Shake dropped the coil of light 10-mm twisted-nylon rope near his right leg and found a position that would hopefully give him a clean shot across the helicopter's fuselage. His timing would have to be nearly perfect, but if he got really lucky, the line just might be snatched up by the bird's un-caged tail rotor and cause enough flight control problems for the aircrew to abandon further efforts.

He saw the nose of the Mi-8 dip as the pilots brought it in line for another run through the pass. Shake checked the coil of line for kinks and was once again grateful that the two Korean Marines were well-trained professionals. The line looked like it would run clean behind the arrow he had notched in the bow. To his left Sgt. Jun pointed skyward and then concentrated on his rifle sights.

"Here they come!" Shake pulled the bow to full draw and focused on the inbound aircraft swooping toward them with its nose pitched down for maximum acceleration. If the pilots kept to this flight profile, they'd be too high for an effective shot. He was hoping North Korean helo pilots were the same sort of frustrated fighter jocks he'd encountered in long years of experience with the breed. That's where Stokey and Sgt. Park came into play from their position below and to his right. If he sent them now, the helo crew might dive on them like a hawk chasing a fleeing squirrel.

"Go, Mike—now!"

Shake kept the bow at full draw and his eyes focused on the helicopter. The main rotor system would likely just shrug off a line fired at it. He needed to hit within the tail-rotor fan and that meant the helo would have to pass by him at fairly low level. He heard the rattle of his Swedish K and caught movement out of the corner of his eye. Stokey and Sgt. Park were running and tumbling down the slope like kids out of school on a snow day. The helicopter jinked to line up on the running targets and Shake heard Sgt. Jun cut loose with his M-4. The helicopter swooped low concentrating on the chase as the door gunner triggered a burst that blew snow and rock shards all over the stand of boulders.

It was now or never. Shake ignored the incoming fire, aiming at a point just aft of the helicopter's engine fairing. When he
saw the big pine tree on the other side of the pass appear
through the rotor-wash, he fired and rolled out of the way so the
line would run free. He saw Sgt. Jun still pumping rounds but
there was no return fire. Shake crawled back up the slope to see
the entire coil of line had disappeared. Where it went and
whether or not it did any good were open questions.

In the cockpit of the helicopter, the pilots felt their cyclic
controls begin to vibrate. They couldn't see the long length of
nylon line that had wrapped around their tail rotor hub where it
was causing a major friction fire but they could feel the aircraft
going into a hard right yaw. The pilot mashed hard on the
rudder pedals but nothing seemed to help. The helicopter was
starting to spin out of control as he jerked on the collective and
added power clawing for vital altitude.

At the base of the hill, Shake saw Stokey and Sgt. Park crouched
behind a snow bank. Stokey waved and pointed. The helicopter
was streaming smoke from the tail-boom and beginning to spin
wildly beneath the main rotor. As he watched in amazement,
the Mi-8 soared straight up and then plunged into the earth like
a huge snow dart sending up showers of debris as the main
rotors shattered. The aircraft shuddered and gyrated wildly for a
few seconds and then exploded into an ugly orange fire ball.

* * *

Senior Sergeant Sun was vividly cursing his officer's lack of
professionalism as he led the patrol toward the plume of black
smoke on the horizon. There was no question in his mind that
the smoke and flames in the distance near the mountain pass
marked the wreck of the helicopter sent to fetch them. The
pilots had reported they were chasing a group of four or five

unidentified men and then shouted that they were going down with some sort of mechanical malfunction. Sun heard an exchange of gunfire as his officer was listening to the radio and he was convinced that the crash was more likely due to fire from the infiltrators they'd given up on finding. Now his unit had a serious problem and no guarantee that any help would be forthcoming given the situation in Pyongyang.

Heads would roll when they returned to headquarters and Senior Sergeant Sun sincerely hoped one of those heads would belong to Capt. Cho, but that was a concern for later. Right now they had to focus on catching or killing the infiltrators. He shouted for his soldiers to spread out into a skirmish line and increase their pace heading for the crash site.

* * *

Lee was strapped to a lightweight folding mountain rescue stretcher that Sgt. Jun was professional enough to include in his mission-essential gear. Jun and Park were on either end of the tubular frame and doing their best to keep from further injuring the wounded man as they struggled up and over the mountain pass. Shake decided it was worth the risk to put as much immediate distance as possible between them and the helicopter crash site. There was no telling whether or not the NKPA would send another bird assuming they got some sort of distress call, but he was sure that any patrols in the area would be running toward the scene of the wreck.

As they descended the slope on the other side of the pass, Shake was searching for a place that would provide some sort of edge if it came to a fight. Sam Jackson was on the left about halfway up a slope where he could look for any pursuit, and it didn't take him long to spot a unit of North Korean soldiers gliding uphill in their direction on snowshoes. He counted about 15 men spread out on line and making enough speed to catch up with a slow-moving party carrying a casualty. Sam focused binoculars on the pursuers and spotted one man carrying a radio with a tall whip antenna waving in the wind.

The man didn't seem to be transmitting but that didn't mean he hadn't already called in a request for air support or reinforcements. It looked to Sam like they might have to fight and it was clear from what he could see that they were badly out-gunned.

"We've got company!" Sam plowed down the slope and caught up with Shake Davis. "Looks like a Special Forces outfit from the gear and weapons. They're heading upslope on snowshoes and making good time."

"That's a problem, Sam." Shake motioned for the others to keep moving and stopped to look around at the slopes on either side of their route. There was nothing but snow and rocks leading toward a narrow cut that he'd hoped to get through before a chase started. "Even if we find some place to make a stand, they'll just trade rounds with us until help arrives."

"We haven't got much choice, Shake." Sam stepped off in the direction of the cut. "We can't afford to get caught by those bastards, it's still a long way to the Yalu and they're making better speed than we can. Best we get past that chokepoint up ahead and find a place to shoot it out."

"We just need to buy some time." Shake was looking at the steep slopes on either side of the narrow pass. Something Sam said about chokepoint was giving him a vague notion. "You gotta believe with all the problems their military is facing right now, they might not expend a lot of manpower and effort chasing a bunch of unknown infiltrators through the boondocks."

Shake retrieved the binoculars and focused them on a stand of boulders about a hundred meters up the snow-covered slope on the right side of the cut. "Who's the best mountain man on your team?"

"Either one, I guess." Sam stared at the spot that Shake was scanning with the glasses. "Maybe Park has an edge. He was an instructor at our Mountain Warfare Training Center. He was born in the mountains, and he's supposed to be an Olympic level ski-jumper."

"Push everyone through the cut as quickly as you can. Then send Park back here to me."

As Sam rushed ahead, Shake grabbed a handful of snow from the base of the slope and examined it carefully.

* * *

Captain Cho gave the hand signal to Senior Sergeant Sun. Pick up the pace and mold the men into a file to speed through the narrow cut in pursuit of the infiltrators. There was no response to his spot report concerning the helicopter shoot-down, but that was a concern for later. The key was to stay in contact with the fleeing infiltrators and get a grip on a situation that was rapidly growing more critical. He was fairly certain his unit would overtake their quarry, but he needed to have the enemy agents in hand or splayed out dead when help arrived.

"No, no!" Captain Cho shouted at Senior Sergeant Sun and pointed toward the cut where his NCO was starting to send flankers up the left and right slopes. "Just push through. We'll engage on the other side." Cho snatched at his radio operator and headed for the narrow mountain pass. The NKPA Special Operations patrol melded into a file from a line and charged toward the narrow pass which required them to close up and pass through one by one.

* * *

Shake Davis fought to catch his breath and nodded at Sergeant Park. They were panting in a position about 90 meters above the narrow cut in the mountain pass where they'd rushed with a glimmer of an idea in mind. "Loose snow and a bunch of it—what do you think?"

Sergeant Park studied the three boulders above the cut below them and picked up a hand-full of snow. "It's wet below the surface; wouldn't take much to cause a slide." The Korean Marine mountain warfare expert understood what Shake was proposing. "We could use some demolitions."

"And that's what we don't have." Shake spotted what he hoped was a key rock on the slope face and pulled a length of climbing rope off his shoulder. "If we can haul that rock out of position..." He pointed at a boulder beneath a clump of snow-covered rocks. "...we might get this whole thing to go."

"No time." Sgt. Park snapped a loop of line into one of the carabineers on his equipment rig and pointed at a tree 20 feet above the boulders. "Belay yourself onto the line and then secure it to that tree." As Shake headed higher on the slope to establish a life-line for them, Sgt. Park pulled a small entrenching tool out of his gear and began to dig furiously at the base of the key rock. Below them Shake could see Sam Jackson, Stokey, and Sgt. Jun struggling with the stretcher-bound Lee and forging clear of the narrow cut. The lead NKPA soldier was approaching the defile and the entire formation was beginning to bunch up as they proceeded with understandable caution.

When Shake returned to the rock formation, Sgt. Park pointed at the pile of snow he'd cleared and slapped a hand on the rough surface of the tall granite chunk. "I think we can dislodge it now." They began to shove at the huge stone but only succeeded in rocking it slightly. Below them the first three NKPA soldiers were inside the narrow passage. "Something is blocking it!" Sgt. Park grabbed his small shovel and began to flail away at the base of the stone. Shake scooted around to the down slope side and began to desperately dig in the snow with his hands. The patrol spotted him immediately and began shouting a warning. Shake ignored it and dug steadily into the snow at the base of the rock. They were running out of time. The North Koreans would now realize what was happening on the slope and power through the narrow area to get clear.

He heard gunfire and glanced down to see Mike Stokey firing controlled bursts at the patrol with the little Swedish K. Mike waved from behind a snow bank. He was trying to pin the NKPA patrol in position while Shake and Sgt. Park worked. The North Koreans were stopped and crouched behind whatever cover they could find in the pass. Shake and Sgt. Park had a little more time to work on the slope above them—but not much.

Shake went back to digging in the snow and finally spotted the blockage. A relatively small granite slab was squeezed up against the base of the rock and holding it in position on the slope. He scrambled around to retrieve Sgt. Park's entrenching tool and a smaller rock that he could use as a fulcrum for a lever. "Keep pushing," he shouted and slammed the shovel as deep as he could beneath the granite slab. "If I can move this I think it will go."

He spent a few precious minutes digging for purchase while Stokey exchanged fire with the patrol. A few of the North Korean soldiers stalled in the pass below began to fire at him. Sgt. Park was covered by the rocks, but Shake suffered through several whining ricochets as he struggled on the front side of the boulder. When he had the crude lever and fulcrum set, Shake stood, balanced for a moment and then jumped on the handle of the shovel. The granite slab lifted slightly and he stooped to dig the lever more deeply under it as a ricochet caromed off the rock and cut into the meat of his right arm. He ignored the pain as he felt the larger rock beginning to give under Sgt. Park's pressure. He stood and jumped again on the handle of the shovel.

Shake felt the rock begin to roll and then the entire hillside seemed to slip from under his feet. In a blinding shower of snow, he caught a glimpse of Sgt. Park tumbling down slope behind the rolling boulder. He slid downward in a cascade of snow and loose rock until he was painfully jerked to a halt by the belaying line. He had only moments to cover his face with his forearms before he was buried by the avalanche.

* * *

Shake Davis was alive and thankful for the arctic warfare training that kicked in when the avalanche started. There wasn't much a man could do to escape cascading snow but the drill was to cover your face to provide some breathing space and wait until the moving snow stopped. If a man was very lucky and not buried too deeply, he might be able to survive until someone arrived to dig him out. Shake shoved upward but the heavy blanket of snow didn't move. He could breathe behind his crossed arms but it wouldn't be long before the extreme cold shut down his system. He was trapped and very quickly turning into a block of ice with no idea if the avalanche had buried the North Koreans as effectively as it had him.

His ears were stuffed with snow, but he thought he could feel something happening above and he shouted, hoping that if someone was digging for him it was friend rather than foe. He shouted again and thought he saw a flash of light in the inky darkness overhead.

Sgt. Jun followed the belaying line to a point about halfway down the slope and found Sgt. Park struggling to free himself. He helped his friend stand and checked him for any serious damage. Park was airborne behind the key boulder when the snow slide started and that saved him from being buried too deeply. He seemed unhurt and smiled when Jun pointed toward the bottom of the slope where the avalanche had wiped out nearly all traces of the North Korean patrol. "Buried them all…" Jun slapped his shivering partner on the back and pointed at two bodies lying in the snow just beyond the narrow pass. "…except for those two. We nailed them on the run." Jun turned and waved at the men further up the slope tramping through the fresh snow.

Sam Jackson followed the belaying line down slope, pulling it free of the snow until it finally stopped and then he shouted for Mike Stokey. "Here! He's under here." Mike struggled toward the spot and called for Park and Jun to assist. Jun arrived with an entrenching tool and they began to dig at the spot in the snow where the belaying line ended.

They had to clear three feet of snow before they saw Shake's legs and part of his mid-section. Stokey and Jun shifted their efforts and lifted snow until they saw Shake's arms crossed over his face. "Shake! Can you hear me?" Mike desperately dug at the snow surrounding his friend's head. "C'mon, man, talk to me."

"I'll talk when you get me out of this goddamn deep-freeze." Shake sat up painfully with Sam Jackson pulling on his shoulders. When he was finally able to clear the snow from his face and see the rescuers gathered around, he gulped a lungful of fresh air and pointed downward. "Did we get 'em?"

"All gone, Shake." Stokey helped him out of the trench that was very nearly his grave. "If you're through playing in the snow, we need to get moving."

Ministry of the People's Armed Forces, Pyongyang

"The helicopter apparently crashed, Comrade Marshal." The senior aide pointed at a message form on Marshal Kim's desk. "The air controller monitoring the mission indicates they reported some kind of mechanical problem."

"And the Special Forces patrol?" Marshal Kim was distracted by the schedule of inaugural events that needed to be finalized in the next couple of hours.

"There has been nothing from them since the initial report that they were heading toward the crash site. We are continuing to call for updates. They are likely pursuing the infiltrators spotted by the helicopter. Radio transmission in those mountains can be spotty."

"If they make contact, have them continue the pursuit." Marshal Kim turned his attention to a list of military and civilian dignitaries that would need to be assembled in the capitol. "We'll just have to do without them for a while. Keep me informed."

"Of course, Comrade Marshal." The senior aide placed another message form on the cluttered desk. "And the team at Wonsan reports they are ready for the tests."

"As soon as we conclude the ceremonies, we'll turn our attention to that project." The Marshal plucked the message form from the top of a pile and stuffed it in a bulging folder. "Make arrangements for a trip at the end of the week."

"Do you need me to come down?" Tracey Davis slumped into a chair beneath the wall phone extension in the lab of the Woods Hole Oceanographic Institute where she worked. Her father had apparently gotten himself in some kind of jam overseas—again—and she was worried about the tension she detected in her step-mother's voice. "I've got some time coming and I can be on the road tomorrow morning."

"Better not." Chan Davis chuckled hoping she sounded more relaxed than she felt. "He'll probably have a fit when he finds out I called you anyway. You know your Dad. Last thing he wants to do is worry his daughter."

"Uh-huh." Tracey wanted more details about the situation but understood that Chan couldn't say much on the phone. "He doesn't seem to have much trouble worrying his wife, does he?"

"Good Lord, girl, you'd think we'd both be used to it by now, but I can tell you I was not happy with the circumstances surrounding this little trip. I guess the important thing is that he's OK. I just wanted to let you know. I'd have called earlier but—well, one of us going nuts is one too many."

"So, he's, uh, out of immediate danger? And heading home with a certain asshole buddy of his in tow?"

"A text came in about three this morning. He's headed home via Seoul as soon as he can get a flight. And that pal of his is going to be *minus* an asshole when I get through with him. I don't have a lot of detail, but I'll email you what I know today."

"If he calls, ask him to give me a ring, Chan. I'm going to have a few words with my Dad about the meaning of the word *retired.*"

"Yikes! Then he'll know I blabbed. We'll both be in hot water."

"I've still got my reserve commission, you know. If necessary I'll lock his heels and issue a direct order."

"I'd like to be there for that. Gotta go, honey. Love you."

"Bye, Chan. Keep me posted." Tracey Davis hung up the phone and walked to the other side of the lab where remnants of the Boston Globe were strewn on a counter. She shuffled in the mess and found the news section filled with items from Pyongyang and Seoul. What part did Gunner Shake Davis and his buddy Mike Stokey play in all these newsworthy events? She thought about the close call they'd all had in the Palaus just two years earlier and realized her father was anything but retired as he'd promised after Peleliu and once again playing around with stuff that could very well get him killed. She picked up a phone and called the Woods Hole administrative office where she put in for two weeks of vacation.

After recovering the submersible carrying the rescue party, the skipper of the Son Won II class sub that spent nearly a week loitering in the disputed waters of the northern Yellow Sea gave orders to take her deep and run south. He had a flash message in hand directing him to bypass his operating base at Yeonpyeong Island and make best speed for the South Korean Navy base at Chinhae near Pusan on the opposite side of the peninsula. The boat was slipping carefully and quietly out of North Korean waters, but he would dial on the speed once they were further down the west coast. The submariners had all heard about the death of Kim Jong-Il, and everyone aboard understood their country was now under a serious security alert. The captain thought the orders to report directly to Chinhae likely had something to do with that.

The crew had been at quarters most of the time near the mouth of the Yalu, kept on edge by diving and dodging a flood of NK patrol boats that suddenly appeared all over their holding station. That much activity was unusual in the captain's experience, but he put it down to the northerner's paranoia after the death of a dictator responsible for starving and oppressing his countrymen. Everyone aboard was fairly exhausted except for the passengers he'd brought aboard just two hours earlier. For some reason the captain didn't quite understand, the two Americans and four Koreans retrieved from the mission inside North Korea seemed calm and collected despite their wounds and the rigors of what must have been a nerve-wracking experience.

There was a moment of tension when he discovered that one of the Koreans that dropped into his boat from the submersible was a northerner. The *Angibu* operator with the odd occidental name pulled him aside and explained the man's presence and importance to the mission. Shortly after his leg wound was treated by the sub's senior medical corpsman, Sun Myung Lee, the English speaking school teacher from the north, became one of the most popular people on the boat. Everyone wanted to drop by the sickbay and get his take on the situation north of the DMZ. The Captain stopped by the navigation station to check their position and decided he'd be very glad to end this mission. The delicate situation in Korea was changing and he expected new orders that might take him and his boat into a final showdown with the communist north.

Shake Davis winced as the Korean Navy medical corpsman deftly stitched the rent in his right arm like a Seoul seamstress working on a new suit for a high-dollar customer. The ricochet had torn a quarter-size chunk out of his triceps, but it was no big deal and the corpsman was more interested in the other bullet and shrapnel scars revealed when Shake shrugged out of his undershirt for treatment. "Lotsa bullet you!" The corpsman poked at the scars and grinned. "Lotsa bullet me," Shake responded. "Other man lotsa bullet more." The corpsman laughed and took another suture as Mike Stokey and Sam Jackson ducked into the tiny sickbay.

"Just another dent in the fenders." Mike examined the wound critically. "How many Purple Hearts does that make, Shake? Seven? Eight?"

"They don't give Purple Hearts for wounds suffered in an effort to rescue idiots from enemies who have every reason and right to blow said idiot's ass away." Shake shifted on the operating table so the corpsman could apply a bandage over the sutures. "What are we gonna do about Lee?"

Sam Jackson shouldered past Stokey and offered Shake a cup of fiery Korean brandy. "I talked to him. Naturally he's worried about his wife and son. That's understandable, but I'm fairly certain we can get them out of the north. If it was up to me, I'd say we wait until the situation up there stabilizes and then we re-insert via the Yalu and just pluck the wife and kid out the same way we got out of there. It's not that big a deal."

"Unless you're Lee." Stokey swallowed his own tot of brandy and slumped against a bulkhead. "I owe that guy a bunch—cash and everything else—and I don't want to leave that debt unpaid."

"We'll handle it." Sam Jackson helped Shake off the operating table. "It won't be the first time we've hauled friendly northerners out of their country. And I think I can guarantee that his cooperation won't go unrewarded." He pointed at Stokey. "If you write up a solid after-action report, my government will do whatever's necessary to make it right with him and his family. I can promise that."

"So we're headed for Chinhae, according to the Captain." Shake got off the treatment table and shrugged into a shirt. "Mike, it's your deal, but let's start knocking together a report about that stuff you found at the Chosin Reservoir. Those bastards are up to something. I don't know enough about the science but I do know that EMP is a threat. Question is—what do they intend to do with it?"

"Just the fact that they're working on it is enough to give me worries." Sam Jackson led the way aft toward berthing spaces forward of the main propulsion plant. "Everybody's been so concerned about nukes that we weren't looking for anything else. And now that Kim Jong-Il has passed on, I'm fairly sure the Nork military sees this as a perfect time to make a major move."

Stokey dropped onto a crowded little bunk and dug in his gear. "I've got some pictures in a thumb drive that I'm mighty anxious to have examined by somebody who knows what he's looking at. There were nuclear warning symbols on some of those generators, and I don't get the connection."

"It could have something to do with the power source or like that." Shake carefully shrugged out of his bloody shirt and searched his pack for a clean replacement. "But if there's radioactive stuff involved, how come the UAV sensor package never picked it up?"

"It has to do with the containers, I think." Mike inserted the thumb drive in a laptop they'd borrowed from the navigator, found the file, and opened it. "Take a look at some of the wider shots. It's hard to tell since I was using IR illumination but I'm pretty sure those big boxes were lined with lead or something similar that would block anything the sensors were looking for."

Sam Jackson scrolled through some of the shots Stokey had taken in the truck park near the Chosin Reservoir hydroelectric plant. "They just look like regular international shipping containers—the kind of stuff you see stacked up on every merchant vessel in every ocean."

"Yeah, they do." Shake Davis squinted at the pictures and had a sobering thought. "If I was gonna hide a weapon capable of producing EMP, a regular shipping container might be a damn good choice."

"The thought occurred to me." Mike Stokey selected an image and pointed at it. "See the markings on the side of that container? You see that kind of thing in every storage yard in every port in the world. It's how practically all cargo shipped by sea moves these days. Load a bunch of those things on a standard civilian cargo carrier and you'd play hell finding anything out of the ordinary."

"Until that cargo carrier got within range of a target and fired up the generators to produce an electro-magnetic pulse." Shake picked up his phone and checked for reception. There was none. Apparently, even the CIA's ultra-high-tech communication gizmo was no good aboard a submerged vessel. "Soon as the skipper gets us into the clear, we need to upload this stuff onto a bird and get it to Bayer. He needs to bring the brains in on this thing."

"Don't forget the deal, Shake." Sam Jackson pointed at the thumb drive sticking out of the computer. "My government gets a crack at all this—share and share alike."

"Don't worry, Sam."

"I have to worry. Suppose they've got something with this thing. Who do you think they'll target?"

Wonsan, Democratic People's Republic of (North) Korea

Marshal Kim Jun-Yi stood on the bridge of the Najin class light frigate rolling softly in the swells off the coast of Wonsan and focused the big, high-powered binoculars on the barge anchored about a mile off their port beam. There was not much to see. The target vessel looked like a simple cargo carrier or garbage scow except for a steel container that filled the deck. Inside that container was a very expensive array of precisely-copied transformers, communications and electronic equipment—all of which would be turned into useless junk if the test was successful.

With yet another hour before the test was scheduled to begin, Marshal Kim reached for his phone and then remembered he'd been advised to leave it on shore. He was told that any unshielded device might be adversely affected by the test, so he surrendered both of his cell phones and the new Casio G-Shock digital watch that had been a present from his wife. He was no sailor and would have preferred the test take place on land, but his science advisors told him that would be too dangerous. There were apparently still questions about the focus and collateral effects of the new weapon that needed to be answered. The chief scientist insisted that the device should be tested under the conditions proposed by the government for its initial employment, and so Marshal Kim agreed to make a trip to Wonsan even though events in the capitol demanded his attention.

There were the nervous Chinese to deal with and the capitalist lackeys in the south were making yet another set of silly overtures in an effort to ingratiate themselves with the new Supreme Leader and subvert the long-range plans for the only possible reunification: A single Korean nation under the banner of the communist party. *Of course, the meddling Americans are behind all this distraction*, Marshal Kim mused as he left the bridge and headed for the pre-test scientific briefing, but if the weapon worked as advertised, the Americans would be the very next target following the initial employment.

In the meantime, young Kim Jong-Un would bask in his new-found notoriety and do precisely as Marshal Kim told him to do. That was the agreement struck between the deceased Supreme Leader and the powerful players of the North Korean military establishment. The son may accede to the throne without challenge, but the power behind that throne would always rest with Marshal Kim, the young man's uncle by marriage.

On the open deck of the frigate, he nodded to his aide and they stepped gingerly through a maze of thick power cables leading to a line of three cargo containers aligned end-to-end on the flight deck. Marshal Kim put his hand on one of the containers but he felt nothing other than cold steel. It was still hard for him to believe that inside those common-looking boxes was a device that could generate enormous power and focus it in such a way that the digital heart, electronic brains, and microwave arteries of an enemy would be instantly destroyed.

* * *

"I apologize for the technical nature of this briefing, Comrade Marshal." The chief scientist of what his team insisted on calling Project Digital Dragon tapped a computer key and shut down the PowerPoint presentation he'd been droning through for the past 15 minutes. He'd noted the familiar, stony expression in previous briefings for the Minister of the Peoples Armed Forces. It was time to either switch to plain speech or suffer another blizzard of tough, impossible-to-simplify questions. "Let me try to save time by explaining what we hope to accomplish with the scheduled test."

"I will appreciate your effort to explain it to a simple soldier." Marshal Kim waved a hand for the scientist to continue and lit a cigarette in an attempt to curb his impatience. He was familiar with the basic science from his study of nuclear blast effects as a young officer. "Focus on the difference between the EMP generated by your experiments and those generated by nuclear weapons."

"Beyond the obvious things such as an absence of blast effect and radiological contamination from a nuclear detonation, the electro-magnetic pulse we can now generate differs in no appreciable way from that generated as a result of a nuclear event. The pulse is of such strength that virtually all electronic based devices, all microwave communications, all unshielded computer circuitry, networks, and memory banks would be—I believe the word is *fried*."

"Fried..." The Marshal smiled and lit another cigarette, "...as in an egg? All electronics rendered inoperable? All data rendered irretrievable?"

"That is the idea, Comrade Marshal. Until our work with the Marx generators on a very large scale, the problem has been directing the pulse. In a nuclear event, the EMP generated has virtually the same radius of effect as the blast. It is, in other words, uncontrollable and merely a welcome subset or consequence of the primary intended damage. What we were tasked with developing is a device that can generate a destructive EMP that is directed in a relatively narrow, controllable way at a specified target."

"A sniper rifle rather than an artillery round." The Marshal nodded. "Continue."

"We have succeeded in amplifying the pulse produced by Marx generators by using certain nuclear materials in the power chain. By linking several of these specially-designed generators in series, we create a powerful EMP that is of relatively short duration but capable of extreme destruction to enemy infrastructure without the collateral damage to human life."

"Yes," the Marshal blew a cloud of smoke at the overhead of the little shipboard briefing space. "The enemy does not die in the nuclear inferno. Rather, he dies in the chaos created when his computer-based infrastructure is fried. I understand."

"The problem has always been directing the EMP. I believe we have solved that problem by controlling the—well, the simple way of saying it is the *width* or the effective dimensions of the EMP pulse. We will test that effect this afternoon. You have seen the target barge. Within the container on the barge are systems replicating those used by the American New York Stock Exchange, the Japanese Tokyo Stock Exchange and most importantly at this point, the Korean Stock Exchange located at Pusan."

"And the control for the test environment is the corvette anchored just ahead of the barge?"

"That is correct, Comrade Marshal. If we can fry the electronics on the barge without affecting those on the corvette, we will consider the test a success."

"Good. Let us proceed." The Minister of the Peoples Armed Forces crushed his cigarette and stood to go back on deck. In the companionway, he encountered his senior aide who pulled him aside for a private conversation. "The ship has been procured, Comrade Marshal. It's on the way from Mogadishu. The vessel is virtually untraceable—owner of record is an import-export firm in Jakarta, and it is operating under a Liberian flag. The firm will be defunct by the time the ship arrives at Wonsan. From there, it proceeds to Taiwan to load a shipment of textile products bound for Pusan. It is all arranged, Comrade Marshal. The crew is minimal and expendable. The captain has been paid the first installment of his fee."

And very shortly after the attack, that ship will be sunk by one of our submarines, Marshal Kim mused as he headed back to the bridge where he could observe the EMP test. *And no one will be the wiser concerning the source of the attack. A second vessel will be procured and outfitted for the follow-on operation against the American infrastructure.* He didn't share his thoughts on those longer-range plans. Not his most trusted aide—not even the new Supreme Leader had the need to know about all that just now. And Marshal Kim was a cautious man.

* * *

The test was controlled by the chief scientist's Digital Dragon team monitoring banks of shielded electronics deep within the belly of the frigate. Although he'd been warned that there would be nothing dramatic to see, Marshal Kim decided to observe from the bridge. He had suffered through the briefing, but he was not about to spend time staring at blinking dials and computer screens. When the weapon was eventually employed, all that testing and control equipment would be reduced to a simple power switch and a single firing control located on the bridge of the vessel. The plan required the ship carrying the generators to maneuver into a specific pre-plotted position in relation to the target. At that point, it was simply a matter of pressing the right buttons in the proper sequence. The captain and crew would have no idea what they were doing beyond following orders for which they'd been well paid. They would also have no idea about the large, devastating explosive devices which would guarantee obliteration of evidence once a torpedo was fired into the vessel.

A series of yellow flashing caution lights throughout the frigate was the only indication that the test had begun. The lights extinguished in less than five minutes, and the Marshal dropped his binoculars to look at his aide. The aide simply shrugged. He'd seen nothing and heard nothing except for a powerful, low-level humming as the controller poured power to the generators inside the containers on the flight deck. The barge had not moved. There was no smoke, no fire, no flash, and no visible indication of an attack. The Marshal supposed that was intended, but he couldn't help feeling a little disappointed.

"It was a complete success, Comrade Marshal!" The chief scientist appeared on the bridge leafing through a sheaf of computer print-outs. "All systems were rendered completely inoperable, and it appears from initial indications that no stored data could be recovered. We will have a more detailed report as soon as we can run diagnostics."

"What about the corvette?" The Marshal pointed at the vessel holding position forward of the target barge. "Do they report any damage to their systems?"

"None whatsoever, Comrade Marshal." The frigate captain replaced the receiver of his ship-to-ship radio and smiled. "And all our systems survived intact—except for one." The captain pointed at the ship's chronometer mounted on the bulkhead at the rear of the bridge. What had been a bright LED screen displaying large illuminated numerals was now black and lifeless. "I believe our electronics technicians failed to adequately shield our clock."

* * *

At 28,000 feet above the Sea of Japan and approximately 12.5 miles due west of the North Korean coastline, an American Navy P-3C Orion aircraft conducting an aerial reconnaissance exercise suddenly experienced a complete and catastrophic systems failure. One minute everything was operating normally and the next it all simply went black. The Orion suddenly had no sensor inputs, no read-outs from any system, and no communication of any kind inside or outside the aircraft. There was no way to let anyone know they had a very serious problem. When the flight controls and engine inputs to the four big Allison T-56 turboprops began to go spastic, the normally unflappable command pilot suddenly got very nervous.

Screaming and scrambling to communicate with each other, the pilots and crewmen went through every drill in the book and tried a bunch of fixes that weren't in any NATOPS manual trying to restore their blind, deaf, and dumb aircraft and keep it flying. Nothing worked. The crew had no fixed bearing, no way to determine a heading and no idea how much fuel remained in their tanks. After flying aimlessly for about 20 minutes on best-guess navigation, the controls ceased to have much effect on the Orion's flight attitude. The command pilot sent one of his flight officers to pass the word. They were going to ditch.

He didn't have much confidence that the emergency tran-
sponders or locator beacons would work given the failure of
every other system aboard, but they were rapidly running out of
altitude, airspeed, and options. The digital watch on his wrist
was as black and uninformative as all the other instruments, but
the last time he'd checked they were in the last two hours of a
scheduled six-hour mission. That meant in another three hours
or so someone from VP-8 would start looking for the missing
bird. If they survived the ditching and bobbing around on life
rafts in the frigid waters below, he was going to have some
serious discussions with the Lockheed tech reps.

T he second to last person Shake Davis expected to see when he crossed the gangway from the moored submarine to the dock at the sprawling Korean naval base was the man who calls himself Bayer. The last person he expected to see was the lovely woman standing next to Bayer wearing his old field jacket and a pissed off expression.

"*Sawadee*, Spouse—how you doing?" Shake dropped his rucksack and tried what he hoped was a disarming smile. Chan Dwyer Davis threw herself into his arms and hugged with a fervor that made him hope recriminations would be brief and relatively painless. Over his wife's shoulder, he noticed Mike Stokey trying to sneak off the docks and escape notice. Chan stiffened for a moment and pointed a finger at him.

"Don't disappear, Mike Stokey! I've got a few thoughts for you."

Stokey froze next to Bayer who was eying him with a mixture of anger and amusement. Stokey pointed at his CIA boss and shrugged. "I think you're gonna have to get in line for that, Chan. Good to see you again, by the way."

Shake gave his wife a kiss and watched her expression melt. "Are you here in a domestic or professional capacity?"

"Both." Chan picked up his rucksack and grabbed for his hand. "Bayer called when we got the initial report and the stuff Mike sent from the submarine. The defecation hit the oscillation in the community and suddenly there was a requirement for DIA to get into the game. He didn't have much choice but to bring me along with a bunch of tech-intel people. But that's for later. We're gonna have a very serious talk about your career options, buddy."

"Many thanks, Shake." Bayer approached and shook his hand. "Outstanding job as usual. We need to get our heads together on this thing soonest. The Korean Navy lent us some secure spaces here at Chinhae. You guys are booked into the VOQ with Stokey." He checked his watch and looked at Sam Jackson and the Korean Marines standing on the dock next to Lee who was leaning on a pair of aluminum crutches. "Chan can take you both over there. How about we meet in two hours?"

Shake nodded and turned to look at the Koreans. "That sounds OK, but I think there's someone here you need to meet in person." He introduced Bayer to Sam Jackson and named the others standing around wondering what to do. "I don't know how the system works, but I'm gonna press you hard to get these folks some kind of formal recognition. They damn sure deserve it."

"Mr. Jackson, I've been in contact with your people since I arrived. Our deal remains in place, I assure you." Bayer turned and pointed at two Korean Navy HUMVEEs parked at the entrance to the docks. "Those vehicles are here to take you to a debriefing. I'm sure we'll be seeing more of each other in the next few days."

"Thank you, sir. I'm looking forward to it." Sam Jackson smiled and gave Shake a friendly, painful punch on his wounded arm. "First I'd like to meet the woman who tamed this beast."

Chan was gracious as always and charmed Sam by greeting him in Korean. "I can't thank you enough, Sam." She smiled and clutched at her husband's arm. "He's a real project as you know from experience. I'm so glad you were there to spoil his efforts to get himself killed—this time and the one before that."

"He's a good man despite his many faults. We'll get together before you leave Korea. I'd like for you both to meet my family." Sam motioned for Sergeants Park and Jun to follow him toward the waiting vehicles. Lee stumped along looking around at the dockside buildings and warehouses like a country bumpkin dumped into Times Square.

"I brought a bottle of Jack." Chan led Shake and Stokey toward a waiting staff car. "You each get one drink." She nodded at Mike Stokey. "And then you disappear."

* * *

Mike Stokey was toweling off after a very pleasant and long-overdue shower in the Korean Navy Visiting Officers' Quarters when he heard the knock. He wrapped the towel around his waist and padded to the door expecting the clothes he'd sent out for laundering. Bayer stepped into the room without a word and slumped into a threadbare chair in one corner of the little sitting room. "Get some pants on, Mike." He pulled a silver flask out of his pocket and placed it on the table. "I've got a meeting with the analyst team in thirty minutes and we need to talk."

When Stokey returned in more presentable shape, Bayer poured scotch neat into two glasses and took a healthy belt. "I've got two things to say. Number one is congratulations on an outstanding mission even if you did violate the hell out of direct orders and damn near put me into cardiac arrest. The stuff you sent is serious business. We believe the Norks have developed an EMP type weapon and given the nature of the fanatics in Pyongyang, there's no telling what they intend to do with it. That's what I brought the DIA wonks over here to try and find out."

Mike sipped his whiskey and nodded. "I wondered why you came to Korea instead of pulling everybody back to Washington. I'd guess the cat's out of the bag over the UAV deal."

"That cat remains in the bag. The oversight people know we're working on a serious threat but they have no idea how we got the lead. That's the way it stays if we don't want the Chinese assets calling in some serious markers and refusing to work with us again. The reason I brought the brain-trust over here is because of a deal I was forced to make about sharing information with the South Koreans. There's gonna be a bunch of speculation going on in the next week or so, and I don't want to do that kind of thing long distance. It's opsec, pure and simple."

"OK, that's thing one. What's thing two?"

"You're through, Mike." Bayer slipped the flask back into his jacket and stood to leave. "I don't want to argue and I don't have time to get into all the reasons. You're on the inactive list as of now. You can put in formal retirement papers when you get back home."

Stokey looked down and pondered the inch of scotch in a cheap bathroom glass. He knew the day would come but he didn't think it would be while he was barefoot and half-naked in a dingy South Korean billet. There should be something more to it than that. He'd never expected a parade or much in the way of formal recognition, but he always thought he'd retire when he wanted to and not when the company said so long and don't let the door smack you in the ass on the way out.

"I'm not gonna argue about it." Stokey polished off the drink and gently set the glass on a rickety, cigarette-stained coffee table. "I'm not going to tell you I'm happy about it either. I've got some good years left in me and you know I get the job done when a lot of other people can't or won't. That said, it's your call." Stokey got up and walked with Bayer toward the door.

Bayer paused and stuck out his hand. "You're a good man, Mike. I'm sorry it's got to end this way—but there it is. Like you said—it's my call. Let me know your plans."

"That's easy." Stokey shook the outstretched hand and opened the door. "I plan to take that kid who went with me to the Chosin Reservoir back up the Yalu so he can get his family out of North Korea. And since I'm no longer in your employ, if you don't like it you can kiss my ass."

Mike Stokey slammed the door and went looking for his shoes and a shirt. Now that he had a plan, he could focus on immediate goals which included finding Lee, Sam Jackson and a bottle of whiskey.

* * *

"You know Bayer is cutting him loose." Chan snuggled next to her husband and inhaled the aroma of sandalwood from the soap they'd used to scrub away the remnants of a very passionate love-making session. "He wandered off the reservation one time too many."

"In one way I can understand that." Shake reached for the drink he'd left unfinished on the nightstand when they fell on the rump-sprung bed shortly after Stokey left for his own quarters. "Mike has been Bayer's ace in a very dark hole for a long time. He may bitch and moan about the guy's cowboy style, but he really likes Mike. I don't think he wants to see him get killed."

"There's a lesson for a certain someone there." Chan plucked the drink out of Shake's hand and finished it. "You want another one of these?" She got up to find the bottle of Jack Daniels she'd left in the bathroom. "You might need it if you're determined to sit through the meeting. We brought some geeks who can bore you to tears."

"One more." Shake sat up and swung his feet over the side of the bed. "And thanks for not making this too tough on me. You know I had to go after him. And you know why."

"I know all that, Shake, and I understand it." She handed him a fresh drink and then began to fish around in her bag for fresh clothes. "That doesn't mean I'm not going to be a nag. This kind of thing has got to stop. You're too old for it and I'm too young to be minus a handsome and loving husband. When we get home Stacey and I will be tag-teaming you like a couple of banshees. She's planning on buying you those wood-working tools you want and I'm going to throw in a set of leg-irons."

"Thanks for letting her know, by the way."

"Oh, get your head out of your ass, Shake. What was I gonna do? What would I say to Stacey if you screwed the pooch somewhere up in North Korea? That girl loves her Dad and she's certainly seen you do asinine things before. You should have called her before you left anyway."

Shake stood and stretched feeling the ache of the sutures in his arm and delighted that Chan hadn't made too big an issue of it once she peeked under the bandage. She'd seen a lot worse during her own time in uniform, and it wasn't a relatively minor wound that prompted the tirade she launched shortly after they arrived in the VOQ room with Stokey in tow. Chan Dwyer Davis vented her spleen for a few minutes while the men meekly mixed the drinks. Her bottom line was fairly simple once she'd run out of initial steam. They both needed to get a grip and start acting their advanced ages. With that fine point put on the issue, she relaxed.

"So, how come the DIA gets all dialed in on this thing?" Shake laced his boots and decided he was as presentable as he was likely to get until he could recover some of his baggage that was being sent down from Seoul.

"When Bayer got Stokey's initial reconnaissance report and took a look at the photos, he pulled in a bunch of tech-intel guys from DIA as the duty experts on EMP and the like. When they saw the reference to Marx generators, they got their panties in a twist. Apparently, DIA has been following the whole EMP-as-weapon concept for some time, but nobody thought it was practical. The Norks may have overcome that problem and suddenly it's a major deal. Given the situation in North Korea, they're convinced the commies up there are going to make a move in the very near future. That's about all I know. I'm here to help guess what they might have in mind doing with it. I've got a bunch of reference material and scientific wild-ass guesses that I'll be briefing this afternoon."

* * *

"The key to enhanced power flow is this element." Senior DIA weapons analyst Dr. Rick Lavers aimed his laser pointer at the enlarged IR photo of the markings Stokey had found on the equipment at the Chosin Reservoir. "Cesium 137 is the radioactive isotope of the element. It's normally used in medical applications or in industrial gauges. Employed with the relatively mundane Marx generator, it neutralizes the space charge that builds up near the cathode, and in doing so, it enhances the current flow. That facilitates a huge increase in power output. You'll note the other numbers shown. Each generator is apparently capable of producing two megavolts or two million volts in a surge.

"Given the number of Marx generators observed," Lavers snapped off his pointer and concluded what had been a mind-boggling lecture for many of the non-scientific types assembled in the spacious, high-security briefing room, "we speculate that the North Koreans intend to assemble a number of the generators in series for use in producing an EMP that would equal or exceed that generated by a standard nuclear detonation. We're working on the equivalency numbers now."

"Thank you, Dr. Lavers." Bayer looked around the room at the American analysts and Korean intelligence executives from their Agency for National Security Planning. "Are there any questions before we proceed?"

One of the senior Korean members raised a hand and spoke in clear, concise English. "We have been researching reports from the EMP Commission of the U.S. Nuclear Strategy Forum which warned about North Korean experiments with what they called a Super EMP device as far back as 2004. Is it your opinion that this is what we may be dealing with here?"

"I believe this is a different thing." Dr. Phil Hamer, Director of the DIA's Technical Intelligence Division Nuclear Analysis Team, got the nod from Bayer to field the question. "The forum was speculating about EMP generated as a result of a nuclear detonation, most likely in the atmosphere over a selected target. They basically concluded that *non-nuclear* EMP attacks were not practical. The problem has always been controlling and directing the pulse which is a very tricky problem in advanced physics. It's a little early to speculate, but we are inclined to think the North Koreans may have defeated the problem—very likely with some high-priced help from Chinese or Russian scientists—by controlling the dimensions of the pulse and employing it in short-duration, very high-intensity bursts of power."

"We concur." The questioner looked at the four other Korean intelligence analysts seated next to him on one side of a huge polished conference table. "EMP attacks are well defined within Russian and Chinese military doctrine which is the same as saying they are part of North Korean doctrine for attacks on enemy facilities. Unfortunately, too many allied nations—ours included—have done nothing to prepare for this sort of attack."

"Obviously, if we accept that the North Koreans have developed a functional non-nuclear EMP generating weapon," Bayer stood and checked his watch, "we must determine several things in short order." He began to tick items off on his fingers. "Will they use such a weapon? If so, what are the most likely targets? How would an EMP attack be conducted? And what can be done in very short order to prevent any such attack? We'll be breaking down into working groups on those questions after lunch, but before that I'll call on Dr. Chan Dwyer Davis of the Defense Intelligence Agency for a very sobering threat analysis that she's prepared."

Chan opened a file on her laptop and clicked a PowerPoint presentation into action. She stood and walked toward the screen at the front of the room. "I hate it when briefers just read what's on the screen." She was gratified to get some nods and chuckles from her audience. "So I'll let this presentation run while I talk. The facts and figures you see are sobering and they speak for themselves.

"EMP has always been the great equalizer. The country that can trip the trigger on an effective EMP generator immediately tips the scales of international power and influence. EMP is a weapon of choice for asymmetric campaigns and most probably *the* weapon of choice for any attack against the United States or any other large-size technically-dependent country. It is, in effect, the only way an adversary—or coalition of adversaries—could attack, create lasting havoc, and remain anonymous long enough to escape counterattack. We believe this element in the equation is what makes it so attractive to a nation like North Korea.

"Following a successful EMP attack, recovery could take up to ten years and would be entirely dependent on the production and supply of up to three hundred major transformers that are keys to operation of a nation's power grid. Considering that these transformers must each be specifically designed and built for the purpose intended, it could take more than a year and millions of dollars to replicate each one of them. We estimate that within twelve months of an EMP strike on America, for instance, as much as two-thirds of the population might die as a result of accidents, starvation, exposure, disease, and anarchy." Chan paused and looked around the table at the sober expressions on both Korean and American faces staring back at her.

"Of course, that data assumes a massive pulse that affects the target nation's general power grid. If the North Koreans have developed an EMP weapon that can be more precisely directed, it might not be as bad. On the other hand, it might be worse depending on what targets they strike. We'll be working on that issue after lunch." Chan returned to her seat in a deathly quiet room. She'd clearly hit home with her comments and everyone at the table seemed lost in their own thoughts.

Bayer stood and dismissed the assemblage for a catered lunch in the local cafeteria. Shake Davis cornered him before he got to the door. "Mike should have been here for this."

"No he shouldn't—and you know why." Bayer nodded at a few stragglers who were gathering their notes and heading for the door. "We've got his full report and he's not in a really good mood. Our last meeting ended rather abruptly."

"Does that surprise you? Christ, Bob, this stuff has been his whole life and you just jerked the rug out from under him. He's got no wife, no home, no family except for his sister, and no life outside the company."

"Mike's gonna be fine. I'm not about to let him just wander off into the sunset. I'll help him get a job and see that he's got enough money to do whatever he wants. We owe him that much."

"We owe him a damn-site more than that and I'll be in the mix to help him out so you can count on hearing from me on that matter." Bayer just nodded and started around Shake to reach the door. "There's just one thing."

"What?" Bayer checked his watch. "I'm due to meet with the Director of the Korean ANSP in twenty minutes."

"Mike told me that the trucks hauling these generators were from some Nork Navy outfit based in Wonsan. He said Lee recognized the tac-marks on the fenders. I think you guys should be focusing on ships."

"Interesting." Bayer pursed his lips and re-checked the time. "I don't remember seeing that note. I'll go back over his report and maybe call some people in the Navy. I've got some contacts at CINCPAC that might be helpful."

On the bridge of the MV *Rabat Milestone*, her Korean captain felt the uneven throb of the ship's ancient engines through the deck plates as his undermanned power-plant crew tested their repairs. He turned to look over the starboard side and noted the last of the North Korean Navy technicians were heading ashore with their instruments and tool-kits. He lit a cigarette and then walked out onto the bridge wing to look forward where six standard containers in various commercial colors had been loaded by dockside cranes.

At their next port of call in Kaohsiung, Taiwan, the ship was scheduled to load ten additional containers, but the captain figured that light cargo load wouldn't stress the old panamax container vessel too much despite her decrepit engines and sluggish handling. *And even if it did*, he thought as he pulled a paper out of his pocket to check the figures once again, *it will be some other sailor's problem*. The wire transfer notice from his bank in Shanghai informed the captain that 50,000 U.S. dollars had been deposited into his account. As soon as his mission was complete, a matching amount would be transferred and the captain could retire in comfort and style. If all went according to plan, this would be his last long-distance voyage.

As the underway conning crew manned stations and the deck gang below started the process of singling up their mooring lines, the captain made a quick trip to his cramped little office just aft of the bridge and shuffled through the paperwork on his desk looking for his file of cargo manifests. His eyes ran over the old ship's registry papers, and he wondered why his last voyage had to be aboard a balky old rust-bucket that had sailed under at least four names and three times that many registered owners. He found the folder he wanted and scanned it.

According to the manifest, the containers currently on deck were filled with automotive electrical assemblies. The captain knew that was nonsense and he didn't care. As with the manifests he had for containerized textiles waiting for pick-up at Kaohsiung, it didn't matter. What mattered—what the captain cared about—were the controls recently mounted on his bridge under a locked steel safety cover. He picked up a chain holding the only key that would unlock that safety cover and slipped it over his head.

When his first mate called from the bridge indicating the harbor pilot was aboard and all stations on the MV *Rabat Milestone* were manned and ready for sea, the captain headed for the bridge. He was thoroughly briefed and half his fee was safely deposited. It was time to embark on the first leg of his last voyage.

T he dinner with Sam Jackson's family at an intimate little waterfront place was spectacular and certainly worth the drive from Chinhae. It was clearly a favorite of the Jackson family, and the staff treated everyone like royalty. Sam's son got leave from the Naval Academy to attend, and his daughter flew down from Seoul for the event. Mrs. Sam Jackson turned out to be a petite, feisty character who spoke broken English well enough to let everyone know she was in charge of the menu and was determined that everyone try a long list of Korean delicacies. Before the second course was served, she and Chan Davis were old pals and commiserating about their wayward husbands.

It was close to midnight when the son and daughter took leave after being alternately entertained or bored by the wild stories told by their father and embellished by Shake and Mike Stokey. Mrs. Jackson and Chan were sampling a platter of iced deserts when the three men retired to the restaurant bar overlooking Pusan Harbor. Stokey had a bellyful of local whiskey and seemed in a good mood for a man who had just been fired.

"Nothing lasts forever." He circled his finger over their glasses and waited for the bartender to respond. "It's been a good run, right? I'll find something to keep me occupied. There's lots of shit I've been meaning to do—so now I'll just do it."

"I've got some thoughts about that." Shake tasted his drink and decided the Korean distillers still hadn't quite got the hang of Kentucky bourbon. "I've been thinking we ought to write a book or two, you know? Tell some tall tales and make a bunch of money. How's that sound?"

"Sounds like a plan if I've ever heard one. I can barely write my fucking name but we'll give it a shot—just as soon as I get one last thing done."

"You can't kick the shit out of Bayer."

"Not that—as much as I'd like to—what I need to do is get Lee squared away." Stokey turned to Sam Jackson. "You sure we can get his family out?"

"Not right away," Sam nodded at the bartender and lowered his voice. "There's too much going on right now. I talked to Colonel Soon and he says when the heat is off, he'll arrange for another trip up the Yalu. Sergeant Park and Sergeant Jun said they'll go along to keep you out of trouble. It's not a big deal. We'll get it done."

"Well, I'm staying right here in Korea until we do. Where's Lee now?"

"My guys have got him in a very comfortable isolation area at Chinhae. He's never had it so good, believe me. The medics are all over him, the Intel wonks are treating him like a king and he gets whatever he wants to eat—when they can pry him away from the TV."

"I've got a bunch of company cash I want to leave for him." Stokey poured the remnants of his drink into a fresh one. "Can you handle that? Set up some kind of account for him or something so he's got what he needs to get started once the family is down here with him?"

"I'll handle it." Sam checked on the women and decided they didn't need tending or attention. "We'll get it all made right once we deal with this other thing."

"I told Bayer he needs to be watching ships—seemed to surprise him." Shake flopped on a barstool and had second thoughts about Korean bourbon. It wasn't bad after the first six drinks. "I've been thinking about those tac-marks on the trucks. The Nork Navy is involved somehow. I'm betting if they've got this new deal, they'll wind up putting it on some kind of destroyer or something like that."

"Too simple." Sam Jackson shook his head and pointed at the bustling harbor outside the bar's picture window. "They drive a destroyer anywhere near this—much less San Diego or somewhere like that—and we'd blow 'em out of the water."

"Well, that's what the brain-trust is here to figure out. And they can do that without me." Shake grappled momentarily with Sam Jackson over the bar-tab and lost. "I have a plan."

"We gonna head up to Seoul and hit some of the old haunts?" Stokey polished off his drink and turned to leave. "Or would Chan frown on something like that?"

"She's gonna be tied up with Bayer and the boys. Meanwhile, I've been invited to spend some time with the MARSOC detachment at Chinhae." Shake threw an arm around Stokey. "You want to come along and meet some of the new breed of bad-asses?"

"Given the size of the generators and the power source required," Dr. Rick Lavers cleaned his glasses and stared myopically around the table at the other analysts on the targeting team, "I'd say air or surface vehicular platforms are not where we should be looking."

Pak Chun Lee of the South Korean ANSP threat analysis bureau nodded and shuffled through a stack of diagrams they'd developed approximating the size and possible shape of Marx generators. "That's right, I think." He punched up a picture on his laptop and spun it so the others at the table could see. "This is an artist's conception of what we believe the Russians have developed. It's called the Club K container missile system. It's a modification of a standard 40-foot cargo container that effectively transforms any container ship into a missile launching platform."

"We've been monitoring that." Chan Dwyer Davis tapped the familiar image with a fingernail. "As you know, Lee, it's designed to carry up to four cruise missiles. We've pretty well agreed that we're not looking for a device that uses a missile as a platform given what we believe about size, et cetera. That said, I agree that the North Koreans may have taken a cue from the Club K concept for their EMP device. It makes sense to me that we should be focusing on ships—container ships in particular."

"And I think we can take it for granted that the Norks wouldn't be sailing such a ship or ships under their own flag, right?" Rick Lavers scribbled some notes and looked around for confirmation.

"Mr. Bayer is calling in some experts from the U.S. Navy to give us a little better read on that whole issue." Chan picked up a plastic coffee urn from a side-table and looked around to see if any of her teammates needed a re-fill. "If we're agreed that the most likely platform for an EMP weapon of this size and capability is a ship, let's talk about potential targets."

"Let me speak to that for a moment." Pak Chun Lee looked to his right where the only other Korean member of the targeting team sat silently taking in the conversation. "Dr. Seung Ji and I had some discussions about potential targets at lunch and I'll ask him to expound on that momentarily." Lee picked up a mechanical pencil and examined it for a moment as he gathered his thoughts. "While I certainly understand the concern of our American colleagues, I believe the most likely potential target for this weapon is not the United States, at least not in the short-term. As we are all painfully aware, the North Korean leadership has declared Kim Jong-Il's son the new Supreme Leader of that country. And only yesterday we got the news that Kim Jong-Un has also been seated as leader of the North Korean Communist Party.

"That all seems fairly straightforward to those who don't know the North Koreans the way we do. It is anything but straightforward, I assure you. Despite the titles and declarations about Kim Jong-Un, the power in Pyongyang rests with the military. All the rest of it is charade. And so, we should consider potential targets from the North Korean military perspective. What are their immediate needs? What do they consider the most pressing threat? What do they want more than anything?" Lee held up his right fist and began to count the answers to his own questions. "First, they are desperate for food, facilities, and commodities not available in the north. Second, they believe our nation is a continuing and pressing threat to their status—even their very existence given our capable military and our backing by the United States. Finally, they want a unified, communist Korea under control of Pyongyang. The most likely target is my country—South Korea."

Dr. Seung Ji waited a moment for his colleague's words to register and then he leaned forward to speak for the first time since the meeting began. "My background is economics. For the past several years I have been employed by my government to study the economic situation in North Korea. It has been a difficult task since the economic situation in the north is nothing short of chaotic and dismal. There are, of course, relatively simple ways in which Pyongyang could solve their problems, but that would require them to abandon the communist-socialist model and mirror what we do here in the south." Seung Ji paused to sip tea and look around the table.

"Given the leadership—some call it hard-headed ignorance—in the north, they continue to cling to outmoded, failed concepts and the people suffer. Pressure mounts from inside and outside the North Korean nation to abandon these concepts and copy the economic plans of China and other nations adopting the capitalist model. When the death of Kim Jong-Il was announced, there were those who thought such a momentous change might be stimulated. I am not one of those. With Kim Jong-Un as successor to his father and the military firmly entrenched as the real power in Pyongyang, no such economic or social progress can be made.

"On the socio-economic front, the North Koreans are faced with a dilemma. They can either change their ways or they can attempt to bring down the competing system they despise. As pointless and as ineffective as it would be in the long-run, I believe they will opt for the latter course of action. I believe they will strike at us in an attempt to destroy our infrastructure and leave the Republic of South Korea open to conquest."

"I understand your thinking, Dr. Seung Ji." Chan Davis was following the economist's reasoning and thought she could see where he was going with it. "But any such move on the part of the North Koreans would bring on a war, wouldn't it? Surely, the United States and other allied nations would step in to prevent it or help you resist any such actions."

"The problem, of course, is China." Pak Chun Lee nodded at the map displayed on a nearby wall. "Does your country want to challenge China given your own economic obligations to that country? And what if it came to a military face-off? History tells us America under-estimated Chinese commitment to North Korea once before with disastrous results. I think you will grant that your current administration is focused on domestic problems and more than a little war-weary after a decade of fighting in the Middle East. We would be left quite on our own, I'm afraid, to deal with the North Koreans."

"That is correct." Dr. Seung Ji leaned forward in his chair and thumped his knuckles on the polished table. "But it presumes a conventional military conflict. That will not happen. North Korea can't afford to commit international suicide. To succeed in conquering my country they must create vulnerability. They need to disarm and distract us so that we are vulnerable to more clandestine incursions. Most importantly, they must shield themselves from blame. That is what I believe they have in mind for the new weapon."

"So you think they will use this weapon to strike at your country's power grid and then make some kind of take-over move in the resulting chaos?" Chan was confused about what she was hearing. "I can't speak for the administration in Washington, but I think the United States and all your other allies would move quickly to help you prevent chaos. Or am I missing something?"

"You are missing what I believe is the intended target, Mrs. Davis." Dr. Seung Ji rose and walked to the map on the wall of the meeting room. He tapped a spot on the eastern coast of the Korean Peninsula about 40 kilometers due west of where they were sitting. "Here at Pusan is the economic heart of my country, our international stock exchange. Imagine what might happen if that economic heart was destroyed by a massive EMP strike."

* * *

The man who calls himself Bayer sat in a cramped, borrowed office at the Chinhae Navy Base re-reading Chan Davis' committee report and waiting for his phone to ring. Not that he needed any more phone time after a blistering 45 minute harangue with the Director of Central Intelligence who was feeling more than a little miffed about being kept in the dark concerning recent developments on the North Korean front.

When the DCI finished venting and going over the threat projection Bayer sent earlier in the day, he hung up with terse final instructions.

"Just sit on it for a while and keep developing the intelligence," the DCI directed at the end of their secure-circuit conversation. "I'm gonna have to brief this to Congressional Oversight, State, and probably the White House. Don't make any moves or any promises without checking it with me." When he finally disconnected, Bayer put in a second call to Vice Admiral Jeff Ault at CINCPAC Headquarters, Pearl Harbor. Ault was an old friend from the Laos and Peleliu operations who had maintained a back-channel connection with CIA during his rise to a high-level desk on the staff of the Navy's Commander in Chief, Pacific.

Ault wasn't in but an aide put Bayer on a priority call-back list. While he waited, Bayer compiled the salient points of their assessment report and sent it along to the Admiral's classified communications address. Hopefully, Ault would get the picture they were painting and lend a hand in planning what to do about it.

It was becoming clear that when the time came—and no one had any idea when that might be—they should be looking for a container ship, but there were hundreds of those vessels plying the Pacific. Bayer didn't know how or under what authority his people—either American or South Korean—might be able to stop internationally-flagged vessels operating legally on the high seas and conduct searches. It was a thorny question, and no doubt he'd wind up calling in the lawyers to argue about it before long.

Bayer scrolled through Chan's report to the last section on likely targets and re-read the assessment she included from the South Korean economist. He had little doubt that the committee was correct in projecting South Korea as the most likely target, but he'd completely missed the potential for a strike at the South Korean stock exchange. *If they succeeded in something like that*, Bayer realized as he poured himself another cup of rancid coffee, *the chaos throughout international markets would be devastating.*

And he'd damn sure have to come up with some serious evidence that Pyongyang was behind any such an attack. Failing that, the bastards would be free to try it again, and Bayer didn't want to contemplate what kind of disaster a similar strike on the New York exchange might cause. The U.S. had enough economic problems without a complete collapse of the stock exchange's ability to conduct business. A thing like that would make the great crash of 1929 look like a minor glitch.

His cell phone vibrated and Bayer snatched it up to check the caller ID. Vice Admiral Ault was returning his call despite the late hour. "Hello, Jeff. Sorry to ask you to get back to me so late, but we've got a problem and I could really use some Navy advice."

"It's no problem, Bob. I've read the file you sent. Is this thing for real?"

"Way too damn real, I'm afraid. We need to start looking at ships, and I need help figuring out how to do that without causing a bunch of international incidents."

"Yeah, I see the problem. Listen, I've been talking to some people here at Hailawa Heights and I have some thoughts. We had a weird aircraft incident about ten days ago and I'm beginning to think it could be connected. Where are you now?"

"I'm at Chinhae, the Korean Navy Base near Pusan."

"OK. Sit tight for a day or two. That's within our Pacific command purview. I'm gonna check with the boss and then fly out to see you. We need to talk."

"Great, and Jeff—if you've got a sea lawyer on staff that knows all about international maritime law, you might want to throw him in the baggage compartment."

* * *

"Looks just like a bunch of fireman sliding down the old brass pole." Mike Stokey stood next to Shake Davis watching a team of Marine special operators fast-rope from a helicopter hover-ing some 70 feet off the ground at a remote Korean exercise area. "What was wrong with the old rappelling method?"

"Couple of things, Mike," Shake pulled on a pair of leather gloves with thickly-padded palms and pointed at the U.S. Army UH-60 Blackhawk helicopter speeding away from the insertion site. "When shooters are rappelling, it takes longer to insert them. The helo remains vulnerable in a hover for too long. Plus, the guys are hooked to the rope and hampered by a rig and 'biners which can take time to de-rig once they hit the deck. And the rope gets blown all over the area by rotor wash. That's why they developed this technique. It's officially called Fast Rope Insertion System."

"And you've done this before?" Stokey pulled on his own gloves and watched as the helicopter maneuvered for a landing to pick up a second section of Marines plus two strap-hangers: Gunner Shake Davis and Mike Stokey who had spent the better part of the day running and gunning through a shoot-house with the MARSOC Detachment at Chinhae and accepted an invitation to try fast-roping.

"Yeah, we were experimenting with this stuff before I retired. It's nothing new, except possibly for an old fart like you. I'll talk you through it." They got the signal to board the helicopter from Gunnery Sergeant Hugh Morgan, known to the MARSOC community as Huge Organ, who was the Team Leader and Rope Master for the exercise. He bumped Stokey on the shoulder and they started toward the Blackhawk. "Just be sure you've got a good grip when you initially get on the rope, set your feet to work as brake and speed control and slide."

"You gonna be OK, Gunner?" Gunny Morgan herded them into the helicopter. The MARSOC Marines wore huge grins as they watched the two older guys crawl into the cargo space and step over the thick ropes coiled on the deck. "We're gonna put eight men on the deck; four on each rope at three-meter intervals. Goal is to get everybody down in less than thirty seconds."

Shake pointed at Mike who was looking a little dubious. "I'll coach him through it. Where do you want us?"

"Last men on each rope," Morgan shouted over the rotor noise and hopped into the helicopter giving a thumbs-up launch signal to the crew chief. "I'll have a couple of my guys on the ground to police up the parts if you crash." He thought that was hilarious. Mike Stokey did not.

When the helicopter was airborne and circling the insertion site, Shake picked up a length of the heavy rope attached to an overhead anchor point in the helicopter's cargo bay and leaned toward Mike so he could be heard. "It's an inch-and-a-half wrapped nylon." Shake ran his hands over the irregular surface of the line. "It's not smooth like regular climbing line and the wrap makes it easier to grip with your hands and feet. The rope is heavy enough so it doesn't get blown around by rotor wash. Once you're on the rope, keep your eyes on the ground. It comes up faster than you think. When you're ready to land, let go with your feet and get ready to take the landing with your knees flexed. You got it?"

"What does not kill me makes me strong." Stokey glanced around at the watching Marines and tried a confident smile. "Anything else I should know?"

"Just one thing." Shake scooted out of the way of the Marines who were maneuvering toward the door. "Don't stand around on the ground admiring your skill. The ropes are too hard to recover, so the crew just drops 'em after the insertion. That much weight falling from seventy feet can knock your dick stiff in a hurry."

The helicopter pilots pulled the aircraft into a hover as Gunny Morgan and the crew chief kicked the ropes out the door. The first two Marines were on them immediately and disappeared out of sight as two more mounted the ropes in rapid succession. Morgan grabbed a rope and looked back to see that his last men out were ready. When he disappeared, Shake glanced down to judge separation and then gripped the rope. He nodded at Mike and then swung out to get a purchase with his feet. As he started the rapid slide, he saw Stokey descending at about the same speed.

They hit the ground within seconds of each other. Stokey examined the palms of his gloves and then looked up at the departing helicopter. Shake grabbed him by the elbow and hustled him off the zone just in time to avoid the plummeting ropes. "How cool was that?"

Stokey grinned and shook his gloved hands. "I thought that rope was gonna burn right through my gloves. What a rush!"

"Not enough friction with your feet." Shake was recalling the exhilaration he'd felt on hundreds of drop zones or insertion points after the always dicey business of getting into the fight via aircraft that don't land. "It takes a little practice."

Gunnery Sergeant Morgan ran up to them pointing at his watch. "Twenty-eight seconds, gents. Not bad. I'm gonna call a school circle, Gunner. Would you mind saying a few words to my Marines?"

They were fairly familiar with the grinning faces that stared up at them from around a semi-circular formation where the Marines were kneeling and waiting for their exercise critique. Once the MARSOC Marines found out who Shake was and got a little background on Mike Stokey, they'd peppered both visitors with questions and requests for war stories all day.

"Well, I thoroughly enjoyed it." Shake grinned and pointed at Mike. "I can't speak for my partner here as that was his cherry drop by fast rope."

Mike grinned and tugged at his gloves. "Yeah, yeah, it was just slightly less stimulating than getting laid. Carry on, Gunner Davis." When the chuckles died, Shake took a knee and pointed at the departing helicopter.

"You guys don't need any words of wisdom from me. I've been around MARSOC enough to know how sharp you all are—a damn site better than Mike and I ever were. I'm proud of that, proud to be a part of your history, and confident that you'll get any job done, anywhere and anytime. There's maybe one thing I could say. It occurred to me when I was dragging this old dinosaur off the zone out there. Those of us who jump out of airplanes, rappel and fast-rope all the time, can get a little wrapped around the axle with the insertion techniques and forget about what comes next. I've seen it with the Army airborne quite a bit. They get so excited about jumping that they forget it's only a way to get them into the fight. It can become more about jumping than about fighting and that's a deadly mistake. If I was gonna presume to have any advice for you, it would be to remember it's the fight that counts and not how you get there." He stood and nodded at Stokey. "Mike, you got anything for these hard-chargers?"

Stokey stared at his boots for a long moment and then moved around the semi-circle shaking hands. "I'm just an old, crusty grunt, but I want you to know how proud I am of all of you. Just thinking that I once wore the same eagle, globe, and anchor that you do is a genuine thrill. Maybe even a bigger thrill than sliding down that damn rope a few minutes ago. Thanks for the ride. We owe you a beer or two the first time we get together again."

A Korean Marine HUMVEE was waiting to haul them back to the Chinhae VOQ. Shake climbed in and cocked an eyebrow at his old friend. "What did you think?"

"I needed something like that, Shake. Thanks."

"You're welcome, partner. Kind of restores your soul, doesn't it?"

Back in the quarters, Chan called while Shake was mixing drinks and let him know she'd be late and he was on his own for dinner. He offered Mike one of the drinks, slumped onto a couch, and propped his boots up on the coffee table.

Stokey grinned and leaned over to slap the muddy boots off the table. "Does Chan let you do shit like that at home?"

"I don't usually come home with muddy boots anymore. Did you read the report she compiled?"

"Yeah, I read it. They got it right, I think. The Norks are gonna put this thing aboard a ship, there's no doubt in my mind. And I'm buying the initial target as South Korea. What got my attention was the business about striking at stock exchanges. That's a new wrinkle."

"Makes sense to me. They create a regular shit-storm and hurt the ROKs much worse than any kind of conventional or even nuclear attack. The question is how would we find that ship among all the other commercial vessels in the area and stop it."

"One thing I don't understand is how the hell do they aim something like that to have any kind of assurance it hits the target?" Stokey retrieved the bourbon, poured refills and put the bottle on the table between them. "I mean you blast that much power out into the atmosphere and it does what it does, right? It goes all over the damn place."

"Apparently, they've got a handle on that. Chan says the scientists are thinking it's a matter of putting the weapon into a pre-determined relationship with the intended target—kind of like lining up for a golf shot before you swing."

"So it's some kind of fucking ray-gun? Seems kind of iffy to me."

Shake shrugged and then reached for the cell phone that was vibrating next to the whiskey bottle. He listened for a few minutes and then glanced over at Mike. "Yeah, come on over. Mike's here and we're just having a drink. OK, I'll let him know." Shake exchanged the cell phone for his glass. "That was Bayer. He wants a meeting. I told him you were here. He said you could stay or not—your call. Can you behave yourself?"

"I will be the very soul of discretion and decorum," Stokey said as he reached for the bottle, "as long as we don't run out of booze."

* * *

Jeff Ault was carrying a little more weight and a lot less hair than the last time they had seen him out in the South Pacific islands, but he seemed like the same jovial sea-dog as he pushed past Bayer and barged into Shake's room headed directly for the whiskey bottle.

"Rank has its privileges!" He grinned and pointed at the three silver stars on his shoulder boards. "Where's my glass—or do I have to chug from the bottle with you two lowlifes?"

Stokey headed for the bathroom and an extra glass as Shake gave Ault a hug and looked over at Bayer who was grinning over his little surprise. "You could have mentioned you were bringing a brass hat; I'd have stocked up on booze."

"Jeff said he wanted to surprise you." Bayer set a paper bag on the coffee table and stripped it away to reveal a quart of scotch. "I learned a long time ago not to argue with admirals."

Stokey returned with extra glasses and grinned at Ault. "Three stars? It seems like only yesterday you were still shitting boot camp chow, Jeff. Guess it won't be long before you're CNO."

"Fortunately, the Navy has not lowered standards that far." Ault offered a toast to old friends. "I'm probably on a twilight cruise at CINCPAC. They don't have enough stars to keep me in harness if I've got to sail a desk for the rest of my career."

"Welcome to the club." Stokey tilted his glass toward Bayer. "I've just become homeless myself."

They played catch-up for half an hour and then Bayer brought the conversation around to the problem at hand. "I asked Jeff to give me some advice on the ship deal. We've just about agreed that when the Norks decide to field this EMP thing it will be on a container ship and everyone seems to think the target will be something here in the south; likely the power grid or the stock exchange at Pusan. The most pressing problem is how we would identify the ship that may be carrying the weapon."

"I brought CINCPAC's expert maritime law guy with me. I left him over at the Chinhae officer's club with my aide so I could let my hair down a bit with you guys..." Ault rubbed a hand over his bald head, "...not that I've got any hair to let down. Anyway, we talked on the flight over and he says it's a bitch-kitty of a problem from a legal standpoint."

"Fucking lawyers." Stokey splashed more whiskey into a glass and shook his head. "You can't even wind your watch these days without one of those bastards writing up a legal liability assessment." Stokey took a drink and pointed a finger at Bayer. "I'm telling you, if you let the lawyers determine how to do this thing, you'll wind up with fried targets and anarchy before they file the first brief."

"Take it easy, Mike." Shake put a restraining hand on his friend's elbow and nodded at Ault. "Let's hear what Jeff's got to say. He's the expert."

"I'm all for flooding the Sea of Japan with every ship we've got, stopping every container vessel we find, searching them all at gunpoint and devil take the hindmost. Unfortunately, it's not that simple." Ault reached into the briefcase at his feet and plopped a thick, blue-bound book onto the coffee table.

"That's just the more pertinent passages of maritime law covering cases like this. I'd have brought the rest of the books but there wasn't room on the plane. The bottom line is if we do something like that—or if the ROK Navy does—there will be more protests, lawsuits, international incidents, and saber-rattling than you can shake a stick at. The Norks know that as well as we do, which is likely the reason they'd put it on a commercial vessel operating under a known and familiar international flag—like Liberia or Panama to name the most common. Plus, if *we* wanted to do it, we'd need White House approval—and you all know how likely we'd be to get that with the current administration in worldwide apology mode."

"The techies are saying the Norks would likely have to line the ship up with the target for max effect." Bayer stood and shrugged out of his coat. "Assuming that's right, wouldn't they bring the vessel inside South Korean territorial waters? If they do that, the ROK Navy could claim some kind of probable cause and board it, right?"

"Maybe." Ault refilled his glass and checked a computer print-out. "I got this from the Vessel Traffic Services Office. According to their figures, between the ports of Pusan, Chinhae, and Pohang right here on the east coast, there is something like five hundred ships coming and going at any time. On those ships is something like seventeen thousand containers with approximately eight hundred thousand tons of assorted cargo. Just limit it to Pusan and you're looking at the sixth busiest commercial port in the world."

"I had no idea." Shake took a look at the print-out and shook his head. "That's a hell of a lot of commercial ship traffic."

"Yes, it is." Ault tapped his finger on the bottom line that showed the billions of dollars estimated to move through the port yearly. "Look at that figure. Even if we just turn it over to the ROKs as their problem and lend a hand where required, they're gonna have big issues with slowing down all that traffic and losing all that money while they search every ship that enters the north or south inner or outer harbor."

"The alternative would be worse." Bayer sighed and emptied his glass. "Surely, they'll understand that. What option do they have?"

"The option is to find that damn ship and stop it before it gets anywhere in range." Shake refilled his whiskey glass and tugged at the laces of his boots. "The biggest glitch right now is how we can identify the ship."

"About that range thing." Ault pulled another piece of paper from his briefcase. "Our vessel carrying the EMP weapon might not need to get very close to do significant damage." He passed a Navy message form to Bayer. "That's a report of a ditching by one of our P-3 Orion's last week. We recovered the crew after a very chilly couple of hours bouncing around in rafts in the Sea of Japan. The aviators are saying it's the damnedest thing they've ever seen. In fact, none of the accident investigation guys have ever seen anything like what happened to that bird."

"Fucking Nasal Radiators." Stokey was feeling no pain but behaving himself in general. "Shit happens and they've got to convene fourteen boards to find out why."

"That's the nature of their beast, Mike." Ault pointed at the report that Bayer had passed along to Shake. "However, in this case it's what the brown-shoes call unprecedented—and I agree with that assessment. The Orion experienced a complete and utter shut-down of all systems. Everything electronic went bat-shit all at once up to and including the crew's digital watches. One of the very, very few things that could make that happen is an electro-magnetic pulse."

"Holy shit!" Shake leaned forward and put his glass on the coffee table. "So you think they might have already used this thing?"

"What new weapon do you know of that's never been tested before employment? The aircraft was patrolling just over twelve miles east of Wonsan, and we have reconnaissance reports of two of their frigate-class vessels operating in that area at the same time. Could be they targeted that aircraft. Or it could be they were testing this thing and it didn't perform exactly as advertised."

Bayer slumped back on the couch and wiped the frosty glass across his forehead. "Well, that jacks everything up into over-drive. Now we've got to assume they are going to use this thing sooner rather than later. And it could be that even the Norks don't know how it might perform once they pull the trigger or trip the switch or whatever. Even if we found it, they might hit the switch and do all sort of damage outside what they intended."

"Could be." Ault re-packed his briefcase. "I've got an im-portant meeting with my ROK Navy counterpart tomorrow morning. We're gonna have to get a lot of assets involved in this thing, surface and air, ours and theirs. First priority is to identify that damn ship."

"Well, we can't just backtrack. They won't be dumb enough to send it south directly out of Wonsan." Shake stood to shake Ault's hand and walk with him to the door. "It's really good to see you again, Jeff. Let me know if there's anything I can do to help."

When Admiral Ault was gone, Shake turned to Bayer and glanced at Stokey nodding in a chair. "I know you shit-canned him but you need to bear in mind that Mike's the only guy who has actually seen any of these containers."

* * *

"So, here's the plan." The man who calls himself Bayer looked around the conference room and paused. Staring back at him were movers and shakers from the U.S. Pacific Command, the ROK military and various intelligence agencies of both countries formed into an emergency task force. "We are now operating on the assumption that the North Koreans intend to conduct an EMP attack on a target or targets here in South Korea. Beginning tomorrow morning, we are in a max effort to locate what amounts to a needle in a haystack." He scanned to see if the Korean members understood the metaphor. The nods he got indicated they hadn't missed the meaning.

"Mission One is to find a commercial container vessel that we believe is carrying a North Korean EMP weapon that may be used in an attack on the Pusan area or some other vulnerable target along the eastern coast of the peninsula. A synopsis of what we know about the weapon is included in your briefing folders. We have no idea about the flag that vessel may be sailing under, and we also have no idea what port it might be sailing from to conduct such an attack. What we do know—or what we believe given the evidence—is that such an attack from the sea is being planned and may well be in the offing right now.

"Since we are legally precluded from stopping commercial vessels on the high seas without demonstrable and credible cause, we will have to rely on best guess and any suspicious elements we may spot. That's very vague and I apologize, but there's nothing we can do about it right now. Our focus will be on vessels bound from this list of Pacific ports." Bayer paused to pass around a list of the area's busiest commercial harbors. "Any container vessels bound for ROK ports—particularly Pusan, Chinhae, or Pohang—will be subject to increased scrutiny. Vice Admiral Ault and his ROK Navy counterpart Admiral Kim have been designated joint task force commanders for the search efforts, so I'll let them brief you on the specifics of that plan."

Jeff Ault got the nod from the Korean Navy Admiral at his elbow and rose to address the team. "We're pulling out all the stops on this one, folks. We have satellite reconnaissance assets diverted to focus on this part of the world's oceans as well as a flight of RQ-4 Global Hawk UAVs that will be almost constantly on station over the Sea of Japan. Both American and Korean reconnaissance aircraft will be supplementing those assets. We have both American and Korean Navy ships moving into the area now, and they'll be on stand-by to intercept any suspicious vessels that enter Republic of Korea territorial waters. We also have both Navy and Marine Corps Visit, Board, Search and Seizure Teams from both nations on stand-by here at Chinhae if we need a quick reaction force. That's about it, I guess. Both Admiral Kim and I will be on hand here at task force headquarters to coordinate the efforts."

Bayer stood and swept a hand around the banks of computers and TV monitors lining the walls of the huge space set aside for the task force headquarters. "As you can see, our technicians have got us set up here fairly well. You've all been given specific duty assignments and we'll be analyzing live video feeds, sensor data, manifests, and international ship movement schedules around the clock. Right after lunch, we'll post the watch schedule and specific team break-downs. You analysts and imagery folks need to be particularly sharp and very suspicious. As I said, we don't precisely know what we're looking for, so don't ignore anything that strikes you as out of the ordinary."

Bayer dismissed the assembly and then caught Vice Admiral Ault's elbow. "Did you talk to Honolulu, Jeff?" Ault help up his cell phone and shook it. "Spoke to the PAO people just before this meeting. They're issuing a press release in the morning. It will look like a routine drill for anyone that's overly interested."

Bayer thanked him and waved at Chan Davis as she headed for the door. She waited until he caught up with her and then led the way down the hallway to a small office located some distance from the main task force operating area. "The technicians got the video feed set up this morning and I told both of them to meet us here." She opened a door to reveal Shake Davis and Mike Stokey slouched in a pair of swivel chairs and staring at two huge plasma TV screens.

"You guys are the filters behind the filters." Bayer indicated the display screens. "You'll get all the images that come in—satellite, drone and airborne camera feeds. Just monitor all of it." He pointed at Shake. "I need your brain and gut reactions." Bayer turned to Mike Stokey. "And you are *temporarily* reactivated for this one endeavor. If you see anything that looks familiar, pick up a phone and let me know right away."

* * *

Chan Dwyer Davis shoved aside the cargo manifests and sailing schedules for container vessels heading for Pusan out of Singapore, Yokohama, Honolulu and Shanghai. They were a mix of foreign-flagged ships of varying sizes and capacities that they'd marked for closer scrutiny. Each vessel had made a stop at a North Korean port as a leg of their Pacific voyages, but there was nothing ominous about any of them.

She was feeling frustrated as were most of the intelligence analysts and maritime experts on the team. They'd been at it for a full week now and had nothing but a long list of vessels that the Korean military and Port Authority officials were promising to intercept and inspect the very moment they entered Korean territorial waters. What they needed was some sort of clue—even a gut instinct would be helpful—to narrow the focus on the commercial traffic in the Sea of Japan, the western Pacific and the South China Sea. It was time for one of her frequent visits to the office down the hall where Shake and Mike Stokey had built themselves a little man-cave to screen all the visuals coming in from satellites and drones combing the areas of interest.

On her way toward the door, she stopped occasionally to peer over the shoulder of one analyst or another watching and checking on vessels headed their way from Kwai Chung, Hong Kong, Kaohsiung, Ho Chi Minh City, and Macau. It was like watching summer sitcom re-runs. Except for size and paint schemes, all the ships looked the same. The 40-foot containers on their decks were all brightly painted and carried the logos of a number of familiar international shipping companies, but there was nothing about any of it that looked out of the ordinary.

"You guys got anything?" Chan stuck her head inside the door of the little satellite office and wrinkled her nose at the smell of stale coffee, cigarette smoke, and dirty socks. Shake was staring at a plasma screen. Mike Stokey was crapped out in a bunk they'd installed along one wall of the cramped little space.

"Nothing so far." Shake turned from an aerial view of a container ship out of Kobe, Japan and looked at his wife. She was showing the strain. "Mike, relieve me here. I'm going to take the spouse to lunch. It looks like she could use a break."

Stokey stirred and rolled off the bunk. He nodded at Chan and dropped into the chair Shake had just vacated. "Anything on this one?" He pointed at the ship showing on the screen.

"Nothing that I could see, but you maybe should zoom in on the containers. When I get back from lunch we'll go over the rest of the tapes." Shake grabbed Chan by the elbow and led her toward the cafeteria.

The Captain of the MV *Rabat Milestone* was not happy and neither was his short-handed crew. The ROC Customs and Maritime officials delayed his departure by a full day fooling around with his passport and master's papers before clearing the ship for departure from their major port on the southwest coast of Taiwan. The crew worked overtime and expedited the loading of ten 20-foot containers filled with textiles hoping for a little shore liberty in Kaohsiung. They got none.

What they got was a promise of bonus pay and a week of regular shore rotations once they reached Pusan. The Captain would pay the bonuses, but he was not about to cozy his ship any closer to the South Korean shore than the exact coordinates the technicians at Pyongyang had pre-programmed into his GPS. That's when he would hit the switches to complete his mission and trigger the remaining half of his payment. He knew there was some kind of high-tech weapon in one or more of the containers they took aboard at Wonsan, but that was none of his concern. The paymasters assured him that no one would ever know his ship was anything but an innocent merchant-man. His North Korean countrymen had been good to their word so far, and the Captain was determined not to worry needlessly.

He ordered a course change to the northeast and had his engineers wring best speed out of the wheezy old engines as MV *Rabat Milestone* swung toward the East China Sea. He'd likely have to deal with an even sulkier crew and maybe pay them yet another bonus when they discovered he did not intend to offload as scheduled at Pusan. When he'd done what his contract demanded, the Captain intended to turn for open water and make directly for his homeport at Shanghai. After that, he would promptly disappear and the owners could deal with the undelivered cargo in his deck containers. That's why they carry all that expensive insurance.

Checking his position and radar repeaters, the Captain stepped up to the console where the special controls were mounted, pulled the keychain off his neck, and inserted the key in the lock. The lid opened easily and he checked the two switches marked in Korean *hangul:* **Power** and **Connect.** They looked the same as they always did: One bayonet switch and a single red button mounted to the right of it. He closed and locked the safety lid, smiling at his helmsman and first officer who had watched him do the same drill every day since they left Wonsan. They had no reason to doubt that the controls were not what the Captain said they were: An experimental degaussing system to assist in keeping the vessel's old bottom clean. The Captain re-checked his position and estimated about three days sailing at current speed in what was predicted to be deteriorating weather all the way to the Korea Strait.

Pyongyang, Democratic People's Republic of (North) Korea

"What is all this nonsense?" Marshal Kim Jun-Yi looked up from the intelligence report and stared over his reading glasses at his senior aide. "Increased air activity over the Sea of Japan, American ships steaming toward the region? I don't like it."

The senior aide reached into his agenda folder and withdrew a sheet of paper. "This is a translation of a news release from the American Pacific Command in Honolulu, Comrade Marshal." He placed the paper on the desk and walked around to read over his boss' shoulder. "It may well explain everything." The Marshal re-seated his glasses and began to read.

FOR IMMEDIATE RELEASE: Honolulu, Hawaii-The U.S. Pacific Command today announced the start of an international military readiness exercise called RIMPAC (Rim of the Pacific) which will involve air and naval forces from allied nations around the world. Ships and aircraft from the U.S., Great Britain, New Zealand, Australia, Canada, South Korea, and Japan will all be involved in the exercise which is expected to last for two months.

Increased air and surface operations throughout the Pacific can be expected as forces cross-train and familiarize themselves with operational techniques used by their allies. Exercises are planned in aerial reconnaissance, anti-submarine and carrier task group tactics as well as higher-level strategic conferences between allied military leaders.

For further information on RIMPAC or photo coverage, please contact the U.S. Pacific Command Public Affairs Office.

"This RIMPAC exercise is not unusual or unfamiliar to us, Comrade Marshal. We've seen several such exercises over the years. It's flag-waving or saber-rattling, depending on your perspective. It's nothing to be worried about."

"I will remain worried until our Operation Digital Dragon is complete." Marshal Kim dropped his glasses on the press release. "I'm told the ship was delayed in departing Kaohsiung."

"I blame typical Nationalist Chinese paranoia, Comrade Marshal. Something to do with the Captain's papers, I'm told. At any rate, the cargo was loaded successfully and the ship is now transiting the Luzon Strait. Our people estimate three more days before it arrives in Pusan."

"Good. That gives me some time to prepare our new Supreme Leader. Order the submarine to proceed at once."

The senior aide returned to his office and picked up a phone to contact the Naval Submarine Base at Mayangdo on the east coast. His instructions were terse and expected by the officer in command. Three hours after the orders were passed down to the docks, a former Soviet Whiskey Class submarine, configured for extended range and armed with four acoustic wave-homing CHT-02D torpedoes, slipped out into the Sea of Japan and submerged, heading for a clandestine intercept of the course being sailed by the MV *Rabat Milestone*.

The Skipper of the Oliver Hazard Perry Class guided missile frigate USS *Reuben James* (FFG-57) got word of the unusual contact as he was looking into a turbine repair with his Chief Engineer. Submarine contacts in this part of the Sea of Japan were not that unusual, in fact hunting subs was what the ship was primarily designed for, but his CIC officer thought the boss might want to take a look at this one.

Commander Ralph Bartlett made his way topside and stepped into the darkened Combat Information Center where his sonar and fire control technicians were gathered around one of the repeaters showing returns from the frigate's AN/SQS-56 sonar system. "We just finished running the tapes, Skipper." The Chief Sonar Technician handed over a computer print-out and pointed at a pattern of repeating lines. "There's no doubt about it. It's one of the old Soviet Whiskey Class boats."

"What the hell is he doing out here?" The captain steadied himself against the roll of his ship. They were heading into some inclement weather blowing in from the Japanese mainland, and he needed to get the turbine repairs completed before it got too rough for his crew to work.

"Beats me, sir," The Chief pointed at another computer screen, "but it's definitely not Russian or Chinese. Best guess is it could be one of the North Korean boats. Sound signatures are pretty similar to the other ones we've got on file."

Commander Bartlett turned to the surface search radar and scanned the screen. "Is that the new surface contact?"

"That's him, sir. Designated One Three Echo. He's the new guy among the twelve others we've been tracking." The radar tech on watch brought up another screen and scrolled through it for a few seconds. "The IMO has it listed as the MV *Rabat Milestone* out of Kaohsiung bound for Pusan."

"Keep me advised regarding all contacts. Stay with the sub as long as you can and be sure I get regular updates, especially on the container ships." Commander Bartlett headed for the bridge and ordered the Navigator and OOD to keep the ship on a track parallel to the courses being steered by the clutch of merchant vessels they'd been following. He'd rather chase subs than shadow merchantmen but his orders from the task force at Chinhae were clear. Any container ship transiting this area got priority and special attention. His next stop was the communication center where he ordered a report sent to Chinhae regarding the sub contact and the new container vessel they'd spotted.

V ice Admiral Jeff Ault hung up the phone and stretched. When he felt his stiff muscles start to relax, he walked over to a station in the task force command post and asked the analyst on duty for the list of ships in the area that they'd gotten from the International Maritime Organization. It took just seconds to find the MV *Rabat Milestone*, a container ship sailing under Liberian flag, registered owner—some outfit called Butang Export-Import of Jakarta, Indonesia. The vessel was bound for Pusan out of Kaohsiung, but there was no record of it having made a call at any North Korean port. He was about to ignore the report from the Reuben James when something caught his eye. The captain had a Korean name.

Ault hauled the thick folder over to a Korean Navy Captain who was the duty ROK watch commander and pointed at the name. "Is there any way to tell if this man is originally from the north or the south?" The Korean officer tapped on his laptop for a few minutes, found what he was looking for, and studied the document on his screen. "I think this is what you would call a shady character, Admiral. His master's papers have been revoked at least once while he was investigated in Singapore for illegal cargo transfer. The information I have here indicates he was born near Hungnam."

Admiral Ault merely nodded and returned to his desk. There was something tickling at his spine. He jotted a note and called for a nearby yeoman. "Take this over to the comm center and have it sent priority to NAS Atsugi, Japan—personal for Admiral Farnsworth. Acknowledge receipt requested."

His old Naval Academy classmate had been aching to launch one of the Navy's new Boeing P-8A Poseidon reconnaissance aircraft on a real-world mission. There were at least two of them on stand-by at Atsugi and Freddie Joe, the cowboy aviator, wouldn't miss a chance to show what the birds could do. They'd have a close and critical look at the MV *Rabat Milestone* in short order.

He picked up the phone and got a secure line to the Communications Watch Officer. "This is Admiral Ault. Pass directly to the *Reuben James*: Send hourly position and status reports on merchant vessel contact designated One Three Echo. Recon aircraft out of NAS Atsugi will conduct aerial survey. Direct liaison authorized. Sub contact is secondary priority."

Admiral Ault strolled across the command center and leaned over the DIA desk where Chan Davis was on duty. "I need you to run a check on Butang Export-Import out of Jakarta." He glanced at the registry and spelled the name of the company while Chan took notes. "They're listed as registered owners of a container ship called the *Rabat Milestone*. Let me know what you find out—quick as you can."

Command Pilot Lieutenant Commander Ron Staff re-trimmed the aircraft as it bounced through a series of thunderheads west of Atsugi and waited for the navigator to send him a new course. His co-pilot was having a ball in the right seat and enjoying the flight time in the Navy's newest long-range patrol aircraft despite the dog-shit weather. For his part, Ron Staff thought it was a hell of a day to send a valuable new aircraft out to take pictures of some stupid hog-hauler. He'd mumbled something to that effect when Rear Admiral Freddie Joe Farnsworth personally ordered the recon flight, and Lieutenant Commander Staff promptly got his ass handed to him.

"Commander, I'm in a somewhat better position to judge the gravity of this mission than you are." Admiral Farnsworth spit tobacco juice into a Coke can and pointed his finger at the gold wings embossed on Staff's flight suit. "You are apparently a Naval Aviator. Now get your ass into that aircraft and aviate!"

Thirty minutes later they were airborne out of Atsugi and headed west just ahead of a storm that was sweeping over southern Honshu. Staff glanced down at the heading display where the course numbers were clicking into place from the navigator's station behind the cockpit. "Here come the numbers." Staff pointed at the screen and nodded at his co-pilot. "You got it. Set us up for a direct intercept." He relinquished the flight controls, hit the all-stations button on the console between the pilots' seats, and began the crew brief.

"We're inbound on the target, guys. Estimated time to intercept is thirty-four minutes. We're looking for a container ship called the *Rabat Milestone*. This will be a dual-axis pass at three differing altitudes with video, stills and sensor package active on all passes. All stations make sure you've got a solid link for live-streaming. No cock-ups on this one, people. I want to get this done and get back to Atsugi before weather forces us to divert."

The Boeing P-8A Poseidon beat the ETA to the airspace over the MV *Rabat Milestone* by eight minutes due to a tailwind and set up for the high pass port to starboard and then stem to stern over the merchant ship plowing through the whitecaps below. They were slated to make two additional passes over the vessel at continuously lower altitudes while still photos, live video, and all sorts of sensor data was transmitted to the emergency task force at Chinhae.

Lieutenant Commander Ron Staff steered the aircraft through choppy air, got all-systems fully functional reports from his crew-dogs, and hoped Admiral Farnsworth choked on his ever-present lip-full of chew.

* * *

Aboard the USS *Reuben James*, the captain was just coming onto the bridge from dinner when the Intercom next to his chair buzzed. He picked up the handset and wedged it between his ear and shoulder as he zipped up his jacket against a chill blowing in through the ventilators. "Skipper, go."

"CIC, sir, there's something weird about that sub contact we had earlier in the day." The watch officer sounded like he wasn't sure what he wanted to say.

"Spit it out, Ensign." Bartlett grabbed the clipboard containing the watch schedules and noticed that his newest officer, still in training for full qualification, was on duty in the CIC. "Or do you want me to talk to the Chief?"

"That's not necessary, sir." The ensign's voice took on a more confident timbre. "I've been sending regular course and pos-reps on the merchantman as ordered, and we are in contact with the aircraft out of Atsugi that's airborne over the ship."

"You called about the sub, Ensign. What's up with that?"

"Well, sir—I know you declared the sub a secondary concern, but the damn thing seems to be holding position right in the merchantman's wake. Every time the container ship makes even a slight course change, the sub is right there holding position aft of it. It's almost like the sub is ghosting on the ship. It just seemed unusual and I thought I should report it."

"You did fine, Ensign." Commander Bartlett pushed up out of his bridge chair and looked into the gloom off his port quarter where contact One Three Echo was steaming at about twelve knots amid a cluster of other commercial vessels all heading into the Korea Strait. "I'll be down in a minute."

Commander Bartlett spoke directly to the orbiting P-8 aircraft once he reached the CIC and checked the radar picture against the sonar returns. The Command Pilot was not happy about it, but he agreed to another pass aft of the *Rabat Milestone* with his sub-hunting gear engaged and looking for the subsurface contact that *Reuben James* was monitoring. Sure enough, the aircraft's sonar men confirmed a submarine contact that seemed to be ghosting on the merchantman. The Skipper asked his aviation counterpart for a download of the aircraft's data on the subsurface contact and then released them for return to base.

Commander Bartlett nudged a radioman out of his station and sat down at the keyboard to peck out a personal report to the task force directing his ship's activities. He wasn't sure if the connection between the sub and the merchantman was significant, but it was unusual enough to report as a priority for the attention of someone at Chinhae who knew what the hell was going on out here.

Chinhae, Republic of (South) Korea

B y the time the man who calls himself Bayer reached the task force command center, Admirals Ault and Kim were gathered around one of the analyst stations where Dr. Rick Lavers was staring at a stream of sensor data. Bayer shrugged out of his jacket and poured a cup of coffee from the communal urn before he joined them.

"I was half-asleep when you called." He stared at the swath of figures on the video screen. "What's up?"

"We got some strange reports coming in from one of our search assets." Ault patted Lavers on the shoulder and led Kim and Bayer away in the direction of his desk. "That stuff that Dr. Lavers is examining is sensor data. It doesn't tell us anything much, but he's going over it looking for increased electrical activity—shit like that. What got me and Admiral Kim concerned was a report from the USS *Reuben James*, one of our frigates monitoring thirteen container ships in and around the Korea Strait. First reports came in a couple of hours ago."

Admiral Kim reached for a sheaf of message forms. "The frigate initially reported contact with a submarine in the area. Admiral Ault ordered them to keep an eye on it. They reported that the submarine appeared to be shadowing—or ghosting—one of the merchant ships: MV *Rabat Milestone*, Liberian flag, out of Kaohsiung and bound for Pusan with a load of textiles and automotive electronics. We ran a check on the registered owners—Butang Export-Import of Jakarta—and they've been out of business since the middle of last month. No indication that they sold or transferred ownership of the vessel."

"If that's not fishy enough for you, I noticed that the captain of the vessel was a Korean and had him checked out." Ault picked up the commentary. "He's apparently born in North Korea and he's got a fairly sordid record, so I asked a buddy of mine in Japan to send up an aircraft to take a look at his ship.

They over-flew the area, shot pictures, and confirmed the sub seemed to be following in the wake of the container ship."

"So, did this ship make any stops at North Korean ports?" Bayer sipped at his coffee and considered the implications.

"No stops at North Korean ports on the routing reports we have," Admiral Kim shook his head and reached for his cigarettes, "but that doesn't mean much. The ship might have stopped anywhere with no routing report from owners who don't exist. That's one thing. The other is the sonar returns from the *Reuben James*. The signatures match a Whiskey Class submarine of the same type we know is being operated by the North Korean Navy out of Mayangdo."

"So we've got an apparently ownerless container ship heading for Pusan with a North Korean submarine following it." Bayer began to see the picture being painted by the two senior Navy officers. "Why would they do that unless they wanted to keep a clandestine eye on that container ship? And why would they want to keep an eye on a container ship unless it was carrying something they were very interested in, does that just about match your thinking?"

Admiral Ault glanced at Admiral Kim and nodded. "That about sums it up, I guess. The *Rabat Milestone* is in the Korea Strait east of Cheju Island and west of Sasebo, Japan. What do you think?"

"Let's go run the pictures." Ault was heading for the door with the two Admirals following. "I want Shake and Stokey to take a closer look at the containers on that ship."

* * *

"See anything that looks familiar?" Shake Davis nudged Mike Stokey and pointed at the plasma screens in their small satellite office. Video was rolling on one and stills were flashing on the other as Shake shuffled through a stack of enlargements of the IR photos Stokey shot in North Korea.

"It's hard to tell. If you've seen one shipping container, you've seen them all," Mike looked over his shoulder where

Admirals Ault and Kim crowded in next to Bayer watching the video sent from the aircraft over the MV *Rabat Milestone*. "Best I could tell under IR and in pitch dark was that all the containers that night were painted a flat black or OD. IR doesn't give you much in the way of colors, but I'm fairly sure none of them were red or green." Stokey pointed at the deck cargo which looked like stacked dominoes in bright colors on the fore and aft decks of the container ship.

"They could have painted them." Ault squinted at the screen containing the close-up views of the ship's deck cargo. "I mean you wouldn't put the damn things aboard a civilian ship carrying military markings or warning signs."

"Those up forward on the bottom row are all marked Maersk Shipping." Admiral Kim pointed at one of the oblique stills on the left-hand screen. "That's the most common thing we see at all our ports these days."

"I want to know about that submarine." Bayer stepped out of the crowd around the screens and dropped onto the bunk in the small office. "Is that thing just screwing around on an exercise, or what?"

"I don't think it's an exercise, Mr. Bayer." Admiral Kim moved toward an overflowing ashtray on a nearby table and shook his head. "The North Korean Whiskey Class subs normally don't operate this far away from their base. This is not a sophisticated, long-range patrol boat."

"Give me a minute." Shake reached for the remote control and played with the perspective on a series of low-level stills taken by the Navy reconnaissance aircraft. "Look here between the stacks on the forward decks. What are those things right there? Are those air hoses or could they be power cables?"

"There's no reason in hell for air hoses to be routed to container cargo." Admiral Ault sat and stared at the screen. "Looks to me like those are power lines—and damn big ones at that."

Shake adjusted the perspective, tracing the dark lines on the cargo decks from one end to the other. They all seemed to join and disappear through a vent in the container ship's weather deck. "It looks to me like they lead from something below decks out to the containers."

"It could be refrigeration or something like that for a perishable cargo, couldn't it?" Bayer was manipulating the contact list on his phone. "Is that a possibility?"

"Could be, I guess." Ault took another look at the nest of thick cables running across the deck of the MV *Rabat Milestone* and through a trough between the container stacks. "But I don't know what kind of cargo on the ship's manifest requires refrigeration. When I checked, she was supposed to be carrying automotive electrical parts and textiles." Ault pointed at the screen. "Shake, let's see if you can zoom in some more. Maybe we can get some numbers off those containers."

"I can only read the numbers on the first container." He scribbled on a notepad and handed the paper to Ault. "Does that mean anything?"

"It might give us a little more info. Maersk is a Danish outfit; probably the largest commercial container shipping company in the world. We could ask them to check this number."

"Chan, I need you to do something for me right away." Bayer held a phone to his ear and reached for the paper Ault was holding. "Get hold of Maersk Shipping, Copenhagen, Denmark. See if you can get them to run a check of these numbers off of one of their containers." He read the numbers into the phone and confirmed Chan's read-back. "That's it. Have them run those numbers. We want to know what's in that container, what ship it's supposed to be on, where it's headed and anything else they can tell us about it. Thanks."

"That's gonna take some time, you know." Ault checked the clipboard containing the course, speed and position reports sent by the *Reuben James*. "The *Rabat Milestone* could be offshore here by noon tomorrow or thereabouts at her current speed."

"The weather in the area is turning nasty." Admiral Kim watched Stokey manipulate the computer controls searching for different angles and a closer look at the containers stacked on the ship's deck. "Its sea state five out there and moving toward six. They will probably have to reduce speed and alter course to the east to keep their bows into the wind."

"I can't be dead certain," Stokey pointed at the blurry image of a container in the bottom row of two stacks on the *Rabat Milestone*'s forward deck, "but I think this may be our boy. That crushed corner right there looks very much like the damage I saw on one of the containers at the Chosin Reservoir."

* * *

"I got hold of the Maersk people in Copenhagen." Chan Davis hung up the phone and checked her notes. "They're checking the numbers in the company database but it's going to take a while." She looked up at Bayer who was pacing in front of Admirals Ault and Kim. "Apparently these containers are all over the world and they often pass from company to company without a whole lot of control."

"That's about what I figured," Ault grabbed for a clipboard hanging off a wall behind his desk in the emergency task force command center and scanned it. "It was worth a shot, but we're running out of time if we want to stop this guy before he gets any closer to the Korean coast."

Admiral Kim nodded his agreement. "We need to get some people aboard that ship. And we don't have to worry about dealing with protests from the owners, do we?"

"Let's get over to the comm center," Ault signaled for Bayer and Admiral Kim to follow him. "I need to talk directly to the *Reuben James*."

Korea Strait, West of Cheju Island and East of Sasebo, Japan

"It's rougher than a cob out here, Admiral." Commander Ralph Bartlett pressed the radio handset to his ear and steadied himself against a bank of radar repeaters on the bridge of the *Reuben James*. "We're somewhere between a sea state six and seven, and the wind is picking up significantly from the east. There's no way I can launch a helicopter in this mess."

Bartlett listened for a while and then checked the screen showing an isolated plot on the MV *Rabat Milestone*. "He's turned easterly into the wind and reduced speed to approximately eight knots, sir. I'm showing the vessel at fourteen hundred meters off my port bow." There was a lengthy transmission and Bartlett frowned as he listened to his orders from the three-star admiral in Chinhae.

"Yessir, I've got a trained VB team aboard and I'm fairly sure we could get them onto the merchantman with one of our inflatables—but doing it is gonna be a bitch in this weather. I'm inclined to maneuver for an intercept and then order him to prepare for boarding. If I can get him to heave-to, it will reduce the risk to my crew."

"Roger, sir." Bartlett carried the handset toward his laptop near the navigator's station and scrolled through his email menu. The flashing icon told him he'd received the threat briefing Admiral Ault promised to send. "I see the message, Admiral. We'll commence moving in his direction right now. Aye, aye, sir—*Reuben James*, out."

"I have the deck and the conn!" Commander Bartlett announced to the bridge crew and then ordered his ship into action. "Bring the ship to full speed on both engines. Come left on a course to intercept Contact One Three Echo. Gator, plot the numbers to bring us alongside. OOD, bring all hands to general quarters. Muster the VB team at the port launch station and get Chief Garcia up here to see me on the bridge."

While the *Reuben James'* navigator plotted a course to bring the 4,100-ton guided missile frigate close alongside the MV Rabat Milestone in rolling seas, Commander Ralph Bartlett read through the threat briefing sent from the task force at Chinhae and tried to figure out how to explain what he was about to order his Master At Arms to attempt. An old-school hard-ass like Chief Roberto Garcia was very likely to think there was someone issuing orders that had too many stars, too few brains and not enough sea time to know the risks involved.

"You wanted to see me, sir?" Chief Garcia's broad-shouldered form nearly filled the bridge access hatch. He was rigged in his boarding party gear but not carrying a weapon. The Chief was an old hand at these things and he'd decide what weapons his team needed once he got the word from the Skipper.

"Chief, we've got a tall order from the task force at Chinhae." Bartlett pointed at the laptop showing the threat brief and watched the Chief read for a while. "Obviously, we can't launch a helo in this crap, so I'm gonna maneuver alongside the merchantman. Your guys will have to put the RIB in the water and board as soon as I can get him to heave-to."

Chief Garcia raised his dark eyebrows and glanced at the rain pelting against the bridge enclosure. "Naturally, it's gotta be now, and it's gotta be in the middle of a frog-strangler of a fuckin' storm."

"There it is, Chief. I did my best to talk some sense into them but we've got orders and we're gonna carry them out— just short of getting any of our people killed. You read the brief, what do you think?"

"Beyond this being a risky fuckin' thing do do, Skipper, I'm not sure what to think." Garcia pointed at the laptop screen. "It says here we're supposed to be looking for some containers on the foredeck, especially one with damage to a corner, and all of them are linked up with some kind of power cables. They want us to board, segregate the crew, take the captain into temporary custody, then check out what's in them containers and report back. Is that the way you read it or am I missing something?"

"That's the way I read it, Chief. I guess we'll get further orders depending on what you find in the containers. Get your guys ready to go. I'm gonna come alongside and see if I can get him to heave-to. When he does, your team goes aboard."

"What if he don't heave-to, sir? You gonna want us to try and get aboard while he's underway?"

"Let's worry about that if it happens. Get your people ready to go before this weather gets any worse."

"Aye, aye, sir." Chief Garcia spun to depart the bridge and Commander Bartlett looked through the gloom at the container ship now coming up directly abeam of the *Reuben James* off the portside. "XO, try to raise him on VHF Channel 16. I want to speak to the captain personally."

Admirals Ault and Kim returned to the emergency task force center and found the man who calls himself Bayer on the phone giving an update to his CIA superiors. The sour look on his face told the senior officers it wasn't a particularly pleasant conversation. Ault held up a cautionary finger, jotted a quick note, and shoved it in front of Bayer.

"I just got an update from the military commanders out here." Bayer scanned the note and nodded his gratitude for what appeared to be a glimmer of good news. "We have a ship very close to the *Rabat Milestone*. They're going to board shortly and then we'll know what we've got. Absolutely, I'll call you immediately after I hear from them." Bayer listened for a moment more and then disconnected. He looked up at the officers and took a deep breath. "That was the DCI with the National Security Advisor on speaker. They were calling from the White House Situation Room. Does that tell you anything?"

"It tells me we need a Plan B with that kind of high level interest." Ault walked over to the wall map and tapped a spot off the southern end of the Korean Peninsula. "The ships are close to Cheju Island right about here. Admiral Kim, what have you got out there?"

"Not much in terms of material support." Admiral Kim approached the map and pointed to a place on the southern coast of Cheju. "We've been trying to build a navy base here at Gangjeong, but we ran into stiff resistance from what I believe you call tree-huggers. We haven't been able to make much progress. There's a small detachment there; about twenty men, I believe."

"Have they got fuel and a landing zone?"

"They have both. We often send helicopters out there and they refuel at Gangjeong before returning to the mainland."

"Good. Let's get a few of our stand-by VBSS Teams launched for Cheju and put them on stand-by to assist the *Reuben James*. If we go now, we can get them on the ground before the weather gets much worse."

* * *

"As an unmarried and recently unemployed individual, I don't have a problem," Stokey shrugged into a flight jacket and climbed out of the Korean Marine HUMVEE idling near the Chinhae airstrip, "but Chan is going to cut your balls off when she finds out about this."

"Sometimes you eat the bear and sometimes the bear eats you." Shake Davis grabbed a gear bag and led Stokey toward an adjacent hangar. "We've both got a ton of sweat-equity in this damn thing, Mike, and I want to be in on the finish."

"Yeah, well, it's probably pissing in the wind anyway. Ault said they've got a frigate closing on that ship right now. They'll probably board the bastard and we've wasted a trip."

They barged into the hangar and spotted Gunnery Sergeant Hugh Morgan shepherding a team of MARSOC Marines out a side entry toward a line of CH-53 helicopters. "Hey, Huge!" Shake waved at the NCO and trotted over to join the ranks. "You're gonna have to make room for two more."

Gunny Morgan squinted at the two men headed in his direction and shook his head. "What's up, Gunner? I got no orders about any attachments."

"It's all good, Gunny. You guys need people who know what to look for if you have to go aboard that ship." Shake pointed at Mike Stokey. "He's the one discovered all this shit up in North Korea in the first place. Admiral Ault knows all about it."

"Uh huh." Gunny Morgan counted heads and looked out to the flight line where a crew was cranking up the engines on one of the Sea Stallion helos. "And I guess if I was to give him a quick call, he'd verify all this, right?"

"You could do that, Huge," Shake grinned and shook his head, "but you'd likely piss the Admiral off. He was going to hit the rack when we left."

"Gunner, this will likely cost me a career and I'm gonna swear you lied and pulled rank on me." Gunny Morgan returned the conspirator's smile. "But no balls, no blue chips, right? And fortune favors the bold?"

"There you go, Huge. Can we borrow a couple of weapons and some gear?"

After they were kitted up and walking toward the idling helicopter, Stokey pulled a phone out of his pocket. "Last chance to save your ass, Shake. You should give her a call."

"She was just off watch and sleeping when I left, Mike. If it goes as planned, we'll be back before she knows we were gone."

"He keeps saying 'no speaka da Eeenglis' or something like that, Skipper." The Executive Officer of the USS *Reuben James* turned to his captain and pointed at the container ship steaming steadily into growing chop and whitecaps off their port side. "You know that's gotta be bullshit. They just don't want to heave-to as ordered."

"And we don't have anyone aboard who speaks Korean, right?" Commander Ralph Bartlett tried to decide what to do next. He wasn't quite ready to launch his boarding team in the heaving swells, so he stared for a moment at the data sheet they'd downloaded from the IMO. "It says here the captain is a Korean. It doesn't say anything about the nationality of anyone else aboard."

Boatswain's Mate First Class Fester Bonchek looked at a sheet of notebook paper he pulled out of his pocket. "Skipper, we ran a check. We got ten that speak Spanish, two that speak Tagalog, one that speaks Japanese and a guy that says he can communicate in Cajun French. I got 'em all on stand-by."

"Get 'em up here and the XO will put 'em on the VHF. I want to exhaust all possibilities before we put the boat in the water."

The XO sidled up next to his captain and lowered his voice. "Skipper, you know all these merchantmen have mixed crews, but there's always somebody aboard that can communicate in English. I mean, some cook or deckhand would know enough to understand we're telling them to heave-to. He's just being an asshole—or he's got something to hide."

"We'll exercise due diligence, XO. Try every language we can speak and then we're going aboard that sonofabitch one way or the other." Commander Bartlett turned to the Boatswain's Mate of the watch. "Fester, break out our emergency signaling device and then get down to comm and find me a radioman that remembers enough Morse to send blinking light."

Bartlett stepped out into the rain and biting wind on his port bridge wing and focused his binoculars on the bridge of the container ship. He could clearly see an Asian individual staring back at him. The man he thought was likely the captain of the MV *Rabat Milestone* looked like he was on the edge of panic. Bartlett stepped back into the warmth of the bridge enclosure, "XO, give all of our foreign language speakers a shot on Channel 16 and send him heave-to on blinking light as soon as we're ready."

As a Chicano sailor began calling in Spanish for the MV *Rabat Milestone* to heave-to, the Skipper of the *Reuben James* eyed a line of grinning sailors waiting for their turn on the microphone and pointed at his XO. "Put Chief Garcia and the VB Team on Ready Five but don't lower the RIB until I give the word."

* * *

The captain of the *Rabat Milestone* had been listening to the repeated calls from the American Navy to heave-to and stand by for boarding for the past 20 minutes. He was sweating heavily despite the chill air blowing across his bridge. He ignored a call on Channel 16 that blared through his VHF speaker in what he thought was probably Spanish. He understood the first call in English perfectly well, but he needed to buy time. As he watched a signal light begin blinking from the warship's port side, the captain realized he'd have to do something in a hurry and he needed guidance.

He snatched an IC handset off the bulkhead and buzzed for his Chief Officer who was down in the radio room waiting for a response to the signal the captain sent to Pyongyang. A standby helmsman tapped him on the shoulder and pointed at the American ship. "They are about to put a boat into the water, Captain. Look at all the guns!"

"Any response to my signal?" The captain shouted as soon as his Chief Officer answered the call. "Nothing, Captain, not even an acknowledgment. We should heave-to." The Chief Officer of the MV *Rabat Milestone* repeated the plea he'd been making for the past half-hour. He had no idea why the captain was refusing to comply with the American ship's instruction and he was in no mood to face an armed boarding party.

"I'll make that decision! Re-send the message to the address I gave you—and make it an emergency request this time." Another voice blared from the VHF speaker in what the captain recognized as Japanese. He looked around at the faces of his bridge crew. The fear and confusion was obvious. None of them understood why he was refusing to comply with the American orders. None of them knew what was at stake. "Shut that damn thing off! Maintain course and speed!"

The captain focused his binoculars on the waist of the warship and saw a small boat being lowered into the choppy water between his ship and the American vessel. He counted at least ten heavily-armed sailors standing by to board it. Even if he increased speed and turned away, they would easily chase him down and come aboard. He'd seen enough films of American sailors in action to know they had the skill to do it. And there was no instruction from his controllers in Pyongyang—not even a message saying they understood what he was facing. He was looking at a long stretch in prison if the Americans found what was in the containers on his foredeck. The captain was on his own with a crew that might begin to disobey his orders at any moment.

When the small craft carrying the armed American sailors was bounding through the chop headed in his direction, the captain of the MV *Rabat Milestone* made a decision that he hoped would allow him to escape this dangerous dilemma. He had no idea what the weapon in the containers was or what it was designed to do, but the North Korean Navy wanted it activated near the port of Pusan and that told him it was designed to do some kind of serious damage. Even if it just bought him some time, he could steer for the nearest coastline and get off of this damned devil ship in a lifeboat.

The captain pulled the keychain off his neck and walked toward the locked cover on the forward bulkhead. When the key turned and the metallic cover opened he took a deep breath and then pulled the bayonet-switch marked **Power** from off to on. There was a momentary flickering of the standing lights on the bridge but nothing else. He took one last look at the American warship looming off his starboard beam and then mashed the button marked **Connect**.

* * *

"What just happened?" Commander Bartlett looked around the bridge of the USS *Reuben James* and saw expressions as shocked as his own. "XO, contact all departments and get me a status! Run the emergency damage control sequence!" The Skipper turned to the helmsman who was banging his fist on a completely darkened bank of course and speed indicators. "Have we still got engines?"

"Beats the shit out of me, sir." The helmsman looked like he was about to cry in frustration. "Everything is black as coal. I've got no indicators and no read-outs of any kind."

"No IC, Skipper!" I can't reach any of the departments or stations!"

"It looks like a complete electronic failure, sir! Nothing is working!"

"XO, get down to comm and fire off a message on our situation. Just tell 'em we've got a major problem out here. Don't declare an emergency until I can find out what's happening down in CIC." Commander Bartlett headed for the bridge access hatch and noticed none of the emergency lights programmed to illuminate automatically in the event of power loss were burning. "Fester, find a way to contact Chief Garcia and get that VB Party back aboard!"

Scrambling down a portside ladder past confused sailors looking for orders, Commander Bartlett glanced at his digital watch and noticed it was completely black. He felt his ship sloughing and pitching heavily in the building seas outside the hull. He was fairly certain he didn't have much propulsion and probably not much steering either.

Flashlight beams were cutting arcs through the gloom in the CIC when the captain arrived. Everyone was scrambling around trying to find out what caused the loss of power. He found the watch officer and got a sobering status report. "We've got nothing, Skipper. No radar, no sonar, and no comm of any kind inside or outside the ship. The ETs are pulling the boards now to see if they can find something. We tried re-sets, re-boots, everything—but none of the systems respond."

"Stay on it and keep me informed." The captain tried to sound calm and confident amid the flurry of activity and shouted curses from one station to another as his crew tried to find out what was causing such a catastrophic black-out throughout the ship. He ducked out of the chaos and ran into his Executive Officer heading for the bridge.

"Big problems, Skipper." The XO snapped on the flashlight he was carrying and pointed it back down a passageway toward the communications spaces. "We've got no comm of any kind— can't send and can't receive on any of our equipment. I've got the Damage Control parties checking the ship and we're gonna get you a full report soonest."

"Do that. I'm heading for engineering to see if we've got any engines."

"Save yourself the trip. I just ran into the Chief Engineer. We're dead in the water. He's trying to rig emergency steering, but we've got no power plant."

"Shit! Send a runner and have all Department Heads meet me on the bridge. We're gonna have to figure this out in a hurry."

"Aye, aye, sir." The XO handed the captain his flashlight. "You better take this." He turned to carry out his orders and then paused. "What about that merchantman?"

"Fuck him! We've got a ship to save." Commander Bartlett headed for the bridge racking his brain and calling on all his experience to try and determine why the USS *Reuben James* had suddenly turned into a big chunk of cold steel, isolated, deaf, dumb, and blind—bobbing around in a heavy sea running through the Korea Strait.

* * *

"Something ain't right, Chief." The coxswain of the RIB carrying the VB Team tapped the senior petty officer on the shoulder and pointed at the USS *Reuben James* rapidly falling away to their rear. "They must have reduced speed or something."

Chief Garcia pulled the radio handset off his equipment harness and tried to raise his ship. There was no response after a number of calls on the designated frequency and nothing on the emergency channel either. He took a look at the little portable radio and saw the power and frequency screen was dark. He quickly checked two more radios rigged to the gear vests of his men and saw the same thing. The RIB was bouncing around like a rubber duck in huge swells as Chief Garcia swept his experienced eyes over the frigate. Something was wrong for sure. None of the radar masts were rotating and she was showing no lights of any kind. *Reuben James* was a greyhound and she usually showed a sizeable wake around her bow when plowing through a rising sea. Chief Garcia didn't see anything of the sort as he stared through the blowing spray and spume pelting the RIB and his boarding party. He had no idea why his ship seemed to be dead in the water, and he had no immediate way to answer that question.

"There's a signal going up, Chief!" A second class fire control tech who did collateral duty as a member of the VBSS Team pointed at the flag-hoist aft of the frigate's bridge. "What's all that about?"

"You're supposed to know shit like that, Evans!" Chief Garcia watched the colored signal flags two-block snapping in the howling wind. "That reads November Charlie. It's an international distress signal."

"They ain't the only ones in distress, Chief." The coxswain reduced power and pointed at the container ship to their left. "That merchie is dark as an Eskimo's asshole—and it don't look like he's got any engines either."

Chief Garcia turned to look at the MV *Rabat Milestone* and saw the vessel appeared to be in about the same shape as his own ship: no lights, no power and no apparent forward motion. The only difference seemed to be that the top-heavy merchantman was taking heavier rolls in the storm-tossed water.

"It's like the fuckin' Bermuda Triangle out here." Chief Garcia pointed toward the Reuben James. "Fuck that merchie-bum. Take us back to the Ruby J. I need to figure out what the fuck is going on out here."

* * *

"Captain! What's happening? We've lost all power." The captain of the MV *Rabat Milestone* nearly ran over his Chief Officer as he scrambled down a passageway heading for his cabin.

"I know that—and we've also lost the engines. I'm going below to check on that now." The captain saw the doubt in his first officer's expression and tried a smile. "We've been in worse situations, you and me. We can probably get it fixed. Meanwhile, you take over for me up on the bridge. Have the deck crew rig sea anchors. That should keep us headed into the wind."

"What about the Americans?" The Chief Officer stiff-armed a bulkhead to keep from being tossed off his feet by the heavy rolls the container ship was taking. "They could maybe rig a tow or help us fix the problem."

The captain pushed by and shrugged. "Let the Americans come aboard if they want to so badly. We have more important problems right now." When he reached his cabin, he ducked inside and slammed the door. The captain of the MV *Rabat Milestone* had no idea what happened to his ship or to the American vessel that appeared to be in the same helpless condition. Whatever the weapon in the containers on his foredeck did, it did it to both friend and foe. He would try and figure all that out later. Right now he needed to get off this ship.

Over the past four years of his seagoing career, ever since the problem with the police in Singapore, the captain always knew he might have to make a quick get-away. He kept a bag packed with emergency equipment and supplies in his locker and before he left Wonsan he'd added a Smith & Wesson .38 caliber revolver with 20 rounds of ammunition. He snatched the weapon out of his bag and stuffed it in his belt before heading topside and aft toward the *Rabat Milestone*'s single free-fall lifeboat. If he ran into anyone with serious objections to the captain abandoning ship in an emergency, the .38 would clear that up promptly.

Fighting against the wind and sea spray on his after weather deck, the captain made his way toward the lifeboat station and considered it a lucky omen that the launch rails were located on the port side which would make his escape invisible to the Americans even if they were watching rather than struggling to save their own ship in this storm. The nine-meter lifeboat was easy and quick to launch. The captain reviewed the procedures as he strapped himself into the molded seat nearest the release trigger at the rear of the boat.

He was facing a rough, difficult voyage, but he had enough fuel and navigation gear aboard to reach either Cheju Island or the Japanese coastline in the other direction. The winds and currents would mostly determine his final destination, but any piece of dry land was better than a jail cell. The captain of the MV *Rabat Milestone* reached over his right shoulder, disengaged the launch safety, and hit the release lever. He plowed into the water at a 30 degree angle with enough velocity to give his neck a painful snap. He waited for a few moments while the lifeboat stabilized as much as possible in the churning sea and then moved forward to start the engine.

Cheju Island, Republic of (South) Korea

It had been a rough, jarring ride from Chinhae to Cheju, and Shake took the Crew Chief at his word when he hopped down after landing and said that the big, powerful three-engine CH-53K Super Stallion was probably the only helicopter in the inventory that was tough enough to make the trip.

"And then there's the skill and daring of your intrepid aircrew." The major who was aircraft commander and had done most of the flying on instruments led the way to a small building that was the only structure in sight at Gangjeong bearing military markings. "If we get the launch signal in this horseshit, it's gonna take more than a good bird to get you guys on target."

Inside the building, Gunnery Sergeant Hugh Morgan and a Korean Marine counterpart were going through a translation drill with the ROK Navy officer in charge of the small Cheju Island facility. Morgan motioned for the Crew Chief and pointed at the Korean behind a cluttered desk. "He'll give you what fuel he can afford. You guys want to handle that?"

When the aircrew left, grumbling their way through the blowing rain and wind toward the helicopter, Shake moved up beside Morgan and pointed at the radio transceiver behind the desk. "Any word from Chinhae or the ship?"

"He just sent a message telling Chinhae we're on station, Gunner. They're telling us to stand-by to stand-by. We might as well get comfortable for a while."

"Hurry up and wait—standard drill." Shake dropped to the deck next to Mike Stokey who was absorbed in a Korean skin magazine he'd found in a nearby rack. Stokey eyed the weather outside the over-heated little building and shrugged. "If we get real lucky, the sailors will handle the boarding drill and we can go after the weather clears or head home and watch Chan cut your nuts off. Either would be entertaining."

Shake looked around the building where the MARSOC Marines were crapped out in their assault rigs that included a horse-collar flotation device which made an excellent upright pillow. Like good Marines on mission standby everywhere and on all the other occasions he could remember, they were mostly asleep or staring vacantly into the distance, lost in enigmatic thought.

"Admiral, I don't know what to tell you." The Communications Watch Officer for the Chinhae emergency task force pointed at an array of sophisticated equipment lining the walls of his space. "We've tried it all: VHF, UHF, SatComm, single side-band, email, and even cell phones. There's no contact with the *Reuben James* and we haven't heard a thing from them since the last standard pos-rep at 1315 local."

"Jesus Herschel Christ!" Admiral Ault turned to look at Admiral Kim, the man who calls himself Bayer and Chan Davis. "Anybody got a clue how a U.S. Navy guided missile frigate, equipped with some of the most sophisticated comm gear in the world, suddenly drops off the grid?"

None of them had a clue and Admiral Ault stormed back toward the task force command center with instructions for the comm officer to keep trying to raise the *Reuben James*. They were gathered around the coffee urn when Bayer tapped his cup with a spoon and got their attention. "I had a disturbing thought." He pointed the spoon at Ault and sipped at the coffee he'd been stirring. "If there's no way to reach that ship and no way for that ship to reach us, one might assume it's suffered some kind of massive electrical shut-down. Isn't that what you said happened to that aircraft off Wonsan?"

"You mean some sonofabitch on the *Rabat Milestone* might have fired that EMP weapon and wiped out all the electronic systems on the *Reuben James*?" Admiral Ault set his coffee cup down and ran knuckles over his bald scalp. "I never considered that, but it would explain a lot." He turned to Admiral Kim. "Have the VB Teams reached Cheju?"

"Just one of them, Admiral." Admiral Kim checked a message board. "It's a MARSOC team, call sign Snakebite Two. They are on stand-by at Gangjeong. The other two teams were forced to turn back due to weather."

"How bad is it out there right now?"

"The last report we had was sea state seven and deteriorating."

"Well, it's our call, Admiral, and I think we need to get some eyes out there on the *Reuben James* and the *Rabat Milestone*. I think we send in the Marines. Do you concur?"

"I concur, Admiral. " Admiral Kim turned to head for the comm center. "I'll contact Gangjeong and issue the orders."

"That's risky business, isn't it, Jeff?" Chan Davis pointed at a nearby screen that was showing weather reports from the meteorological team at Naval Air Station Atsugi, Japan. "The storm seems to be moving westward and right toward the Korea Strait."

Admiral Ault grabbed a clipboard from his desk and scanned it for a moment. "Yeah, it's risky, but Snakebite Two is aboard a Marine CH-53K-model, the biggest and most powerful bird we've got. That's likely why they made Cheju when everybody else had to turn back. It's ten of our very best under a veteran Gunnery Sergeant. If anybody's gonna make it happen, they will."

Admiral Kim was nodding and jotting in rapid Korean on a notepad. "We should reinforce that effort, Admiral. I have two destroyers on patrol near Pohang. I am diverting them to the area immediately. I would respectfully suggest you do the same with any American ships nearby."

Chan Davis filled two cups with fresh coffee and walked down the passageway to give her husband and Mike Stokey a little refreshment. She figured they'd be up and following the mission, and she'd rather be with them than sitting around watching Jeff Ault and Bob Bayer dither. She pushed open the door with an elbow and saw the little satellite office was dark. When she found the light switch and flipped it on there was nothing to see beyond two empty swivel chairs and two dark plasma screens.

She set the coffee cups on a table and fished out her cell phone. She hit the speed dial—first for Shake and then for Mike Stokey. In both attempts she got the same response: Number Not Available.

"You assholes," she shouted at the two empty swivel chairs. "I know where you are and if you live through it, I will personally cut your balls off!"

Pyongyang, Democratic People's Republic of (North Korea)

"That idiot actually fired the weapon?" Marshal Kim Jun-Yi stormed around his desk and glared at his senior aide. "Why would he do that? He had no idea what it was designed to do!"

"My assumption is that he panicked, Comrade Marshal." The aide backed up a pace but his boss quickly closed the distance. "He likely assumed the weapon would do some sort of damage, and he triggered it in an effort to keep the Americans from boarding."

"He is a dead man—and I will find his family and make them suffer! We have been betrayed by his stupidity! Where is the submarine now?"

"They dropped back when the American ship closed in, Comrade Marshal. They are maintaining distant contact with the American and our ship. Assuming the weapon worked..."

"Of course it worked!" Marshal Kim kicked at an ornate chair and sent it flying across his office. "And that is all the more reason we can't let that ship be boarded or captured. Order the submarine to sink it immediately and then return to base."

"That might cause damage to the American ship, Comrade Marshal. You'll recall we rigged the *Rabat Milestone* with explosives."

"That is the least of my problems right now. You may tell the submarine captain to try to avoid damaging the American vessel, but he is to sink that container ship regardless!"

"And if there are Americans already aboard, Comrade Marshal?"

"Regardless!" The Minister of Defense for the Democratic People's Republic of Korea crouched in his desk chair and glowered until his senior aide departed to give the orders bringing an abrupt and unsuccessful end to Operation Digital

Dragon. Then he picked up the glowing after-action report he'd been preparing for the new Supreme Leader, complete with recommendations for a second EMP strike on the New York stock exchange, and dropped it into the shredder.

"There they are!" The CH-53K pilot fought buffeting winds as he brought the bird carrying Snakebite Two—plus two—over the area where MV _Rabat Milestone_ and the USS _Reuben James_ were tossing and rolling like lifeless corpses in a whirlpool. "No lights, no nothing, and I can't raise the frigate on the radio."

"I see some people milling around on the flight deck, sir." Gunny Morgan was leaning as far as he could out of the aircraft as they approached the Reuben James. He ducked back inside the cabin and wiped the rain off his goggles. "Can we make a lower pass and shine some light on 'em?"

"We'll give it a shot, but I don't want to get too close in this wind with the way that ship is bouncing around." The pilot maneuvered toward the frigate's fantail while his co-pilot flicked on the xenon searchlight mounted under the helicopter's nose. They immediately spotted a clutch of sailors in foul-weather gear hanging onto lifelines near the ship's hangar bay.

"Look at that guy near the bridge." Shake Davis craned around the right door gunner and pointed toward the ship. "He's sending blinking light."

"Terrific." The pilot added power to try and hold the helicopter stable. "And here I am without my Boy Scout manual. What's he trying to say? Can anybody read that stuff? "

"In distress...no comm..." Shake watched the flashing signal and keyed his microphone. "Come aboard...we can secure aircraft."

"Is he shitting me?" The pilot pulled the Sea Stallion into a wide turn and watched the flight deck on the after part of the frigate surge up and down like a roller-coaster. "Stand by back there. I'm gonna call Chinhae and let 'em know what's happening."

While they waited, Shake and Mike Stokey tumbled to the other side of the aircraft and stared at the container ship wallowing in the waves. It looked as dark and dead as the frigate, but there was at least one man standing on the nearest bridge wing and waving his arms over his head.

"Gunny, are you hearing me?" The pilot keyed the IC switch and heard Morgan acknowledge. "I just got off with Admiral Ault in Chinhae. He says if there's any way at all that we can get it done he wants your guys on that merchant ship. What do you think?"

Morgan looked around at his Marines and decided they were up for an effort. "It's what we get paid for, sir." He signaled for his men to get ready. "If you can make an approach over the bow, I think we can kick out the ropes and get aboard in a hurry. We'll take it from there and you can haul ass."

"Copy all, Gunny. We'll give it a shot, but I'm not gonna be able to haul ass. Looks like I'm the only guy with a working radio out here. Chinhae wants me to remain on station as long as I can."

"Copy, sir. We're rigging to go back here." Morgan and the two door-gunners stumbled to the rear of the helicopter, lowered the ramp, and checked the hard-points securing the ropes Snakebite Two would use to board the *Rabat Milestone*. Morgan had a quick intercom conversation and watched as two crewmen maneuvered forward and then returned with cans of heavy .50 caliber machinegun ammunition. Morgan and one of his Marines worked to lash the ammo cans to the bitter ends of the ropes as Shake crawled over to see if he could lend a hand.

"We got it!" Morgan waved Shake off and pointed at the ammo cans. "We need some ballast with all the wind blowing out there. I'm hoping these cans will help keep the ropes from going bat-shit until we can get aboard."

Shake gave a thumbs-up and shouted over the engine noise as the helicopter staggered through bumpy air, driving right down the centerline of the container ship's foredeck. "Where do you want me and Mike?"

"Same drill as last time. You guys are the last ones out. We gotta do this in a hurry, so don't worry about interval. If we get in trouble or I wave you off, don't go."

Bucking and jinking in the gusting winds, the Sea Stallion roared into the best approximation of a hover the pilots could manage. Gunny Morgan and another MARSOC Marine kicked the heavy ammo cans out the rear ramp and watched as the thick ropes unspooled behind them. Apparently, it was good enough to go. Morgan and his first man mounted the ropes and rapidly disappeared from sight. They were followed in a blur by eight more Marines. Shake slapped Mike on the shoulder and didn't even look to see if it was clear below before he mounted the rope and slid down toward the heaving deck of the *Rabat Milestone*.

The MARSOC boarding party was already scrambling down the sides of the container where they landed when Shake and Mike Stokey arrived. Remembering the drill from his initial experience, Mike shoved Shake toward the edge of the container and out of the way of the ropes that crumpled behind them as the helicopter banked hard left and pulled away from the container ship. Morgan was on the deck with his radio squawking when they reached him.

"Pass to higher...twelve on deck and no problem so far. Snakebite Two is moving to take this sucker down. I'll send you a sit-rep ASAP. Thanks for the ride."

Shake steadied his body against the huge rolls the ship was taking and pulled a water-proofed Canon digital camera out of his gear. He'd bought the expensive little camera at the Pusan PX to replace the one given away in China and tossed it into his mount-out gear just before leaving Chinhae. "Let's go see what's in those containers." He shook the camera at Mike and headed forward, rebounding right and left off the tied down container stacks and stepping gingerly over the huge cables lining the deck. Gunny Morgan waved them on and keyed his Integrated Inter-Squad Radio. "Let's do this by the numbers, people. Complete search and clear, top to bottom. Push me when we've got control of the bridge and then start the sweep.

Segregate the crew in the mess area we spotted on the diagram. I need a head-count of fifteen. Next thing I want to hear is that somebody's got the captain in flex-cuffs."

By the time Gunny Morgan joined Shake and Mike Stokey near the bow of the ship, they had managed to locate the container with the corner damage, cut the seal and pry it open. Shake was shielding the camera lens from the sheets of saltwater spray booming over the bow and flashing pictures wherever Mike Stokey pointed. "What is that thing?" Morgan stared over Shake's shoulder and pointed. "It looks like the guts of somebody's stereo."

"That's what blacked out this ship and the frigate over there." Mike pointed at the U.S. Navy vessel still wallowing in the waves to starboard of where they stood. "This is the stuff I saw the Norks loading onto trucks up by the Chosin Reservoir— same markings and everything. It's called a Marx generator and it's designed to create a massive EMP pulse."

"EMP? Like in a nuclear detonation? Holy shit! No wonder all comm and electrical systems are crapped out." Morgan called for a situation report from his clearing team as Shake and Mike moved onto an adjacent container and struggled to get it open. "If you guys got what you need down here for now," Morgan shouted over the howling wind. "We better get up to the bridge. My guys found something weird."

They followed Gunny Morgan through a hatch on the weather decks and up a series of interior ladders toward the bridge. At a level just below the conning station, Morgan signaled a halt and ducked into what looked like the crew mess. Seated around a long aluminum table were 13 very frightened crewmen of various nationalities. They were frightened because the ship was powerless and rolling violently and because there were two very determined U.S. Marines pointing weapons at them.

"Head count is thirteen, Gunny." One of the Marines motioned toward the crew with the muzzle of his M-4 carbine. "Plus one with Sergeant Macintosh up on the bridge makes fourteen. None of 'em is the captain. At least three of 'em speak English."

"Hold 'em here until I see what Mac's got up topside." Morgan ducked out of the mess room followed by Shake and Mike and headed up the last ladder leading to the bridge.

"This guy says he's the Chief Officer, Gunny." Sergeant Laird Macintosh nodded at the man he'd flex-cuffed to a stanchion near the bridge access hatch. "He says the captain abandoned ship."

"Let me talk to him, Gunny. You got better things to do." Morgan got back on his radio, checking with other Marines searching lower levels as Shake approached the man and motioned for Sgt. Mac to lower his weapon. "You speak English?"

"Yes, of course." He was a slender, swarthy individual and Shake guessed he was most likely East Indian or Pakistani. "I am the Chief Officer. I assure you I had nothing to do with whatever happened to us or to the American ship." He nodded to starboard. "I would like to be released so I can see about saving this ship."

"We're gonna let you get right to that, my friend." Shake pointed the camera and flashed a photo of the startled crewman. "But you need to answer a couple of questions first. You do that—and you answer me honestly—and we'll all get started on saving your ship. Understand?"

"I'll tell you anything I know," the Chief Officer assured Shake, "but I'm very likely as much in the dark as you are. The captain kept his own counsel on this voyage."

"And you don't know anything about what's in the bottom row of containers forward or what happened to blow out all the electrical systems?"

"Our cargo manifest says those containers contain automotive electrical parts, but I doubt that. When they were placed aboard, we were in the port of Wonsan. As far as I know, the North Korean Navy does not deal in automotive electrical parts and they were all over our ship at the time."

"That fits," Mike Stokey approached the Chief Officer, drew his Gerber fighting knife, and sawed at the flex-cuffs. "What happened just before all the lights went out?"

The Chief Officer rubbed his wrist and pointed at the silver lid on the console near the steering helm. "The captain unlocked that device and pressed a button, I'm told. I wasn't here on the bridge when it happened, but a crewman said he unlocked the cover and did something with the controls. The lights flickered for a moment and then everything was suddenly dark—no power, no communications, no engines, nothing."

Stokey staggered to the box on the console and tested the lid. It was locked. "Have you got a key?"

"No, the captain had the only key and he kept it on a chain around his neck. He said the box controlled an experimental degaussing system to assist in keeping the hull clean. Everyone was forbidden to touch it."

Mike stuck the edge of his Gerber under the lid and pried until it popped open. "Look here, Shake." He pointed at the markings on the controls. "I've seen enough *hangul* to recognize Korean when I see it." Shake walked over, focused his camera and took several flash photos of the controls.

"And you say the captain has disappeared?"

"We carry one nine-meter free-fall lifeboat. It is gone and so is the captain."

Shake turned to Gunny Morgan who had a worried look on his face. "Better raise the helo, Gunny. The guy we want is somewhere out in that soup aboard a little lifeboat."

"We got bigger problems right now, Gunner." Morgan turned to head for the ladder leading down off the bridge. "My guys have found two big-ass explosive charges rigged below the waterline. We're gonna have to deal with that and get everybody off this rust-bucket in a hurry."

* * *

At 300 feet below the surging sea, the captain of the North Korean People's Army Navy submarine *Seungli* (Victory) cruised at moderate speed, fighting a surging current and closing the range he had allowed to open when the American warship approached their target. In normal circumstances, the captain would simply obey his orders from Pyongyang and fire one of the wake-homing torpedoes loaded in his forward tubes and be done with this strange mission, but there were other concerns.

His active sonar and the last periscope sweep he made put the American Oliver Hazard Perry Class frigate at some 500 meters starboard of his target vessel, but that separation was closing due to the current flowing through the Korea Strait. He needed to find a firing solution that would do the minimum amount of damage to the American vessel once his torpedo struck and detonated the explosives he'd been told were rigged on the merchant ship.

He needed more information, but there was no way he was going to get it by asking questions. He'd been an officer in his nation's Navy long enough to know that some orders from certain command levels were not meant to be questioned. He'd just have to find the best option, take his shot, and run for home. The key was to insure the target vessel was completely destroyed and sent to the bottom. If there was collateral damage to the Americans, that was their problem.

"Range to target?" The captain studied the plot with his boat as the center icon.

"Five-seven-zero-zero and closing, Captain." The navigator checked the sonar returns and frowned. "Both vessels seem to be stationary."

"Stationary?" The captain looked up from the screen. "What do you mean stationary?"

"The ships are making no speed at all, Captain. No screws or machinery sounds. They both seem to be dead in the water."

There was no reason for that, the submarine captain thought, *especially with the heavy seas running on the surface*. A wise captain would be making steady speed and steering into the wind, especially if he was conning a top-heavy container ship. There was something not right 300 feet above him and a mile distant off his bow. He decided to proceed with caution.

"Find me a course to best firing solution." The captain snapped at his navigator and returned to the screen that showed two fat, sluggish targets drifting toward the South Korean island of Cheju. "Set number one and number two for acoustic tracking. I want to shoot before the range between the target and the American closes much more."

* * *

The pilot of the CH-53K Sea Stallion made a cautious approach to the fantail of the USS *Reuben James* while his co-pilot sent an emergency situation report to the task force headquarters at Chinhae. The major was an experienced rotary-wing aviator, but this approach was beyond anything he'd tried in nearly 20 years of flying. The fuel they'd taken aboard at Cheju Island was nearly exhausted from the power settings required to fly through the nasty weather and he was approaching bingo—the point of no return. In the next few minutes, they'd either accomplish one of the most daring and difficult feats in the annals of naval aviation, or they'd dump a very expensive bird into the drink and if they survived the crash likely lose their wings for even trying.

No balls, no blue chips, the major decided and locked his eyes on the sailor holding a pair of lighted wands over his head in an attempt to give the pilots a target on the heaving deck. He could see a pair of sailors standing on either side of the landing signal man holding sets of heavy chocks and chains. He was confident those sailors would risk life and limb to get him secured to the deck if he managed to get aboard in one piece. As far as he knew, no one had ever tried to land a bird as large as a Sea Stallion on a frigate. He wasn't even sure if the big bastard would fit on the relatively skimpy flight deck. To get a better shot at rotor clearance, he was making a diagonal approach that required him to fly while looking over his left shoulder to judge relative positions.

The major juggled the cyclic and collective delicately and drove the Sea Stallion closer to the heaving deck. He watched the wands since the Optical Landing System was dark and useless. When he judged he had his main gear over the mid-point of the deck, he dropped the collective, dialed off engine power, and stood on the brakes waiting for the crash. The deck rose to meet the Sea Stallion's landing gear with a hard bump, and the major saw *Reuben James* sailors plus his own aircrew rushing to chock and chain the helo against the roiling sea. He needed to get out of the bird and find the captain of this dead vessel, but it was a minute before he could stop the shaking in his hands and ease the cramps in his legs.

"Stay in your seat." He pointed at his sweating, wide-eyed co-pilot and began to unbuckle from his restraints. "Shut down the engines, but keep power to the radios so we can communicate with Chinhae and the guys on the merchantman. I'm gonna find the Skipper of this barge and see what's happening."

An officer wrapped in foul-weather gear pulled open the cockpit door on the pilot's side and stuck out a hand wrapped in a water-soaked glove. "Commander Ralph Bartlett," the man shouted over the roar of the wind. "I don't know how the hell you managed it but welcome aboard the *Ruby J*!"

* * *

The explosive charges were rigged inside two small lockers just forward of the MV *Rabat Milestone*'s main propulsion spaces. They were covered with large tarps stenciled **Emergency Equipment Only** and stuffed behind wire screen doors secured with padlocks. The VB Marines would have ignored them completely if not for an explosives sensor that began to shriek as they investigated the engine room.

"Scared the shit out of me, Gunny," the Marine who found the charges pointed at the sensor suspended from a strap around his neck. "I forgot we were carrying these things until it tripped."

"I'm betting the crew didn't even know these charges were aboard." Shake pulled at one of the screen doors and cautiously lifted the tarp covering what looked like a stack of wax billets wrapped in striped detonation cord. "That's how come none of them had a key to the locks." He pointed at the two padlocks that the Marines had ripped open with their Hooligan Tools. "This is Semtex—and a butt-load of it," Shake felt one of the blocks and traced his finger along the det-cord bindings.

"Get everybody topside!" Gunny Morgan pointed at the two Marines who discovered the explosive charges. "I want everybody including the crew mustered on the weather decks and standing by to get off this piece of shit right now!"

"Hold one, Gunny." Shake motioned for Mike to give him a hand and they carefully traced the detonation cord from one end of a square knot to the other. It made several passes over the Semtex and came to a full circle at the knot. "No cap—no firing device." Stokey snapped a fingernail on the pile of explosives. "This stuff wasn't meant to be command detonated."

"Then why the hell is it here?" Gunny Morgan was switching the freq on his radio to contact the helo. "If it's just contraband cargo, how come the det-cord?"

"Beats me, Gunny." Shake carefully untied the square knot and asked Mike to do the same with the other charge across the heaving passageway. "The relevant point is this stuff isn't dangerous as it sits. You're the man on here and what you say goes, but I'd recommend we just take this shit up topside and toss it over the side. The crew might do some good keeping us afloat and you know Chinhae will be sending ships to give us a hand."

Morgan knelt beside Shake and lowered his voice. "Act like you're the man here, Gunner, and give me your best counsel. How important is it that we salvage this fucking barge."

"The safety of your people comes first in a shitty situation like this, Huge, but I just don't think there's much danger from this stuff. The real problem is staying afloat until help comes our way. If we can manage that, what's in those containers topside becomes real important. It's a hell of a weapon and our people need to find out all they can about it."

"Copy all, Gunner—and thanks." Gunny Morgan hit his IISR transmit button. "Turn the crew loose to do whatever they need to do. Everybody else get down here to the engine room."

* * *

"Range one-three-zero-zero, Captain. Bearing is three-five-three relative. We have a solution." The *Seungli's* conning officer re-checked the figures and decided the submarine was as close as they could get it to a best shot at the target and as likely as not to cause only minor damage to the American tossing off the merchant ship's starboard side. "Confirmed, Captain, you can shoot anytime."

The captain glanced around at his tightly-focused crew and realized that this was the first time for any of them to fire live torpedoes at a target with human beings aboard. "We do it just like in training, Comrades." He breathed deeply and tried to put a touch of good humor into his commands. "Confirm power to one and two and open outer doors."

The *Seungli's* Fire Control Officer checked his instruments and smiled confidently at his captain. "Power is confirmed on one and two. Both outer doors open; flooding both tubes."

"We'll shoot two on impulse mode." The submarine captain rechecked their bearing in relation to the target.

"One and two flooded, Captain. Final shooting check: Outer doors are open, one and two have target data loaded, impulse-mode selected. Both weapons are set for acoustic homing. We are ready to fire on command."

The captain quickly scanned the instruments and decided he was as ready as training and dedication could make him. "Fire one." He felt the slight shudder as the first of two CHT-02D torpedoes in his forward tubes launched. "Fire two!"

"Both weapons away, Captain." The Fire Control Officer listened to his headset for a moment. "Sonar reports two good screws; both weapons running true."

"Close outer doors on one and two, vent tubes," The captain decided his crew had done it by the book. He probably wasn't going to see much through the chop on the surface and the result of his attack would be confirmed by sonar returns, but the temptation to watch his torpedoes strike home was irresistible. "Bring us to periscope depth."

* * *

The captain of the MV *Rabat Milestone* tried again for the fourth or fifth time in the past hour, but he could not get the lifeboat's engine to start. There was simply no power from the ignition control to the engine. The current was carrying him away from his ship, but he needed propulsion and direction. He had neither and the only logical reason seemed to be that the weapon he'd fired to escape had somehow disabled his means of doing it. None of the electronic instruments fitted to the little nine-meter covered escape craft worked. He had nothing but his wits and skills acquired through years at sea to save him. The money safely deposited in his account at Shanghai would mean nothing to a dead man and even if he survived, he couldn't spend it locked up in an American gulag at Guantanamo.

He needed to think—fast and effectively. The captain slumped into one of the contoured chairs and fought the nausea in his stomach brought on by the incessant pitching and bobbing of the lifeboat. He looked to his right through a spray-saturated port and saw his ship drawing away as the current pushed him in what he thought must be a northwesterly direction. The wind was a factor, and if it continued to blow from his right to left, he'd be drifting generally in the direction of Cheju Island. There was not much he could do to influence it. He dug into one of the survival kits on the bulkhead, found a packet of Dramamine tabs, and swallowed three of them.

* * *

"Is that all of it?" Gunnery Sergeant Hugh Morgan had one arm wrapped around a chain stanchion on the forward deck of the MV *Rabat Milestone* as he manipulated the frequency controls on his radio. "Somebody talk to me!"

Shake Davis groped his way toward the VB Team Commander and showed him a thumbs-up. "We got it all, Gunny. Last load just went over the side. Where's the bird?"

"The dumb-shits somehow landed aboard the frigate!" Gunny Morgan waved his hand in the general direction of the drifting American warship. Shake looked through the stormy afternoon gloom and saw the Sea Stallion sitting on the frigate's flight deck at an odd angle with the nose protruding over one side of the ship and the tail hanging over the other. "They say we've got a couple of ships heading in our direction to take us in tow. Think we can stay afloat for a while?"

The answer was lost in a staggering blast that seemed to lift the container ship out of the churning water and sent everyone on the weather decks tumbling toward the bow. A giant sheet of flame erupted and rolled over the MV *Rabat Milestone* sweeping from the fantail toward the bow as the fuel in the vessel's tanks erupted. Shake slammed into Mike Stokey who was caroming off one of the nearby containers and grabbed for his equipment harness as they both banked off a weather deck stanchion and tumbled into the roiling waters of the Korea Strait.

For some strange reason he remembered that it was just eight days until the revered Marine Corps Birthday celebrations on 10 November, which meant that the water they were about to impact would be frigid and their chances of surviving for very long were slim.

* * *

Commander Ralph Bartlett was huddled with the aircrew in the cockpit of the Sea Stallion and talking directly to Vice Admiral Ault at Chinhae. His Chief Engineer hadn't been able to start the *Reuben James'* engines but an innovative damage control crew had managed to restore enough semblance of mechanical steering to keep the ship from broaching in the heavy seas. He was passing that status report to the task force when the horizon off to the portside erupted in a blossom of flame and black smoke.

"Admiral, the merchantman just exploded!" Bartlett cut off Ault's transmission and then sent a description of what he was seeing. "I don't know what the hell happened but the ship just exploded! I'm looking at it right now. There was a huge detonation at the stern and then it looked like the fuel tanks must have blown. It broke her back. The ship is down by the stern and rolling over to starboard."

Bartlett listened for a moment, staring at the spectacle of a dying ship heading for the bottom in a hurry; pushed by the containers on her fore and aft decks. "Last we heard, the VB Team was dumping a bunch of explosives over the side, sir. We're trying to contact them now."

The shocked aircraft commander made circling motions and pointed at the radio. "Sir, the aircraft commander is asking if he should get airborne." Bartlett listened for a moment watching as the MV *Rabat Milestone* rolled completely over on her starboard side and slipped more deeply into the frigid water. "Aye, aye, sir, we'll keep you advised."

"It's your call, but the Admiral doesn't want to risk your aircraft unless it's absolutely necessary. He says we've got two Korean ships and an American destroyer less than an hour away. Let me see if we can get something in the water and search for survivors."

Commander Bartlett tossed the headset to the pilot and ducked out of the helicopter. "XO, get me Chief Garcia."

* * *

The frigid water seemed to be eating away at his feet and legs as Shake bobbed in the trough of a wave. He could feel a burn followed by a frightening numbness crawling from his ankles up to his knees. He wouldn't last long in water this cold. The buoyancy compensator that was an integral part of the VB Team rig he was wearing had worked like a charm and inflated almost immediately after he hit the water, but staying afloat was rapidly becoming secondary to staying alive in the face of rapidly advancing hypothermia.

He tried to maneuver his body and get a look around as a huge wave lifted him but something was tugging on his gear and pulling him off balance. "I got you! Hold still!" Shake got a brief glimpse of Mike Stokey's helmeted head and felt another strong tug on his gear. Stokey spun him around and pointed at the dummy-cord now clipping them together. Bobbing behind Stokey was Gunny Morgan and two more Marines; all of them clipped together by the rescue lines on their assault vests. "Is this everybody?" Shake could see that the little band of survivors included a couple that were nearing shock. "Wait until the next wave and then everyone look around to see if we can spot anyone else."

"Break out your lights and shine 'em around!" Gunny Morgan gasped and pointed at the reflective tape on his helmet. "We should be able to spot the reflectors." Shake reached under the water to pat his assault vest. His gloved hand brushed over a lump in one of the pockets and he hoped the waterproof bag he'd used to wrap his camera was holding. Next to the camera was a high-intensity Brite-Strike flash attached to his vest by a lanyard. He brought the little light up to the surface, snapped it on, and added its beam to the others sweeping the surging water near the little clutch of survivors.

As the next wave lifted them into the air, Shake swept his light quickly over the whitecaps from left to right but didn't see anything in the gloom. "There's Sergeant Mac!" One of the Marines on the other end of the string pointed his light, but Shake couldn't make out anything before they dropped into the following trough. "Everybody kick right!" Gunny Morgan tugged on the tether and the swimmers began to struggle in the indicated direction. On the crest of the next wave, Shake was staring directly into Sergeant Laird Macintosh's startled eyes. He snatched at the man's gear and got a good hold as Stokey fumbled for a dummy cord and added Sgt. Mac to the conga line of freezing men.

They were still searching with the lights every time a wave lifted them when Shake caught sight of the lifeboat. The beam from his light sparkled off the reflective tape running around the gunwale of the little craft but he couldn't see if anyone was aboard it. "There's a lifeboat off to the left!" Shake shouted and motioned. "It's gotta be from the ship. Wait until we go up on the next wave—you'll see it about fifty meters away."

"That chicken-shit captain's probably aboard," Stokey could barely speak his teeth were chattering so badly. "We've got no choice." Shake shook his head to clear saltwater from his eyes. "We've got to get out of the water."

"On the next wave..." Gunny Morgan maneuvered everyone into the semblance of a line. "We do a right side-stroke and kick like hell. Stand by..."

The current helped some as a wave lifted the string of swimmers and they began to claw and kick toward the drifting lifeboat. It was hard to judge distance covered as they constantly dropped into troughs between sets of waves, but the act of swimming gave them a little warmth and a little hope. They were just about out of endurance when a wave brought them within reach of the boat. Shake was actually looking down at the covered craft when he saw an Asian individual emerge from the sheltered interior. "Lend a hand!" He shouted over the noise of the water impacting the fiberglass hull of the lifeboat but the wave dissipated before he could see how the man responded.

As the next wave began to crest, Gunny Morgan looped an arm over the side of the boat anchoring the line of survivors to salvation. It looked like the guy on the lifeboat was going to help them aboard until Shake spotted the pistol in his outstretched hand.

"Gun!" Shake screamed but Morgan was halfway up the side of the lifeboat and too focused on getting out of the frigid water to respond. Two shots drove Gunny Morgan back into the water as Shake kicked hard and grabbed the merchant captain by the gun hand. He leaned back, bracing his legs against the hull of the lifeboat and hauled the shooter off balance. The man managed to fire one more shot so close that it burned Shake's face with muzzle gas before he hit the water.

Shake didn't have much strength left to wrestle, but he managed to get the renegade captain in a reverse headlock that kept him stabilized until Mike Stokey thumped the bastard smartly on the left temple with the butt of his knife. The captain of the *Rabat Milestone* slumped unconscious in Shake's arms. "Let go, Shake!" Stokey was pulling himself over the gunwale of the lifeboat. "Let the sonofabitch drown."

* * *

Chief Master At Arms Roberto Garcia picked up three MARSOC Marines in his RIB and was wrapping them in survival blankets when his bow-hook spotted the drifting survivors. "Lifeboat over on the right, Chief! I see 'em waving at us."

"Stand by to get a line on 'em. We'll tow that lifeboat back to the ship." The worst of the storm had blown through the Korea Strait, but there was still an angry sea running and Chief Garcia had no desire to attempt a transfer of survivors from the lifeboat to his inflatable in the churning water. *At times like these*, he thought as he nailed the bobbing lifeboat in the beam of his six-cell flashlight, *a sailor earns his sea pay and begins to understand what the U.S. Navy is really about.* There were a bunch of youngsters aboard the *Reuben James* who were learning that lesson the hard way.

As the coxswain maneuvered cautiously toward the lifeboat, Chief Garcia spotted two Korean destroyers plowing through the water aft of the *Reuben James* with big white bow wakes showing as they charged after something. *Probably that sub the Ruby J spotted just before the lights went out*, he speculated, and turned his attention to the American ship approaching on the horizon. She was one of the guided missile cans from the Expeditionary Strike Group, but Chief Garcia didn't hear which ship before the captain sent him out to search for survivors. He grinned at the thought of his buddy Boatswain's Mate Fester

Boncheck trying to teach the *Ruby J*'s deck gang how to rig a tow in this mess.

"I've got a Corpsman aboard if you need him." Chief Garcia shouted as his RIB maneuvered alongside the lifeboat. He could see that everyone was wrapped in reflective space-blankets from the boat's survival package, but two of the Marines seemed to be working over another one sprawled on the deck inside the weather shelter.

"I think we'll be OK if you're gonna haul us back to the ship." Shake shrugged out of his blanket and started forward to receive a tow line. "Did you find any others?"

Garcia pointed at the Marines huddled in his boat. "I picked up three. How many do you have?"

"We've got six aboard plus the merchant captain." Stokey pointed at the unconscious form propped up against the gunwale with his hands bound by flex-cuffs. "We're missing three Marines. I don't know if any of the crew got off before she went down."

"We've got a destroyer headed in to take the *Ruby J* in tow." Chief Garcia waved at the sleek vessel now clearly visible approaching from the north. "We'll get you all back and then keep looking. If the weather keeps clearing, we can probably launch helos."

Shake looped the tow line around a forward cleat and maneuvered back to the shelter of the lifeboat. The RIB coxswain cautiously took a strain and then the survivors felt the lifeboat begin to move with a purpose. "How you doing, Huge?" Shake ducked in out of the wind and knelt beside Gunny Morgan who was conscious but obviously in a lot of pain and having a trouble drawing any kind of deep breath. "I'm OK, Gunner. SAPI plate stopped the rounds as advertised but I think I've probably got a couple of cracked ribs. Did they find the rest of my guys?"

"They've got three in the RIB that's towing us. There's a destroyer inbound and they're gonna keep looking for the rest."

"They did a hell of a job, Gunner."

"They damn sure did, Gunny. And I'm gonna be damn sure everybody knows it."

As the RIB towed the survivors toward the accommodation ladder rigged amidships on the USS *Reuben James*, Shake heard a muffled thump, felt a pressure wave lift the lifeboat and looked to see two destroyers launching depth charges and a series of torpedoes. He was too exhausted to ask, but he thought he was looking at a clue concerning what happened to the container ship.

Pusan, Republic of (South) Korea

Shake Davis watched the waitress in traditional Korean dress pour cold OB Lager into two tall pilsner glasses and stretched out in the upholstered massage chair located in a quiet corner of the Pusan air terminal's executive lounge. He had an hour to kill before Bayer's CIA chartered 757 was ready to depart for the States and a lot on his mind.

"They found two more in various stages of hypothermia." Mike Stokey picked up one of the beer glasses and tasted. "One's still missing. They never found any of the crew."

"Did you attach the award recommendations to the after-action report?" Shake tasted his beer and then shifted so that the massage rollers worked on his lower back. "Those Marines deserve to be recognized for what they did, even if the citation does have to remain classified."

"All the paperwork is in, Shake. And Bayer—bless his black heart—covered for us with the MARSOC command. He told the general we went along on his orders so Gunny Morgan is in the clear."

"How's he doing?"

"He's a little shook up about losing a guy and sore as hell around the ribs, but otherwise he's good. He even invited me to the birthday celebration for the Marines at Chinhae."

"You going?"

"Yeah, I guess so. I'm gonna stick around here anyway at least until I get the deal with Lee and his family sorted out."

"What happens now?" Shake checked his watch and signaled to the waitress for more beer.

"What happens about what?"

"You know—what happens about the ship and the weapon and all that?"

"That stuff is way above my paygrade, brother, but if you're asking me to speculate, I'd say somebody in Pyongyang—

initials Kim Jong-Un—is gonna find his balls in a very tight vice. It will all happen behind the scenes and under the media radar, but they've got the captain of the ship, the pictures we took, sworn and notarized eyewitness statements and every other kind of evidence short of the actual weapon that went down with the container ship. The Norks are gonna be under some serious international pressure to behave."

"And you don't think they're gonna scream about that sub that the ROK Navy sank?"

"Not if they want to keep from being branded as the out-of-control warheads that they are. My bet is the ROKs and the U.S. will use the leverage we've got to force Kim The Younger to do some shake-ups in his cabinet and deep-six some of the die-hard commies. It's the perfect opportunity to bring those lunatics to heel. Either they play ball or the good guys take it all to the press and the U.N. and demand sanctions. They can't afford anything like that."

"Well, I guess that's the way the game is played, but if it was up to me, I'd just lay it all out there and watch China roll across the Yalu and annex North Korea. I bet they'd do it in a heartbeat if they knew what the Norks were playing with right under their noses."

"And that, my friend, is why it's not up to guys like you and me." Stokey drained his beer and stood. "It looks like they're ready for you." He took Shake's hand and pulled him into a hug. "Give my love to Chan when you see her."

Shake followed a flight attendant toward the waiting aircraft and tried for a fourth time to reach Chan on the phone. He got her service but didn't bother to leave another message. When he was seated and belted in along with the other Americans on the emergency task force heading home, he pulled her note out of his jacket pocket. He'd read it several times since he returned to the Chinhae VOQ and found it propped up on a pillow but no matter how many times he scanned the words, he couldn't discern the real message. "Called away on another job. See you when I see you. C."

Shake Davis had a long flight ahead of him and no idea what he would discover on the other end of it.

About the Author

D ale Dye is a Marine officer who rose through the ranks to retire as a Captain after 21 years of service in war and peace. He is a distinguished graduate of Missouri Military Academy who enlisted the United States Marine Corps shortly after graduation. Sent to war in Southeast Asia, he served in Vietnam in 1965 and 1967 through 1970 surviving 31 major combat operations.

Appointed a Warrant Officer in 1976, he later converted his commission and was a Captain when he deployed to Beirut, Lebanon with the Multinational Force in 1982-83. He served in a variety of assignments around the world and along the way attained a degree in English Literature from the University of Maryland. Following retirement from active duty in 1984, he spent time in Central America, reporting and training troops for guerrilla warfare in El Salvador, Honduras and Costa Rica. Upset with Hollywood's treatment of the American military, he went to Hollywood and established Warriors Inc., the pre-eminent military training and advisory service to the entertainment industry. He has worked on more than 50 movies and TV shows including several Academy Award and Emmy winning productions. He is a novelist, actor, director and show business innovator, who wanders between Los Angeles and Lockhart, Texas.